# DEADLINE

JACK NOBLE BOOK ELEVEN

L.T. RYAN

LIQUID MIND MEDIA

ltryan70@gmail.com

http://LTRyan.com

https://www.facebook.com/JackNobleBooks

## THE JACK NOBLE SERIES

*The Recruit (free)*
*The First Deception (Prequel 1)*
*Noble Beginnings*
*A Deadly Distance*
*Ripple Effect (Bear Logan)*
*Thin Line*
*Noble Intentions*
*When Dead in Greece*
*Noble Retribution*
*Noble Betrayal*
*Never Go Home*
*Beyond Betrayal (Clarissa Abbot)*
*Noble Judgment*
*Never Cry Mercy*
*Deadline*
*End Game*

**Receive a free copy of The Recruit by visiting http://ltryan.com/newsletter.**

# 1

The sedative they injected into me prior to boarding the Gulfstream G650 knocked me out cold before the flight from Texas to who the hell knew where departed from a private airfield somewhere north of Dallas, Texas. I'd been there twice before. Both times while working for Frank Skinner and the SIS. It seemed fitting that we used it as the first step on a journey to see Frank, presumably for our final meeting.

Waking up hours later as the jet touched down, I felt the full hangover effect of the knockout drug. At least it made it easy to forget about everything that had happened over the past few days.

To forget them.

To forget her.

*Especially her.*

It was futile to dwell on it. The FBI had made Reese McSweeney vanish. She was out of my life. Again. Somehow I always figured we'd meet again. We had one shot. And we'd blown it.

Nothing new there.

We should've left Texline when we had the chance.

I sat in the rear seat of the sedan with an agent on either side. The windows were blacked out, and a divider separated us from the front. I couldn't see a damn thing. The Feds weren't much for conversation, either. They didn't even crack a smile at my recent bad dad joke repertoire. It made it difficult to ascertain where the hell we were. The end destination had been made evident by my brief conversation with Frank. Based on that, I figured we were somewhere in Northern Virginia.

Frank had been placed in charge of the CIA's Special Activities Division, Special Operations Group. Didn't take much of a stretch of the imagination to assume that my escorts were his men, and that we were en route to his office.

One of his offices, at least. The kind of place the rest of the world assumed was a farm, but underneath the barn or the house was a labyrinth of Agency offices and interrogation rooms. I, like others before me, would learn my fate there.

What did Frank have planned for me? We'd last seen each other a few months ago. Our farewell consisted of me holding a pistol to his head. The only thing that stopped me from pulling the trigger was that my daughter, Mia, stood thirty feet away. I saw the fear in her eyes. She hardly knew me as a father. I sure as hell didn't want her to remember me as a monster. So I let Frank live. I knew then that it was a mistake. Things weren't the same between us, and hadn't been for years. Tension escalated every time we were near each other. I could've ended it there. I should've ended it.

I assumed, since my identity had been exposed while in Texas, it had landed me on a watch list. One that Frank had access to due to his position in the CIA. He used resources to determine the credibility of the report, then acted on it. At least he'd left me enough time to clean up the mess in Texline.

I had to be prepared for other outcomes of our pending meeting. I'd pissed off plenty of people over the past decade, and performed enough shady deeds for even shadier individuals that any city, state, or federal agency would want to bring me in. Frank was the only one with a solid motive, though.

Instinctively, I glanced at the side window as the vehicle slowed to a stop for the first time in over an hour. The blacked out glass revealed nothing. One of the men, a bald guy with bushy eyebrows and a tattoo behind his right ear, glanced at his phone. He leaned forward, made eye contact with his partner. They both nodded.

We were close.

A wave of panic traveled through my body, numbing my fingers and toes. I took a deep breath, relaxed my arms, legs, chest and abdominal muscles. The feeling slipped away. I had no control over whatever was about to happen. My job moving forward was to react. Whether that was to an attack, or just information, was to be determined. I prepared for either.

The ceiling vents stopped spitting out cold air. In its place was a warm stream that smelled like gasoline and oil. The men squeezed in close to me. If I started to move, they'd know.

The vehicle turned left and right a few times. I pulled up a mental map of Langley, tried to match our changes of direction with streets, and the accompanying buildings, training facilities, housing. I recalled what was underground as best I could. And hoped that we wouldn't end up down there. It was an exercise in futility. We could have been back in Crystal River, Florida. The turns would line up the same. It was impossible to tell with any accuracy.

The guy with the tattoo lifted his phone to eye level and poked at it with his index finger. After a minute, he lowered it, grasped it with both hands, and typed out a message with his thumbs. He used his hands to block the screen from view. For a few moments the haptic feedback tone was the only sound inside the car. We'd come to another stop. The engine idled quietly.

I counted the seconds in my head. Thirty, fifty, ninety. Tattoo played on his phone, no longer hiding the screen. No need to. Angry Birds was hardly anything to conceal. At least if he was twelve it wouldn't be. His partner stared straight ahead. I didn't bother to ask what was going on. They weren't going to let me know.

The front passenger door opened. The vehicle dipped to the right, then rebounded, swayed side to side for a few seconds. I strained to hear footsteps, couldn't make out any. The inside of the vehicle must've been soundproofed. What else was the car used for? Transporting foreign dignitaries? High profile refugees and asylum seekers? Double crossing agents coming over to our side?

*Our side.*

Made me want to laugh and puke at the same time. I'd reached a level in intelligence where there were no sides. No good versus evil. Just a bunch of bad men doing bad things all in the name of an ideology that no one at the top believed in anymore.

And for a guy like me, one that worked on the inside, and outside, who sold himself to the highest bidder and was willing to do any job, none of it meant anything. Give me an order, pay me enough, and I'd execute any command, and any person.

But the truth was that used to be me. Now, I wanted nothing to do with any of it. I'd reached a point where my only goal was to drift and disappear with Mia. I realized we should have left together, rather than taking a few months to let things blow over.

It all led to me stuck in the back of a government sedan, parked outside of God knows where. Presumably I wouldn't have to wait much longer to figure that part out.

The rear passenger door opened, and I squinted in anticipation of sunlight flooding in. Didn't happen. Dim yellow fluorescent light was the flavor of the day.

Tattoo exited the vehicle first. He stepped out, turned, leaned in, then gestured with his pistol for me to follow him. His partner remained seated, hand hidden inside his jacket. I climbed out and glanced around the parking garage. There were two similar cars parked there, and a Mercedes in the corner. Couldn't fit much else in there. It was smaller than I expected, which meant we were near one of the less frequently used offices.

The kind of place few people like me walked into, but when they did, they were brought out in a body bag. If they left at all.

Four agents boxed me in and led me forward. It wasn't until we neared the steel doors set into concrete walls that I recognized where we were.

It wasn't Langley.

Hell, it wasn't in Northern Virginia, either.

They'd taken me to New Jersey. And I stood in the parking garage of the now-defunct SIS headquarters.

# 2

We walked through the hallway, and into a series of memories. Ones I'd fought to forget over the years. For all the good we did during my time in the SIS, there was no fooling anyone that we were a bunch of choir boys. We had been able to operate without restriction Stateside, and elsewhere. Rules rarely applied to us. I'm sure that made Frank Skinner an appealing candidate to head up the SAD-SOG. He'd run a similar operation with a much smaller budget, and much less backing from the politicians. He was unstoppable now.

The carpet in the corridor had been ripped up in favor of concrete. Chemical-laden air blew through the oversized vents in the ceiling. Overhead lights hummed and blinked on and off at irregular intervals. I figured they hadn't been on since the SIS was dissolved. Of course, I had to question whether it had been shut down after all.

Walking past my old office, I thought of specific missions we'd run. The faces of men, women and children we'd saved. Agents, and friends, we'd lost along the way. The six-by-nine room now stood empty, save for a vacuum cleaner in one corner. Judging by the floor, I doubted anyone had ever used the machine.

We stopped short of Frank's office, which was next to mine. Tattoo knocked on the door, waited a second, nodded, then entered. Two of the remaining agents left us. Coffee, maybe. Readying the interrogation room, perhaps. I hoped it didn't get to that point because it didn't appear Doc's office was occupied anymore. Who'd set their broken bones once I was through with them?

Tattoo emerged from the office, looked past me, nodded at his partner.

"Skinner will see you now." Tattoo took a step back, gestured at me like I was a plane making my way toward the runway. He guided me toward him, then into the office.

Frank remained seated behind his desk. He offered no greeting or handshake. One hand remained on the chair's armrest, the other hidden beneath the desktop, presumably gripping a pistol so tight his fingers turned white. His neutral expression gave nothing away. I might die in the next five minutes, or he could ask me to assassinate a politician in Colombia.

Despite the chair next to me I remained standing.

"Good to see you, Jack."

Was it? I responded with a slight nod. Nothing else.

He lifted his hand from the armrest and gestured toward my waist. "You mind?"

"They checked me out half a dozen times, Frank."

"I'm sure they did. How about you humor me. Please?"

I lifted my shirt a couple inches, turned around. "Good enough?"

"Sure." He scooped a pen off the desk, aimed it at me. "Have a seat."

I sat back in the chair, rested my head against the glass window. It was bulletproof, and when the light in the frame was switched on, no one from the lobby could see in. It'd saved Frank's life once. Unfortunately.

"Comfortable?" he asked.

I'd taken that posture in this very office a hundred times in the past. Don't know that I was ever comfortable in here. Still, I nodded at him.

"Little," Frank said, talking to his agent. "Close the door for me."

Tattoo reached in and pulled the door closed.

"Little?" I said. "Guy's built like a tank."

"Ironic, right?" Frank placed his other hand on top of the desk. He'd left the pistol mounted to the underside. I glanced down at the steel divider preventing me from accessing the weapon. Frank leaned over his forearm. "Jack, what the hell happened down in Texas?"

I waved my hand in front of my face to disperse the smell of his aftershave. "Don't wanna talk about it."

"Can't tell you the feeling in my stomach when your name flagged. I mean, there's only a handful of people in the world who would show up on that report. Damn, we hadn't had anything come up on it in three months. I'll tell you what, Jack, it scared the crap out of everyone around that table. It went all the way to the top. You were included in a daily briefing that usually ends up with someone dying."

"That's why I'm here? My time's up?"

He gnawed on the end of his pen, shook his head.

"Then why mention it?"

"The meeting? Just thought you should know."

"And Texas?"

"Curious is all. I've been getting texts keeping me in the loop about a massive weapons deal supposedly going down soon. There's four different agencies collaborating on this. The FBI, Homeland, DEA, one of those Texas groups. It's supposed to be huge. Hearing we'll take down one of the largest terrorist cells in the southwest."

I said nothing.

He twirled the pen between his fingers, index to pinky and back. "Earned yourself a lot of goodwill with this, Jack."

"That's great."

Thinking about Texas led my thoughts to Reese. Frank had always been perceptive to the inner workings of my mind. Today was no different.

"I understand witness protection had to get involved. Someone you knew, right?"

I held his gaze for a few seconds, wondering where he was headed with this. "Yeah, old friend of mine. Met her during the Brett Taylor mission. Remember that?"

"I do, and I know about Reese McSweeney. Maybe I can pull some strings."

"I figured I was here to die."

"That's up to you."

I straightened in the chair. "How so?"

"The past is the past," he said. "That's how I feel, at least. I understand why you acted the way you did. If the roles were reversed, I probably would have put a gun to my head, too. You had me dead to rights. But you let me live. And, Jack, I'm grateful that you didn't go through with it. Now, don't you think I've totally forgotten about it. I may understand why. I may thank you for not killing me. But I can still get pissed thinking about it. And remember, I could provide enough testimony to put you away for ten to twenty, at a minimum. And we both know you wouldn't last long in a cage."

"So that's it, huh? You don't care, but you do. You'll use everything you have against me, unless you won't." I placed my arms on the table, leaned forward. About a foot of air separated us. I could smell the ham sandwich he had for lunch, and the beer he washed it down with. "Listen up. I've got just as much on you, if not more. We can both go down, for all I care."

Frank leaned back, spread his arms with his palms facing me, smiled. "Sorry, that came off as a threat, didn't it? That's not how I meant it. I really am over the whole thing."

I was growing tired of the game. He was beating around the bush about whatever it was he wanted, making not so subtle threats toward me.

"OK," I said. "Then my answer's no."

Frank laughed. "No to what?"

"Whatever the hell you're about to ask me."

"Let's walk, Jack."

Given the confines of the SIS headquarters, taking a walk was never a good thing. I had little choice at the moment, though.

We left his office and headed down the hallway away from the entrance. All the other offices were dark and empty. Same with the interrogation rooms. Frank and I had spent a lot of time in them, sitting on the same side of the table.

Obviously Frank no longer operated out of this place anymore. No one did. Not regularly. Perhaps it had been left in place for situations like this. Or worse. With the building now being off the grid, it could be used to deal with hostiles in a certain way. One that the politicians generally frowned upon.

The lights in the stairwell barely functioned. They illuminated the area enough to make it down the stairs, but that was about it. There could've been someone hidden on the first landing, and I wouldn't have seen them.

The first sub-level smelled the same as it had five years ago. Which is to say it smelled like two week old squid nachos. We stopped in front of the meeting room where the team used to get together weekly and before any large missions. I expected to be greeted by some of Frank's SOG agents. He reached inside, flipped a switch and the lights cut on. The room was empty.

He took a seat at one end of the large conference table. I sat on the opposite side.

"Other than Texas, what've you been up to?" he asked after settling in.

"That's why we came down here?"

"Things were getting a bit intense upstairs. Figured a few minutes hanging out and catching up might help."

"I've been drifting. Nothing more, nothing less. Saw my family for a day, left without saying goodbye, and started driving."

"Poetic."

"Isn't it?"

"I lost track of you after you left Florida," he said.

He was about to bring up his next bargaining chip. I hadn't fallen for his threat to turn on me in court. Mia was his ace, though. I wanted nothing to happen to my daughter, especially because of me.

Frank continued. "I know you left without your daughter."

I clenched my jaw, shook my head.

"What?" he said.

"Don't say it, Frank. You can hold whatever you want against me, but so help me God, if you bring my daughter or family into this, I will unleash every ounce of my fury against you. Neither of us will leave this building alive today."

Frank rose, walked down the side of the table closest to the hallway. I countered on the opposite side. We stopped in the middle. Four feet of cheap particle board separated us.

"I've got nothing on her, or anyone else in your family, Jack. You know me. That's not how I operate."

"Things change." I could feel my blood pressure skyrocketing, my pulse pounding in my head, against my temples. My ears and cheeks burned.

"That they do." He held out his hand as though he wanted to shake mine. "But I have a few strands of moral decency left. Hell, I'd help you protect them if your ass wasn't too proud to ask. I've got the best operatives in the world working for me. No one asks questions."

"Makes it that much easier, doesn't it?"

"Christ, Jack. I'm trying to help you."

"Think I would risk giving away their position to you?"

"You think I can't find that out anyway?"

"There you go again," I said. "You come across as saying you'll help, but then you have to make those threats."

"You are a paranoid son of a bitch, you know that, Noble?"

He was right. "Aren't we all? How else have you and I survived in this business so long?"

"By trusting the right people." He placed both hands flat on the table and leaned forward. It left him vulnerable. I could lay him out cold before he could move his jaw. And he knew it. "There was a time when you and I had each other's back. Every goddamned minute of the day, man. We didn't always get along, but we sure as hell made sure that we went home alive at night."

"Your point?"

"Trust me that nothing is going to happen to your family. Not even if word of this gets out."

"Word of what?"

He looked up at me with a grave expression I'd only seen twice before. "We should head back up to my office."

# 3

Frank switched off his phone and turned his laptop on after we returned to his office. My gaze fell on the red folder on the table while he messed with his computer. We never used red in the SIS. Maybe in his new job it had something to do with a threat level, or pertained to operational security.

He placed a hand on it. "It was literally all I had in my drawer, and I was in a rush to get over here. Tell you the truth, we weren't all that hopeful that we'd find you after the damn FBI moved Reese. Figured you'd cut rope and bail."

"We?" I said. "Who is we?"

He shook his head. "My guys that detained you. Don't worry, there's no one else involved in this mess."

*If word gets out.*

*This mess.*

What the hell was going on? Why did Frank keep referring to something while continuing to keep me in the dark about it? I could press him on it, but I had a feeling he was building up to telling me. I figured it best to take these last moments and relax because once that folder opened up, things might change.

I caught a glimpse of his laptop as he pushed it back. There were faces on the screen that I hadn't seen in eight or nine years. Former SIS agents. At that time, we were a team that didn't exist, working stateside and on foreign shores. We acted independently and needed permission from no one.

A lot of the things we did were not exactly legal according to most other agency heads. But that didn't matter. We took our orders from the top.

Had some of that information come to light? Were the few remaining living members of SIS about to be exposed? Was that what Frank was referring to when he mentioned putting me away for ten to twenty?

"Haven't seen some of those faces in forever," I said.

Frank nodded, smiled. "Right? I was thinking the same thing. So many good men. You know, outside of you, I haven't spoken to any of the old guys in years. I'm aware of what they're doing, for the most part. A lot went on to contract work and are sitting in that mess in the Middle East right now. Hardy and Scalding started a security business and only work with celebrity clients. I found out they're making close to seven figures each a year now. You believe that?"

I nodded slowly. I was mostly letting the information pass through. No sense in retaining any of it. It was bullshit, after all. I didn't see how Frank could sit there spewing lies when he had allegedly been a part of a mass extinction of former and current SIS agents, among other black ops. I suppose it was possible a few guys slipped through the cracks. All I knew was that several SIS and black ops were terminated in a very short span not too long ago.

Frank adjusted his laptop so I couldn't see the screen. He tapped on the keyboard, then slid the computer to his right. He leaned over the desk, placed his interlaced fingers on top of the red folder.

"You fucked up," he said.

# 4

SUCH A SIMPLE PHRASE CAPABLE OF COVERING A HOST OF SITUATIONS. I NEVER operated by the book, not that we had much of a ruleset to abide by in the SIS. Still, I found it difficult to recall an event that occurred over a half-decade ago or more that would require Frank Skinner to send a group of SOG operators to Nowhere, Texas to find and bring me to the remains of the SIS headquarters in order to hold a clandestine meeting.

Frank took a deep breath, leaned back in his chair. "Actually, we all messed up. But you were the man in the field, so a lot of this falls on you."

"OK?" I said, unsure what the hell he was talking about.

"Our intelligence was garbage to begin with."

"That was often the case."

He waved his right hand over the folder. "Yeah, I know. But in this case, we had it wrong. I mean, big time, Jack."

"Get to it, Frank." I reached for the folder. He grasped the edge of it and pinned it to the table. "Come on, I'm tired of playing this guessing game."

"Katrine Ahlberg," he said. His eyes wavered back and forth as he stared at me, waiting for my reaction. "Remember her?"

"The Scandinavian Princess. Came from a wealthy family in Norway." I stared at a yellow stain on the ceiling. "No, Sweden."

"That's right."

"Father made his fortune in textiles. At least, that was his gig on the surface. Something else to do with human trafficking, if I remember correctly."

Frank nodded, said nothing.

"Katrine married that son of a bitch Saudi, Awad. One of the Crown Prince's two-thousand cousins, right? His dad was an oil tycoon. Awad followed in his footsteps, but spent little time actually working in the family business. When we found him, he was driving around in a gold Mercedes AMG. I mean, the thing was actually made from gold."

Frank shook his head. "Such flagrant waste."

"Intel said that Katrine and Awad had been involved in dealings with terrorists. Funding, recruiting, planning, that kind of stuff. More indirect than direct."

"Good memory," Frank said. "Kinda surprised considering all the lumps you've taken on the head."

I reached back and cupped the back of my skull. Noticed for the first time that the sedative-induced hangover had cleared. "So were we wrong? Were they not involved in those things?"

"No, we were right. Hell, turns out they were more involved than we suspected. We—," he took a sip from his water bottle then cleared his throat, "I should say, you, Jack Noble, did the world a favor the night you assassinated her."

"What's the problem then?"

"You killed her twin sister."

# 5

THE CHAIR BANGED AGAINST THE GLASS AS I ROCKED BACK WHILE THE MEMORY OF pulling the trigger on the fatal shot that took the life of the woman I thought was Katrine Ahlberg played in my mind's eye. I raced through files of information stored in the recesses of my brain for her sister's name, and whether she was involved with Katrine's dealings. With the top of my foot against the underside of the desk, I pulled myself forward, allowing my torso to continue until it collided with the desk.

"The hell you mean I killed her twin sister?"

"You finished the mission. Only problem is it wasn't Katrine. It was her twin sister Birgit. We were purposely fed false information by an informant."

"Son of a bitch." Details of the hit came back in fragments. I placed the pieces of the puzzle in place as they appeared. "And do we know the bastard who sold us out?"

Frank shook his head. "Obviously he wasn't who we thought he was. So far, taking what we know about him, we haven't been able to determine his true identity. He could still be there. That's why you and I are meeting here, and not any of the other locations available to me now. We had no face-to-face with this guy. He could be in the Agency for all I know."

The danger of working with an informant. We vetted them as best we could, but sometimes they arrived through alternative channels, and the information they provided had to be acted on before full compliance could be achieved.

Frank continued. "Our best guess is Katrine received advanced notice of the hit, used that information to set her sister up. She compromised our channels with the bad informant. Gave up her sister's location and her schedule. Think about it, that was probably your easiest job ever. At least, that part of the mission."

"But there were identifying markings, Frank. Hell, I remember taking the pictures of her tattoos."

Frank opened the folder. He pulled out a thick pile of photos, flipped through them and placed two in front of me. At once, I recalled standing over the corpse, snapping the pictures. He slid them to the side and placed what appeared to be surveillance photos on the table. They were of Katrine at the beach. She had on a bikini and nothing else. The markings matched what we had.

"Either the women got the same tattoos," he said. "Or our surveillance was compromised, too. Or it could've been pictures of Birgit. The women were identical, after all."

"Awad is there, though."

Frank nodded, placed two fingers down, one over Katrine, the other her husband. "I've considered that they were altered and what we're seeing are two separate images here. Maybe a picture of Birgit and another of Awad, or one where Birgit's tattoos were superimposed onto her sister. Whatever they did, we were duped."

I studied the photos. Any of the explanations were valid. And they meant little now. This had gone down a decade ago.

"So fast forward," I said. "What's going on now? Has Katrine resurfaced? Is she dabbling in her old businesses again? What's the threat we're facing here?"

Frank flipped through a few more photos, placing them on top of the ones on the table. They were of Katrine. She'd aged, slightly. Looked nearly the same at forty as she had at thirty. Slim, attractive, definitely deadly.

"I don't know if that's the case," he said. "I have the feeling I'm not being told everything."

"How can that be?" I said. "I mean, considering your new position, you should be aware of damn near everything going on."

Frank seemed disinclined to delve deeper into that aspect. "Jack, what I can tell you is that this situation came to light recently, and I was told to fix it. Katrine has to disappear. She can't simply die. Any trace of her, or Birgit, I guess we should say, has to be wiped clean from the planet."

There were things he'd left out. Intentionally, I presumed. Why had this come up now? And why did it require me to be a part of it? It left me feeling like I needed to pass on the situation. Only problem was, I doubt that option would be available.

"You're sure this isn't a setup?" I said.

"I trust my guy here," he said.

"Like the original informant?" I paused to judge his reaction. There was none. He knew he'd screwed up. "Maybe it's not you he's setting up."

"You know how it worked back then, Jack. No one outside of me and the agents on the ground ever knew who pulled the trigger on any of these jobs." He spread the pictures apart, eyes darting one to the next. Then he looked up at me. "And you can stop wondering. You weren't asked for by name. They told me to get whoever I needed and fix this. I could've gone with any of the guys in my group. And you know how them sons of bitches are. They'd gladly do this."

"Sounds like that'd be the way to go."

He shook his head. "No, Jack. Fact is, even if you hadn't been the one to carry out the original hit, I'd still ask you to do this."

"Why?"

"You're the only one from back then that didn't go soft."

I rose out of my seat, placed my hands on the desktop, leaned forward, hovering over him. "I'm the only one still alive. So quit feeding me line after line and let me know what's at stake here."

He pushed away from the desk and stood. His chair continued rolling back and collided with the wall.

"What I said is true," he said. "I got to pick my guy. And we've got a limited amount of time to make this right. Once the goodwill expires, they'll open the file, and everyone involved will be flagged for the spooks."

Now it came together. Frank thought that I'd have a vested interest in resolving this issue. More so than any of his current agents, seeing as how their lives weren't on the line.

I traced Katrine's face in a close up photo that appeared to have been taken recently. She had a wrinkle on her forehead, and some lines in the corner of her eyes. With such fair skin, I'd have imagined there'd be more. How had they screwed this up so badly? And why was it now falling on me to fix it? Well, me and one other person.

"I wasn't alone in this," I said.

"I know," he said.

"Bear—Logan was with me."

Riley "Bear" Logan had been my best friend since recruit training. Even though he was never an official member of the SIS, he had worked with me from time to time after he'd left the Marines.

Frank reached down and grabbed his bag off the floor. It was the same one he'd had the day I met him down in the Keys. He pulled the zipper back and opened it up enough to slide his hand inside. He retrieved a blue folder and placed it on the table in front of me.

"What's this?" I asked without opening the folder.

"Your travel pack. Identity, passport, credit cards, everything you'll need. There's a code to a Swiss bank if you get in trouble. You also have accounts in England, Sweden, and Morocco."

Two of those destinations made sense. "Why England?"

"That's where Bear is living right now. It's all in the folder. You leave out of LaGuardia in five hours. A man will meet you at Heathrow, on the other side of customs."

"Who?"

Frank waved me off with a shake of his head. "No names here. You'll figure it out. He'll give you everything you need: a car, weapons, Bear's location, and Katrine's location." He shuffled the photos in a stack, leaving the most recent ones of Katrine on the table for me. "And Jack, so help me, do not go to any of your friends in British Intelligence. This is strictly a need to know deal, and they don't need to know anything about this."

"What if I get in trouble?"

He reached into his bag again, placed three cell phones on the table. The first was a typical large-screen smartphone.

"Daily use. Traceable. Use it for getting around, general information. Imagine you're a tourist."

He held the second and third smartphones up. "Untraceable. This one is yours." He gestured with his left hand. "The other is for Bear. You communicate with each other on these. GPS your mission routes with these. Call me only from yours. Same number as always. Got it?"

I nodded and collected the phones. "Luggage?"

"It'll be in the car. Two duffle bags. Check one, carry the other."

"Does it matter which?"

"Whichever one has the clothes you like best, carry it on. You're not claiming the other when you get over there." He closed his bag and placed it on the floor. "It's time for you to get going."

I tensed during our walk to the garage, anticipating a team of armed men on the other side. Frank pushed the door open. I held my breath as I crossed the threshold. There was no one there waiting to take me out. Frank remained at the door, stuck out his hand. I took it.

"I'd like to say it was good seeing you again, Frank."

"But it wasn't." He smiled. The first genuine one I'd seen from him in some time.

We grasped each other's hands for a few more seconds, then I hopped into the waiting car, wondering if I'd make it to New York alive.

# 6

We took the Lincoln Tunnel across the Hudson into midtown Manhattan. At one point Bear and I had had several properties spread throughout the city. Now I only had the one apartment, and we were close to it. I hadn't been there in months, and wondered whether the cleaning service had emptied the fridge. Anything I required to disappear forever was only a couple blocks away. I considered persuading the driver to drop me off, figuring it'd be easier to hide for a while out in the open in New York City than the wide open landscape of Texas.

He'd never go for it, though. Frank would be on his ass and would never stop riding it. Didn't matter how much I offered the guy, it wasn't worth it.

I searched for old friends, and enemies, amid the mass of people crammed into the confined spaces of the sidewalks and crosswalks. There was only one person in particular I cared to see. And even if I spotted Clarissa, what good would it do? They wouldn't let me out. I couldn't hug her and make sure life was treating her fair these days.

I pressed the window control on the door. To my surprise, it rolled down. I stopped it half-way, leaned my head back, and took in the aroma of the city. I was inundated with smells from restaurants and food carts, as well as trash and exhaust. A blend that reminded me of everything I loved and hated about the city rushed in through the cracked window. I hadn't ever wanted to stop at a hot dog stand as bad as I did in that moment.

The guy driving coughed a couple times and muttered an indecipherable comment under his breath.

"Something bothering you?" I said.

"That disgusting smell," he said, his voice thick with a southern drawl.

"Guess we need to find a barbecue restaurant for you, huh? Or maybe a place that serves fried catfish."

"That'd be good, man. That'd be good."

"Go to hell."

That was the last we spoke. After I'd seen enough of Manhattan, I rolled the window up and turned my attention to the route ahead. I estimated we'd reach the airport in thirty minutes. It took almost a full hour. Felt even longer.

I hopped out of the car when we arrived at the terminal, grabbed my bags and headed toward the ticketing counter. I checked the bag that looked like it had been packed for a ninety-year-old man. Carried on the other. Surprisingly, I made it through security in a matter of minutes, and reached the gate with an hour-and-a-half to spare.

Once on board, I had a drink, closed my eyes, and nodded off before we'd reached cruising altitude.

# 7

THE PLANE TOUCHED DOWN AROUND TEN A.M. GMT. THE AIRPORT WASN'T AS busy as I'd seen it in the past. Could've been the day of the week, time of day, or any other number of variables I supposed. It only mattered at Passport Control. An overworked Border Force officer was more likely to ask fewer questions. A bored one might want to dig deeper.

I made my way through the sparse crowd of Terminal 2 with my carry-on bag in hand. It only contained clothing. I'd used the cell phone to take pictures of the documents and the photos of Katrine, then destroyed the originals. Everything else Frank had given me was on my person. None of it would arouse suspicion.

There were four Border Force officers working this morning. As I made the long approach, I studied each, and got in line for the woman who seemed to talk the least and moved travelers through the fastest. When it was my turn, she only asked a few basic questions, including the reason for my visit. I gave my standard answer about an aunt having emergency surgery. The woman looked at me once, when she gestured me past. I grabbed my bag and continued through the airport, skipping baggage claim.

The trans-Atlantic flight had left me groggy. Despite my nap, I was on Texas time, which made it 4:15 am. I stopped at Caffe Nero, and bought the tallest cup of coffee they offered. And a shot of espresso. I found a spot along the wall and observed life amid the expansive steel and glass terminal.

I tossed the espresso cup and made my way toward the exit. Presumably Frank had arranged a specific window of time for my contact to wait around. I remained vigilant and aware, using subtle changes to line of sight, and stops and starts to monitor for a tail. Despite the fact that I was here because of Skinner and had to rely on the assets he put in place for me, I couldn't trust the man. The entire assignment had the potential to be one massive setup, placing me as the unwitting target. Death or imprisonment, it was all the same to guys like us. In fact, most would prefer death. I'd escaped detainment enough times, whether on my own or with assistance, that I'd opt for that route.

And whether Frank had true intentions regarding Ahlberg, or if he wanted me taken care of, he had eyes on me.

I identified two who fit the mold amid the thickening crowd trying to exit the terminal. It wasn't their look, or their actions that made them suspect. It was how they carried themselves. How aware they were of their surroundings. When I glanced around the terminal, most travelers were weary-eyed and moped around like zombies. This man and woman were different. They took note of everyone, and did so in a way that was not overt. They quickly surmised the physical capabilities of each person that entered their personal space and then reacted accordingly.

And both held my gaze a beat longer than anyone else in the terminal.

The exits were one turn and another hundred feet away. I prepared myself for the multitude of scenarios that might present themselves outside. Before reaching the final turn, I tossed a quick look around and spotted each of my potential tails. Neither had moved, nor did they appear interested in my actions.

But someone else did.

Nothing stood out about the guy. He looked like an average businessman, probably arriving from Dayton, Ohio, or Freeport, Mississippi, or some other city that was as American as one could get. I caught sight of his reflection in a mirror. Instead of turning toward the exits, I continued on, stopping at a small bookshop. I picked up a science fiction paperback and flipped to the middle, acted like I was reading a passage of the book.

The guy walked past, slowed, stopped in front of a monitor littered with flight information.

I passed the guy after exiting, headed toward the men's room at the end of a wide corridor. Inside the restroom I ran cold water over my hands and rinsed my face. The jolt from the frigid water combined with the adrenaline rushing through my veins banished any remaining grogginess. I grabbed a towel and wiped my face.

And then I saw the guy in the mirror. He stood at a urinal, his back to me. He turned and approached the sink next to me, maintaining eye contact in the mirror. The wall was lined with sinks, yet he chose mine. I readied myself for the eventual fight.

He looked over, nodded. "Should be nice weather here the next couple days." His neutral accent gave nothing away.

I ignored him, stepping past to the air dryer.

"Not one for conversation?" he asked.

My heart rate rose as I crossed the next few feet. I had my back to him now. In such close proximity he could strike before I could react. Why had I put myself in that position? Because I wanted to draw him out. He might land a blow, and it'd likely hurt, but that's as far as he'd get. I hadn't been "retired" so long that I'd forgotten how to handle myself.

He shook the water from his hands and smiled. "Picking up my daughter. She's flying in from her mother's place in Denver. Nerve-wracking waiting, you know?"

I did, in a way. And for a moment I let my guard slide a bit. "Yeah, I can relate."

He walked past, said, "Enjoy your stay in London, or wherever your travels take you."

I remained in the restroom for another minute. Random encounter? I supposed it was possible. But random rarely invited me on board. It seemed anyone who held that much of my attention either needed my help or wanted to kill me.

The janitor held the door open as I exited the restroom. I moved toward the center of the terminal, scanning the area for the man. When I found him, he was headed in the opposite direction his story indicated. I began to doubt his story about picking up his daughter.

I swiped a hat off the janitor's pushcart. It didn't do much to alter my appearance, but in a crowd it prevented me from standing out. A little, at least. People clustered together in the corridor, huddled together the way mobs of unrelated people tend to do as they move through a confined space. I hustled past the first of them, and settled in behind the next in a spot where I could still keep tabs on the guy. He turned down a hall that led to the exits. I stopped at the corner and waited a few seconds before proceeding.

He glanced back near the exits. His gaze swept past me. Had he missed me, or was he trained well enough that he kept his eyes moving no matter what? Did he process each frame as he took it in without needing to stop and analyze?

He stepped outside, and I followed. But amid the bustle of activity on the sidewalk and street, I lost track.

When someone jabbed something in my back, I realized he had found me.

"Just relax, Mr. Noble." He ran one hand around my back, then down my arm. I let go of the bag after he tugged on it. "Just a precaution. Now act normal and start walking."

I felt the small package against my thigh.

"Long stay car park for Terminal 2. Hit the unlock button a few times and you'll figure it out."

I heard a thud on the ground next to me.

"Don't forget your bag."

# 8

The A8 Frank had arranged was loaded to the hilt. And not only with features. I located a hidden compartment in the trunk, to the right of the spare tire. It contained two Sigs, one 9mm and the other a .45, an extra magazine for each, and two boxes of ammunition. The compartment also contained a lightweight Remington Defense concealable sniper rifle, broken down into three parts. The accompanying rucksack, made to look like something a regular guy would carry around, was on the trunk floor.

I had plenty of firepower. More than I'd need for one target.

There were two envelopes on the front seat. The first contained a picture of Ahlberg. There'd be time to deal with that later. I turned my attention to the other envelope, which contained a single sheet of paper with two lines of text.

*Riley Logan.*

And an address.

I punched the address into the GPS and adjusted the mirrors while the computer mapped my route. It estimated the drive at two hours and forty minutes. Good thing I napped on the plane.

Highway miles comprised most of the drive. The M25 led me counterclockwise around the northwest part of London. Traffic was stop and go, even at the early hour. Maybe there was an event that morning. Perhaps the heavy flow was normal. I made it through the herd, hopped on the M1, and drove north, exiting about halfway between Nottingham and Sheffield. From there a series of turns onto increasingly narrower roads guided me to my destination. I wasn't sure which towns I'd passed through on the last leg, or even which city I was in at the moment. Odd how GPS did that to me.

The car idled at the end of a long gravel driveway that led to a large estate house. The tall iron gates stood open wide enough to pass through. Was this the right place? I waited at the edge of the property for a moment, half-expecting a sentry to come out and check my ID. When no one arrived to vet me, I grabbed the piece of paper with Bear's name on it and re-confirmed the address. Things didn't add up. The house looked like it had been built a century or two ago. The well-maintained lot was several acres with an impressive garden through the middle and around the house.

"What have you gotten yourself into, Bear?"

The tires crunched on the gravel as I rolled forward. The driveway curved and circled in front of the house. I took the empty spot amid the four luxury vehicles parked there. All were more expensive than the A8.

It felt as though I was being watched from every direction as I crossed the driveway to the front door. I scanned the area looking for security cameras and rooftop guards. I didn't find any sentries posted, but the four cameras mounted to the house seemed to ignore me.

The double doors were solid oak, each ten feet high and five feet wide. They dwarfed anyone who passed through. I rang the bell and waited as the chimes echoed throughout the hidden foyer.

There were a number of scenarios that could play out here. It hadn't escaped my mind that Frank could've made this my final destination. I waited in anticipation with my hand around my back, resting on the .45.

The door made no noise as it opened. Surprising for such an old house. Sunlight pervaded the space, but beyond that it was too dim to see. A face I hadn't seen in some time appeared. She looked shocked at first, then her eyes settled. She bit her lip.

"Jack? I wasn't expecting to see you any time soon."

Sasha looked beautiful, perhaps more so now than our last encounter. Of course, most of the time I'd spent with her had been while working. Even our casual time together had been in the midst of a job. I recalled the last time we spoke. It was around the time of my incident with Frank. Sasha had asked me to return to London with Mia. She offered to start a life with me.

And I had turned her down.

"It's me," I said. "But, what are you doing here?"

She blushed, tucking a wayward strand of hair behind her right ear. "This belongs to my family."

"Are you done with MI6? I mean, you're looking at a three hour commute from here to Legoland."

"Done? Not exactly. Took a post here. Less stress." She smiled, shrugged. "Less pay, too. But it's worth it."

I nodded, not sure what to say next. The woman lived for the stress British Intelligence put on her. It didn't seem right that she would semi-retire out here.

"I'm sorry, Jack. I just can't figure out what you're doing here. How did you find me?"

"It's not you I'm looking for."

She bit her lip and glanced over her shoulder. Her hair fell across her face as she turned back toward me. She brushed it aside, keeping her finger at her temple.

I could tell by the look on her face that I should've chosen my words more carefully. "Sorry, I didn't mean it like that. It's just, I'm—"

"You're here for Bear."

Almost as if on cue, he lumbered down the hallway into the light.

"Babe, what's taking so long? Need to get the kiddo settled so we…" His gaze swept past her and settled on me. He froze where he stood, arms locked with his hands in front, mouth hanging open an inch. Looked as though he'd seen a ghost. Perhaps that's what he figured me for.

"Big man," I said. "How the hell are you?"

"Jack." He remained still for a moment, then hurried past Sasha, throwing the door open wide.

I couldn't escape the ensuing hug. It didn't matter how we made our living, how tough we were supposed to be, Bear and I had a bond that was stronger than blood.

He moved his paws to my shoulders, and held on as he stepped back, leaving a few feet of space between us. "Damn, it's good to see you."

"You, too."

He let me go and moved to the side. The smile faded as his eyes narrowed. His gaze darted around the courtyard. "How'd you find me?"

"I didn't," I said, hesitant to go into further detail with Sasha standing there.

All it took was a quick glance in her direction, and she picked up on the reason for my hesitation.

"What's going on?" she said. "If you're here for any reason other than a family reunion, I need to know about this."

I looked at her, then Bear, and shook my head. "I wish I could fill you in, Sasha, but I can't. Not at this point. It's—"

"Jack?"

The voice of an angel.

Bear and Sasha both straightened, their eyes fixed on me.

The girl approached apprehensively, looking at me much the way Bear had. What had they been told about me? Were they led to believe that I had died? I studied Sasha for a tell, anything that indicated she was made nervous by my presence. After a few seconds I shifted my focus to the girl I hadn't seen in months.

"Mandy," I said. "I swear you're taller every time I see you. Practically a woman now, aren't you?"

She smiled, said nothing while inching closer.

"Are you living here?" I looked to Bear for confirmation. He nodded. "You going to school here?"

She crossed the final few feet quickly, throwing her arms around me in a hug that rivaled Bear's. "I go to a boarding school that's close enough I'm actually able to spend most nights here. But I'm well-protected there."

"I've taken care of that," Sasha said. "If she's not here, there's security around her."

Mandy handled the situation like a pro. I couldn't see a trace of fear or doubt on her face. In her, I saw a future Fed, if that was the route she wanted to take. And at the same time, there was still a hint of childhood wonder and a softness about her. Balance, I supposed. She'd been through so much. Most people, if they had faced everything she had, would give in, give up, let life harden them to the point they lashed out in ways that led to trouble. Mandy traversed a different path. One uniquely her own. And she was guided by the best man I knew.

Bear grabbed Mandy and Sasha and pulled them close. "Babe, why don't you take Mandy and help her get ready for the week. I think Jack and I need to talk."

Sasha's protests were neutralized as Bear ushered her and the girl down the hallway. He returned to the foyer, leaned up against the banister, draping a large arm over the railing.

"Can't imagine you're here for any good reason," he said. "What do you say we head into town and talk about it over a beer?"

# 9

THE TAVERN STOOD ALONE AT THE EDGE OF TOWN, APART FROM THE LONG TWO-sided row of shops that stretched through the center. One of the two white-haired gentlemen at the bar nodded at Bear. A bald man close by leaned against the opposite side of the bar, next to a line of eight taps. He greeted Bear with a smile, and nodded at me.

I figured the big man was a bit of a curiosity in the locals-only town, so it was no surprise that the three men stared at his American friend. But they weren't a threat, so I ignored them.

Bear led me to a corner table, away from the old guys and the front door. A brunette woman in her early thirties stopped by the table to take our order. She was attractive, in a plain way. Nothing remarkable, and nothing unpleasant about her. She left us, slipped behind the bar, and grabbed a couple mugs. Bear and I sat in silence until she returned with two pints.

I took a sip of an imperial stout so dark it looked black, from a brewery I'd never heard of but which had probably been in existence since the early rule of Queen Victoria. Might've been the best stout I ever had. A couple more, and I might strike up an English folk song I'd learned from my old man with the old guys at the bar.

Bear set his mug to the side, cleared his throat.

I didn't wait for him to start talking.

"So you and Sasha?"

He nodded, eyes aimed toward the front door. "Crazy, right?"

"Yeah, it kind of is, actually."

He took a long pull from his mug, wiped away the frothy head from his mustache, leaving a small piece to trail down his beard before dwindling away.

"Look, Jack, I know there was something between you two. And I don't want you to think I didn't consider that. But, you know, things happen." He turned his hands palms up on the table. "And this just…happened."

"First, there really wasn't anything between us. Yeah, I liked her at one time. And she liked me at one time. You know that. But we were ships that passed on either side of a deadly current. We weren't meant to be."

He held his glass in front of him, stared into it, said nothing.

"Also, I wouldn't have expected you to hold back because she and I didn't work out. I know you're not gonna take pity on someone because I'm an idiot. You deserve happiness, big man. If Sasha makes you happy, then that's great, and I am one hundred percent behind you."

"That's good, 'cause we're getting married."

I wasn't expecting to hear that, but I couldn't let the shock show in my expression.

"Get out of here." I smiled and leaned forward. "When?"

"Six months. It'll be a small thing." He glanced away, his smile faded. He placed his hand on the top of his head, appeared to wince. "And because of that, I have to turn you down. Let's have a couple beers and catch up. But then you have to leave."

I drained the remaining stout from my glass and held it up for the waitress. She came over, took both our mugs and disappeared behind the bar again.

"Am I that transparent?" I said.

He nodded.

"Don't think I'd be tracking you down and coming out here just to check up on a friend?"

"There's no way you should've found me here. I'm using an alias. Mandy goes to school under an alias. There's no record of us entering the UK. We're ghosts, man."

The waitress returned with our beers and a basket of chips.

"So, how'd you do it?" he asked. "Who's involved in this? Am I gonna have to pick up and move again?"

"Depends," I said, popping a couple chips into my mouth. I savored the saltiness for a few seconds. "Frank Skinner is how I found you."

Shaking his head, Bear stared down at the table. "Working for that son of a bitch again?"

"It's a long story."

"Well, I got a fresh beer in front of me. I wanna hear all of it."

I told him about the day I almost killed Frank. How I looked at Mia, and couldn't pull the trigger. Afterward, I left her with my brother, Sean, then drifted state to state for a while. Days turned into weeks. Weeks into months. Eventually I found my way to a small place named Texline, Texas. All because the Jeep died. I explained the events that happened there. Seeing Reese McSweeney again and making plans to disappear together. Only thing was someone made sure that didn't happen.

"So Frank's guys apprehended me," I said. "Flew me out of Texas and took me to him. We met in the old SIS building."

"It no longer exists, right?"

"It never did."

"You know what I mean, man. It's officially shut down."

I nodded. "As far as anyone knows, I guess. It wasn't like the old building was in use, but Frank still had access."

"Why?" Bear said, pushing the empty chip basket to the edge of the table. "Why you? Why now? What's this got to do with me?"

"Katrine Ahlberg," I said.

He searched his memory, shrugged. "Who?"

"The Scandinavian Princess."

A memory flashed in his eyes. "Married to that oil tycoon's kid, uh, Khalid Awad, right?"

I nodded, waited for him to continue.

"They were huge terrorist supporters, and some believed they dabbled themselves. We took care of her."

"We thought we did."

He held his glass inches from his mouth, leaned forward. His eyes were wide, and his brow rose up, creating a dozen wrinkles across his forehead. "What do you mean?"

"Did you know Katrine had a twin?"

He rolled his eyes up. "I don't recall that."

"Yeah, me either. It's true, though. I don't know how we didn't have this information a decade ago."

"Let me guess," Bear said. "The sister's causing problems now and they want us to take care of her."

"Kinda."

"I'm out." He pushed back from the table, and crossed his thick arms over his chest, his beer still in hand.

"Wait a sec, man."

"I'm not gonna rehash the past, Jack. This isn't my battle. Hell, it's not yours either."

"We screwed up, Bear."

He straightened up, set his mug down on the table, lining it up with a previous ring of condensation. "How?"

"We got Birgit. Understand? We took out the twin sister. Blame it on bad intelligence, whatever. Fact is we did it. Afterward, Katrine went into hiding, and eventually resurfaced as her sister. They're saying that she's resuming operations. Anonymously, for now. At least, she thinks she's covering her tracks. Which presents a golden opportunity to Frank and all the other higher-ups who have a lot to lose if this gets out."

"Christ." Bear looked like someone had taken a bat to his stomach. "We took out an innocent woman, and a monster still lurks just offshore."

"Pretty much. And someone's afraid that the wrong person is gonna find out. And if they do, we're all dead."

"Who?"

"I can only guess. It's really not important, though. This needs to be cleaned up. If it's not, Frank is gonna do everything in his power to lay the blame at our feet. He already found you once, so I don't think going into hiding is gonna do any good."

"We executed orders," he said. "They can't blame us for this. There had to be a mole. Someone had to have given her a head's up."

"I agree. Frank agrees. Doesn't mean we won't be fingered for it. This needs to be taken care of and it has to be done quietly."

"Shit." He grabbed the basket and ran a fingertip along the lining, collecting up any remaining salt.

"Agreed."

"Has to be us?"

"You want to stand trial for treason? Or worse, disappear into a holding cell buried deep in the middle of farmland, never to be heard from again?"

He blinked hard a couple times. "Doesn't sound appealing to me."

"Me either."

We sat there for a few moments. I homed in on the music, some kind of modern folk rock. Hadn't heard it before.

"How do I break this to Sasha?" Bear said. "She's not gonna go along with this."

"Be as truthful as you can without telling her the truth."

Bear smiled. "Easy for you. You don't know how her gaze levels me, man."

I felt bad taking him from his new life. I could've managed the job on my own, but with Bear at my side, we were both safer.

"She understands how this all works," I said. "And she got into this relationship with you knowing full well that you worked with me in the past. She knows what you've done. There was always a chance it could come back to haunt you."

"What's to stop her from digging in and figuring this out? Damn, man, if she does that, what'll Frank do?"

"We'll both talk to her," I said. "We can make her understand what's at stake here. It's in her best interest to lay low and not mention anything about this."

"I hope you're right." He held up his glass and the waitress returned to our table with another round. "Let's not talk about this anymore. We'll get started in the morning."

And with that, Bear was in.

All in.

And so was I.

# 10

WE STEPPED OUTSIDE MID-AFTERNOON AMID THE BUSTLE OF RELEASE FROM school. Parents ushered the kids down the street, from the bakery to the butcher to the deli. Some argued, others laughed. Life carried on no matter what. The constant opening of the deli and bakery doors left a lingering smell on the cool breeze that reminded me of New York. I glanced up at the watery sun, hiding behind a veil of gray clouds. It offered little in the way of additional warmth.

"That's odd," Bear said, his eyes loosely fixed on the sidewalk.

I took a quick look around without being too obvious. Noticed it, too.

"Ever seen that car before?" I said.

"Nope," he said.

"Ever seen those men before?"

"Nope."

"Things like this always happen whenever I show up someplace new."

"Yep."

The men could've had a thousand reasons to be parked on the side of the road a half-block away from the tavern. Perhaps it had been coincidence that the driver started the engine after we exited the tavern. Maybe they idled there because they waited on a friend, or one of their wives. But they looked even more out of place than me and Bear.

"You trust Frank?"

"Hell no," I said. "I told you, I would've killed him that day had Mia not been present. The son of a bitch has hung me out to dry on more occasions than I care to recall."

"What's your feeling here?" Bear stopped in front of a store window. The car stood out in the reflection. "I mean, you think he arranged this to get us both in the same place? Take us out at the same time?"

"It's crossed my mind."

"And?"

"He had me in the old SIS building. Alone. He could have killed me there. And disposed of me there. The only people who knew my identity in Texas were either swept away by witness protection, or are now dead. As I sat there in his old office, there wasn't a soul alive who knew my whereabouts."

The car pulled away from the curb. Both men stared at us as they drove past. They didn't go far. A block or so was all before pulling over again. This time the passenger got out and went inside a store.

"And Frank obviously knew where you've been hiding out," I said. "He's head of the SOG now. He could've had someone sitting on you, waiting to take you out when the right opportunity presented itself. My guess is out here that wouldn't have been too difficult to do."

"Maybe those guys over there are SOG," he said, turning toward the sedan, leaning back against the glass.

"Maybe," I said, mirroring his movements. "But instead, he put us together. He knows as well as anyone that as a team, we're damn near indestructible."

He ran a hand through his hair. "I don't feel so indestructible these days."

"Neither do I," I said with a quick laugh. "Pain lingers on a hell of a lot longer than it used to."

"Right. It's like, why won't that bruise go away, or that cut heal? I swear, this getting old shit is for the straights, man."

"Retirement doesn't sound like such a bad idea."

"You'd get bored."

"Have you?"

He nodded. "Sometimes, at least. Mandy and Sasha keep it interesting, though."

I forced a cough, covered my mouth. "He's back."

The guy exited the store carrying a large paper bag. He turned his head toward us for a quick glance. Wasn't more than a second, but in this case, that was a second too long.

"Let's move," Bear said, not waiting for me. The big man picked up the pace and closed in on the car.

What did the guy have in that bag? He could have retrieved a weapon from inside the store, one meant to kill us. Whether Bear had considered that, I had no idea. And I couldn't leave him to face the situation alone. I sprinted across the street and caught up with him.

The man opened the passenger door, threw the bag into the backseat and managed to get most of his body in as the driver accelerated away from the curb quickly. The guy's shoe got caught and was pulled off his foot as the tires fought to gain traction on the road. Their high-pitched scream resulted in a pair of black tracks left behind.

Bear knelt down and tossed the shoe to me.

"Fancy," I said. "Don't find many spooks wearing shoes like this. In fact, I don't think I've met one, even among the mob guys. No one wants to spill blood on a thousand dollar pair of shoes. Let alone try to run away in them."

The car was out of sight. Those who had witnessed the scene moved on.

"Who do you suppose they are?" Bear asked.

"Can't even begin to speculate," I said. "Maybe someone was tipped off to my presence, though I can't imagine how."

"Yeah, right." Bear looked over at me. Did he trust me anymore? It was a genuine question considering how long we'd been away from each other, and how much his life had changed.

"Like I said, if Frank wanted me dead, he would've been better off doing it in that building and not after we were together."

We maintained a heightened sense of vigilance on the way back to the estate. I repositioned the 9mm for quick access, and gave Bear the .45. As the house drew near, it became clear we weren't going to encounter the men again unless they were waiting for us inside.

Bear closed and locked the heavy iron gates behind us. They wouldn't stop someone determined on getting in, but it sure as hell would slow them down and relegate them to approaching on foot.

We stopped in front of the door. Bear leaned against the one on the left, held the handle, but didn't open it up.

"I don't know how this is going to go," he said.

"Probably not well," I said.

"And we're gonna have to tell her to leave here for a while," he said. "I just don't trust what we saw in town."

"Agreed." I glanced back at the road as a white car passed. "Does she have somewhere she can slip away for a couple days?"

Bear nodded. "Let's get this over with."

A few minutes later we were settled at the table, with Bear sitting next to Sasha, holding her clenched hands in his. He told her as much as he could, emphasizing that there was no choice in the matter. We had to leave, and so did she and Mandy.

"Hell no, Riley." Sasha rose, tipping her chair over. It hit the floor with a loud bang. She grabbed her cell phone and shoved it in her pocket.

"Sasha," Bear said, moving in front of her to stop her from storming off. "I don't have a choice. We don't have a choice. Don't you think if I did I'd tell Jack to pound sand?"

Her cheeks and ears were maroon. Her voice wavered. "Then tell me what you're going to be doing."

"You know how this works," I said. "We can't do that."

"I could find out," she said. "I've got more contacts than both of you combined."

"You do that," I said, "and you'll start a diplomatic nightmare that'll get us all detained and likely killed."

Bear reached for her hand. "This is it. This is the last time. After this, we can just disappear. Christ, I've got the money to make it happen."

"I don't want to disappear," she said. "I like our life here. And besides, you've got..."

He brought a finger up, held it between their mouths. They stared at each other without speaking for several seconds. Sasha appeared resigned to the fact that Bear was leaving, and there was nothing she could do to stop him. Having come up through the ranks of MI6, knowing and seeing men who did what Bear and I did, she understood that we couldn't turn down an assignment. Sometimes, the option simply didn't exist.

She wrapped her arms around him, placed her head against his chest. "Keep yourself safe. Jack, too."

"You, too," he said. "I want you to leave town for a bit. Maybe go to the States until I contact you."

She looked like she wanted to argue, but instead nodded, clenching her mouth tight. She turned and walked away without another word. Bear remained motionless as he watched her disappear around the corner. He knew the risk involved, as did she. And both were aware that could have been their last interaction with each other.

"You OK?" I said.

He said nothing.

"I'm sorry about this, man. Trust me, if there was a way—"

"Just stop," he said. "Let's do what we need to do, and then it's over." He turned to face me. "That includes us."

Things had changed for Bear. It had been a process that had spanned the past couple years, starting with Mandy. He'd found a normal life, or at least something that would pass for guys like us. Everything had been leading up to this moment between us. We'd had similar conversations in the past, but now his mind was made up. Mine, too, in some ways. It was best for everyone if we went our separate ways after this.

I'd become toxic.

And no one was safe around me.

## 11

The steering wheel felt cool in my hand, chilled by the vents that sent streams of neutral, filtered air into my face. We were twenty miles away from the house without a clue as to where we were supposed to go. I figured there'd be travel involved, so London seemed the most appropriate destination. I also assumed that Frank was tracking the vehicle and would wait to contact us until we were sufficiently distanced from Sasha.

Ten minutes later, my phone rang.

"Frank," I said.

"Jack," he said. "How'd things go with Logan?"

I glanced over at the big man. He stared out the window, perhaps thinking of everything he'd left behind. The man loved Sasha and Mandy more than himself. Presumably he questioned why the hell he was sitting next to me driving away from them.

"He's with me," I said. "It wasn't easy, but the gravity of the situation isn't lost on him."

"Good to hear. Let him know that I'm going to provide every last bit of support I can for you two. Unfortunately, that can only be intelligence, not men. I can't get any more involved than I already am. They're watching me non-stop right now. You don't know the lengths I have to go through to even get a call out to you. No other US agent can help either."

"Yeah, I got it. You and them, it'd create clutter anyway. Bear and I work best when it's the two of us." I saw him nod, eyes still fixed on the green fields beyond the road. "I have to ask you something."

"OK?"

"We encountered a couple ghouls in town. Dressed nice. I mean, real nice. I'm talking thousand dollar shoes."

"And?"

"They weren't the kind of guys who dressed like that to impress the company board. Got me? They were like us. Any idea who else might be around?"

I could hear Frank tapping on his laptop keyboard. He didn't have to ask me to explain any further. He'd spent enough time in this business that he'd developed the eye for picking out another killer. "I'm not getting anything. You get a good look at the guys?"

"Just one," I said. "He got out of the car. Spanish, maybe Italian. Short dark hair. Short beard. Like I said, dressed nice."

"Coincidence, maybe?"

"Nah, they were watching us."

"You sure Bear hasn't gotten into anything while there?"

I lowered the phone. "Bear, you dealing drugs or weapons or anything like that out here?"

The big man laughed. "Tell Frank to go fuck himself."

"I heard that," Frank said.

"He said go fuck yourself, Frank."

"Yeah, I think I got that." He banged on his keyboard a bit more. "I'll put some feelers out, but right now I'm not seeing any activity out there. Maybe it was a couple crooks who were thinking of shaking you down."

"Us?" I said, picturing the sight of Bear and me on the sidewalk. A linebacker and his defensive tackle ready to gobble up the trash so I can bring down the runner. "You serious?"

Bear and I were the last two people a couple of thieves would look at and decide to rob. But I could see this wasn't getting us anywhere, so I cut it short.

"So what's the deal?" I said. "Where's our girl?"

"I'm gonna text you some information soon. Just keep heading toward London while I finalize your travel arrangements. Trying to keep you out of the air so you can hang onto your weapons and phones."

"In other words you don't have a solid contact for us at our destination."

Frank ignored the question. "I'll hit you up soon."

That was it. The call ended, and we were left waiting for the follow-up from Frank.

After a few minutes, Bear said, "You believe him?"

"About those guys?"

"Yeah."

"I don't know. I mean, they didn't fit the bill for the kind of dudes that'd be after us, and they weren't common criminals. Not with those shoes. Not dressed like that."

"I'm just gonna file it away for now," Bear said.

I agreed. We had to focus on what was ahead of us. If those guys showed up again, we'd deal with it then.

The text arrived from Frank. I read it aloud to Bear. It contained three bits of information.

*Lowestoft. Yacht club marina. Captain Shue.*

A follow-up message a few seconds later said Frank would reach out to us again soon.

In other words, don't attempt to make contact. I wondered who was on his ass over this, and what they would do if we failed. Or worse, if we were caught out here.

"Feels like we're playing a damn game," Bear said. "What's next? Searching an old manor house for a damn butter knife?"

The thought had occurred to me, too. And it left me questioning whether Frank knew more than he let on about the men we saw in town. I know he didn't plant them there to keep an eye on us. He had the Audi to keep track of me. So why were they there? And was their presence the reason why he was doling information out in bits? Did he send me into this mess knowing that the situation was hotter than he'd let on? Fact was we wouldn't talk if caught. And we couldn't if we didn't know everything.

"Wonder how much this Captain Shue is gonna tell us?" Bear said.

"I doubt much, if anything. Probably doesn't know anything more than what Frank told him. I'm guessing he'll ferry us on to our next stop. Another contact. Another bit of information. Hell, we'll probably make our way all across Europe in this manner."

He laughed. "Wait until Sasha finds out. She'll bitch me out for taking her dream honeymoon without her."

"Hear from her yet?"

He nodded. "She texted me on my cell a little while ago. Apologized for the dramatics. Said she understands the position we're in. Said to let her know if we get caught in a bind and she'd put everything she could on it."

That would be a disaster. Not only would that pinpoint our location at the time, but it'd land her in a world of trouble.

"If only we could get away with that," I said. "Frank has someone watching her every move now. The moment she logs onto her computer they'll record every keystroke."

"She knows it." Bear rolled down his window and stuck his hand into the stiff breeze. "And I'm sure she has ways around it. Whatever she does, she'll take care to be clandestine about it."

Bear reset the GPS with our new destination, then found a jazz station.

"You remembered," I said.

He shook his head. "How could I forget?"

# 12

THE YACHT CLUB LOOKED SIMILAR TO ANY OTHER I'D SEEN. THE FEW CARS parked in the lot were upward of a hundred grand each. The few people we saw that weren't front-line employees were dressed in clothing brands I'd never wear. Little whales on their pastel shirts. It wasn't until we got to the marina docks that we saw working men scrubbing decks and hauling gear. Yacht crews hired by millionaires.

A silent wind blew cool air across the sea, disrupting the surface with small white caps. The boats rocked in their slips. Grey clouds bunched together above.

We stopped a worker for directions. "We're looking for Captain Shue?"

He pointed in the direction he'd come from. "Last row, last slip on the right."

"How'd you like to own one of these?" Bear said as we passed what was easily a twenty-five million dollar boat.

"Can't imagine the fuel costs," I said. "And I'm not too keen on having a full-time crew, which you'd probably need on a vessel like that. I mean, I guess you could do it alone, but it'd be a pain. What's the point of having a boat like that if you're not relaxed while on board?"

"I guess I see your point," he said, gaze still fixed on the boat. "Still, it'd be nice to set off in one of those."

I spotted a white and blue catamaran and pointed toward the vessel. "That's more my style. Can sail or use the engine. Big enough for an ocean crossing. Plenty of room for a family. Perfect for the Caribbean and island hopping."

He nodded, staring down at the catamaran like it was a target as we passed. "How much would something like that go for?"

"Probably as low as quarter of a million used, maybe a bit less if you're willing to put a little work into it. If buying new, half a million to a million would get you a pretty nice one."

"You always talk about this, Jack. Retiring on a boat or an island. Why haven't you? Christ, I know money isn't the issue unless you've taken up losing at gambling recently."

"I guess I just haven't had the chance." I glanced up at the thickening clouds after hearing the crack of thunder. "Something always happens. Even when I cut down my ties to no one, something frickin' happens and I'm caught up in a mess like this one. Penance for the crimes I've committed."

"We committed," Bear said.

I shrugged. "Don't take responsibility for me and my actions."

"They were all sanctioned." He held his arm out in front of me as though we were in the car and he'd slammed on the brakes.

I stopped, turned and faced him. "Yeah? What about all those ones we did for the love of money?"

He broke his stare long enough to tell me he didn't truly believe what he said. "Ain't no one we took out that didn't deserve it."

"That's true." I looked out over the sea. It had darkened with the increased cloud cover. "But it doesn't make it right."

Bear rotated his head until his neck popped. Another tell. "If we didn't do it, someone else would've. Better we got paid for taking out the trash. At least that's how I think of it."

"I suppose."

"No supposing, man. That stuff is in the past. You got a little one to think about, just like me with Mandy. We've made a good bit of coin. Put it to use after we finish this. Get away from this life. Far enough away that these people can't reach you anymore."

His thoughts echoed my innermost dialogue. Finish this, then it's time to move on.

"Problem is," I said, "they've got long arms. Long enough to reach anywhere we can travel."

Bear hiked his thumb up and toward the catamaran. "Get on one of those and you're as good as a ghost."

The sun hovered over the horizon to the west, peeking through a break in the clouds. We had thirty minutes or so of light left.

"Look," Bear said with a simple gesture.

I tossed a quick glance toward the sunset again and spotted a car making its way through the parking lot. I'd seen it earlier that day.

"Is that...?"

"Yup," he said. "Sons of bitches from earlier."

"They gotta be Frank's guys then."

"Call him."

I pulled out the phone and navigated to the recent calls list. "Dammit, blocked number."

"You don't have another number for him?"

"Not that I'd compromise this phone by dialing. Come to think of it, the only number I can recall for him is almost ten years old. I'm pretty sure it went away along with the SIS."

The yacht club parking lot had filled up about halfway. The sedan snaked around cars, headed toward the marina entrance. They drove past our position. It didn't appear that they had spotted us.

"You wanna wait on them?" Bear asked. "Or move?"

We were close to the last pier. "Let's move. Maybe we can find this guy before they find us."

"Afraid of a little confrontation?"

"We don't know these guys, Bear."

He laughed. "Never stopped us before. You tired of fighting?"

A little of the Bear I knew had returned. I hoped by morning the rest of him would show up. It'd be easier to wrap this up with my partner beside me.

"I'm just willing to take the door that leads out," I said. "I'm assuming these guys tracked us via the car. Maybe that's Frank's doing. Perhaps Frank's guy in London was a plant."

Bear considered this for a moment. "For who, though?"

"Pick an acronym. Could be British Intelligence, terrorists, I really don't know. Could be on Sasha's payroll and all this is to make sure I'm not in country to screw up any plans. Maybe Ahlberg. It's possible they are Frank's guys after all. But I got a feeling that once we're on a boat out of here, we'll shake free of them for good."

I looked back and spotted the sedan parked in a spot close to the marina entrance. The men hurried toward the building.

"Let's move," I said.

We traveled down the final pier. Most of the boats there were darkened. They rocked amid the small surf. A couple had lights on in their cabins, or string lights illuminating the deck. There was conversation and laughter and drinks being poured and glasses clinking. An elite world oblivious to what was happening around them.

Bear stopped, turned around. He had his hand on the sidearm tucked in his waistband.

"What is it?" I said.

"Thought I heard something," he said.

I looked back, saw nothing. "There's some deckhands up ahead."

We approached the young men.

"Captain Shue," Bear said. "Where can we find him?"

One of them pointed toward the last boat. Right where we expected the man to be. The vessel looked to be about a forty-footer. As we approached, I noticed the stencil along the side. It read Captain Shue. It wasn't a person we had been sent to look for. It was a boat.

"Hello?" Bear leaned against the ramp. The rails creaked and bowed out under his heft. "Anyone up there?"

A man stepped out of the shadows onto the sunset painted deck. He had long, dark hair and a beard to match that covered his neck.

"We received a message from a mutual friend to find the *Captain Shue*," I said.

He reached into his pocket. I grabbed the butt of my pistol. He smiled, pulled out his cell. He swiped the screen a few times, glanced at us, back at the phone and then at us again. Finally, he gestured for us to board.

He jutted his chin toward the end of the pier after we'd boarded. "Friends of yours?"

I steadied myself and adjusted to the rocking. I saw the men hurrying toward us.

"Christ," Bear said.

"They've been following us," I said to the man.

"Then I guess we should get moving," the man said. "Either of you have sailing experience?"

"I do," I said.

"Then you can help me."

There wasn't much needed to get the boat moving. The guy had been expecting us and was prepared to depart. The men following us must've noticed the flurry of activity. They started running, and drew their weapons two slips away. We were already a hundred feet out by the time they reached where we'd been docked. The Italian looking guy extended his pistol toward us. His partner forced the guy's arm down before he could get a shot off.

A few minutes later my adrenaline settled. The men wouldn't catch us now, even if they commandeered a ship. My phone buzzed in my pocket.

"You guys safe on the boat?" Frank said.

"Barely," I said.

"How so? What happened?"

I strained to see the marina in the fading light. It looked like a black bump against a veil of deep purple.

"The guys we ran into in town showed up," I said. "You find anything out yet?"

"Nothing," he said. "We've been monitoring for any kind of chatter, but there hasn't been a single lead."

"You're not screwing with me, right, Frank?"

"You think they're my guys?" He laughed. "You'd be dead already if they were. Hell, I could've taken you out when we met."

"I wouldn't put it past you."

"Jack, take a second and think this through. This snafu doesn't just affect you and Logan. My ass is on the line. Everything I've worked for, that I've built, my new position, it's all on the verge of falling apart. Hell, I'm the architect of the original damn mission. I'll go down as hard, if not harder, than you two. So get this through your thick skull. I am on your side, one hundred percent. You fail, I'm done. I have more than a vested interest in this situation."

I watched Bear take a sip from a beer bottle and gestured for him to grab me one, too.

"And when this is over?" I said.

"We're through," Frank said. "I'm shredding all your files, physical and digital. You won't exist anymore."

"I have your word?"

"Yes, you have my word."

"And what's that worth these days?"

I hung up the phone before he could answer. Trust him one hundred percent? I didn't trust him even half a percent. The phone buzzed in my hand. I ignored it. It buzzed again. And again. Eventually I answered.

"What?"

"The hell you want me to say, Jack? Huh? Want me to apologize? All right, I apologize. I'm sorry for every goddamn bad thing I ever did to you. That better?"

"Yeah, sure."

I hung up again, this time tucking the phone away in my bag.

# 13

I'd fallen asleep about an hour after my last conversation with Frank. Bear and I had managed to catch up for a bit. We took the time as an opportunity to forget about the job for a while. To forget about the woman we wrongly killed all those years earlier.

And to forget that there were two men following us, with obviously bad intentions. I had thought we would be free of them after setting sail. Now I doubted we'd seen the last of them.

I woke as the sun crested the sea, painting the waves red. I exited my small cabin and found the captain standing in the wheelhouse. His unwavering eyes stared out over the barren seascape. I wondered if he had slept at all that night.

Bear greeted me on the deck. The steam from his coffee rose up and quickly dissipated on the blustery deck.

"Where can I find some?" I said.

He pointed to the open door. I found the coffee pot and a mug and filled up. It was cheap grounds, but that didn't matter. I took a swig of the earthy brew. The burn on my tongue continued down my throat. Back on the deck I took a seat opposite Bear. A cool breeze washed over the deck. It sprayed us with bits of foam and water. I licked my lips, and savored the salty taste. Reminded me of fishing in the gulf with my brother Sean and sister Molly.

Bear gestured toward the south with his mug, which read "#1 Pop-Pop." I glanced over my shoulder and spotted a narrow beach in front of a long row of trees.

"Where do you think we are?" I said.

"Belgium? Netherlands?" He shrugged. "Considering we're seeing ocean to the east, I'm guessing we're sitting north of the Netherlands."

Made sense. Would we continue on to Ahlberg's native Scandinavia? Was she hiding out there? Frank had provided limited details. Made me uneasy. Every future move hinged on us making it to somewhere else first. Planning was impossible. We were subject to the whims of others.

"Think we're gonna see those guys when we dock?" Bear said.

I had avoided thinking of them most of the morning. "Can't say either way. Guess if we do, we take care of them."

"Have you considered that they might work for Katrine Ahlberg?"

"It's crossed my mind. I mean, the woman has made it almost ten years without anyone suspecting her to be alive. She has had every resource available to her. I wouldn't doubt that she had a considerable amount of money in a numbered account. Maybe she opened a joint account with her sister before we killed the woman. Would have allowed her easy access to funds in the event she was ever on the run."

He uncrossed his arms, leaned forward, nodded. "Probably bought herself a couple hired hands. Reached out to a few Agency contacts. She had to have friends somewhere, right? All that money. Pretty simple to dole out a couple handouts."

"Sure, she had to have someone somewhere. And one of those contacts probably monitored for her name all these years. Frank's good, but there's better out there in other agencies and even other countries."

"If that's the case, then she knows we're coming for her."

I didn't doubt that someone might've tipped her off about the plan to right the wrong of a decade ago.

"That wouldn't be good," Bear said.

"We'll see how things go," I said. "We don't know what her capabilities are at this point. She's been underground. Her forces can't be that large, if she has any at all. If we need more manpower, we get it."

Bear shook his head. "I think you're wrong there, partner. Frank's decided you and I are the equivalent of John Wayne in this flick."

He was probably right. Frank made it seem like his hands were tied. Whether that was due to those above him or of his own accord didn't matter. I knew if we asked for another team, he'd deny the request.

The boat rocked against a series of waves coming in strong from the north. They smashed against the side of the boat. Water rained down on us, and streamed past on the deck.

The captain came down and told us we were heading to shore. He navigated past the barrier islands off the Netherlands's north coast, and led us to a small town called Eemshaven, close to the German border. I had expected we'd have to swim to shore. Instead, he brought us up to land. We docked at an empty pier that stretched a hundred feet. There was no marina nearby. Just a stretch of deserted coast with a couple randomly placed houses.

The man handed me a key. "It's parked nearby. You'll find some new creds in the trunk to use if you have to cross the border."

"Will we need to?" Bear asked.

The man clasped his hands and leaned back, shaking his head. "I know nothing other than what I told you. I had no part in arranging any of this. I'm simply a ship captain."

"This your boat?" Bear asked.

The man gestured toward the pier without a word.

"How far you think we are from Amsterdam?" Bear said as our boots hit land.

"Maybe two hours," I said. "Sounds right if my geography is correct."

"Think that's where we're gonna end up?"

"Wouldn't be the worst thing that's happened, that's for sure."

He laughed for a moment, then regained his composure. We had to remain vigilant. There were at least two forces at work here. Perhaps more than that. Though we had determined that it was possible the men who had followed us worked for Katrine, it was also possible they were agents for another government. Perhaps we'd stumbled upon something they didn't want us delving into.

"Why so close to Germany?" he said. "He said if we have to cross the border. So, I'm thinking our woman is here. At least according to the last intel Frank received."

"Let's get the car and wait on Frank."

There weren't many vehicles along the stretch of the two-lane road. I pressed the unlock button, and the lights on an A6 flashed. Not as fancy as the last vehicle, but it'd do. I held down the trunk button and it popped open.

"Not here," Bear said.

He was right. We might be under surveillance. At the same time, I didn't want to travel far on the creds I flew with. They could be flagged. If we were pulled over that would result in me being detained.

I found an empty parking lot a couple miles down the road where we stopped and inspected the Audi. The vehicle wasn't configured like the last. Everything was under the trunk flap, set on the spare tire. There were IDs and passports for each of us, credit cards, and a few other things. I hated relying on Frank when I had safe deposit boxes spread throughout Europe with my own documents. Using the credit cards Frank provided enabled him to track our every move, from renting a hotel room, down to buying a pack of chewing gum. If we tried to purchase a phone, he'd know. If we got cash out of an ATM, he'd probably assume we were using it for a phone. It would all lead to more questions, which we didn't have time for. We needed answers. Which was why after going through all the documentation in the car, the missing piece of information pissed me off. There was nothing indicating where we had to go.

Then my phone buzzed.

"You got the car?" Frank said.

"Yeah, and our docs," I said. "But you already knew that."

Frank breathed into the phone, said nothing.

"And there's nothing that says where to go, or who to meet."

"You won't be meeting anyone unless I get some new intelligence," he said.

"Gonna tell me where we should be headed?"

"Katrine's last known location was a hideout about an hour from your current position, between the towns of Apeldoorn and Almelo, a couple miles off the E30."

"All right. Can you be a little more specific?"

"Damn right I can," Frank said, a twinge of excitement in his voice. "I'm going to text the coordinates to you."

"Any specific way you want us to handle things when we get there?"

"Yeah. If she's there, kill her. No questions. And if there are others, well, we don't need witnesses. Got it? No survivors. Take everyone out."

"How many others might be there?"

"According to the intel I received, up to five."

"Can I ask who provided that intel?" I pictured a shadowy figure in the woods, and drones flying overhead manned by some guy back in Northern Virginia popping Altoids like they were crack.

"No."

The line went dead. I paced a twenty foot span of the road. A few moments later, a text arrived with the coordinates. We hopped in the car and Bear punched the destination into the GPS.

"You ready for this?" I asked.

He nodded. "Let's get it done."

# 14

The sun burned off the morning fog as we drove inland. The route Bear chose kept us off the main highways. We made use of single lane backroads. In some cases the road was only wide enough for one vehicle. The route kept traffic — and possible witnesses — to a minimum. Would anyone pay attention to two guys in an A6? I doubted anyone would. At least not until we exited the vehicle.

After an hour on the road, we closed in on the coordinates. The narrow road morphed into two dirt lines. We followed them into a densely wooded area. The thick foliage hindered the sun's attempt to shine light through.

Our destination drew near. The dirt tracks faded as grass overtook the ruts. An old house stood amid a clearing at the end of the path. Weathered wood siding hung at odd angles. Patches of shingles were missing on the roof. Years of sun and wind and rain and snow had taken their toll on the place. The windows were in good shape, even though some were boarded over. The front door was closed. Two rocking chairs on the porch faced us. They moved gently in the breeze.

"Looks abandoned," Bear said.

"Doesn't mean it is," I said. "The door, windows, all in good shape. Look, there's fresh flowers in that tin bucket by the steps. Someone's been here."

"Or is here."

We waited outside the clearing for several moments, watching the house, looking for signs of movement within.

"Think we should back up a bit and approach on foot?" Bear asked.

It had merit. If we pulled right up to the house, they'd know we were there. Then again, the car stood in view at that moment, so anyone watching would have spotted us already. Hell, they likely heard the crunching earth under the tires as we rolled up.

"I don't like the idea of the car being too far away," I said. "What if we need to get out in a hurry?"

"Us?" He laughed. "Having to leave in a hurry? Unfathomable."

"Yeah, I know. Wouldn't be the first time."

Bear cracked his window and took a deep breath. "Wood smoke."

I smelled it, too. "It's not heavy. Seems distant."

He rolled his window down the rest of the way and stuck his pistol out. "All right, pull right up and lets bum rush this place."

I pulled into the clearing and turned the steering wheel hard. The vehicle whipped in a circle and now faced the dirt road. Bear hopped out first, with me right behind him. We split up in front of the house. He went right. I went left. We worked our way around. A simple yell was all it would take to notify the other of danger.

The shrubs along the side of the house were unruly. Appeared they hadn't been touched in years. The grass was long and brown. It was bent in places. Laid flat in others. Animals passing through, perhaps staying for a night. The backyard was no better. There were heavy, rusted chains snaking through the high grass. They were attached to thick iron spikes in the middle of the yard.

Bear stepped out from the corner. His gaze swept the yard. His expression changed as he followed the chains. Looked like his top lip rose in a snarl. We met near the back door.

"Dogs?" He lifted one of the chains with his foot.

"Don't see any other evidence of them." I picked one of the leads off the ground. "Look at the grass here. It's stamped down like the chain has been laying on it for weeks or months."

He pressed against the sliding door, hands cupped around his eyes, positioned on the glass. "Abandoned." He rocked the slider until the latch popped. The door grated as it slid along the dirty track. The smell that emanated from the house rivaled that of a freshly run-over skunk. It burned my sinuses, my eyes, my throat.

Bear backed up, gagging. He bent over, hands on his knees, and dry heaved a few times.

"Christ," he said. "What the hell is that?"

"If I had to guess," I said, lifting my shirt over my face, "I'd say a dead body."

I pictured Ahlberg's rotting corpse on a defiled bed. We wouldn't be that lucky. Never had been. Doubt we'd start now.

A minute or so passed and we somewhat adjusted to the nauseating fumes. With our mouths and noses covered with our shirts, Bear and I headed inside. I took aim at the staircase and shot Bear a hand signal for him to check the downstairs.

"We might as well talk," he said. "If anyone's here — and I doubt anybody could live with that smell —they heard my gastrointestinal pyrotechnics just now."

"I'm going up," I said. "Be on the lookout for a basement or trap door down here. And watch out for traps."

The place had all the markings of a hideaway, which meant whoever stayed here might not want intruders to get to them. I tossed a double glance at every square inch I passed.

The rickety stairs felt like they were going to collapse under my weight. I stepped on the sides rather than in the middle. The putrid smell intensified with every foot higher I rose. A thick layer of dust coated the second floor landing. The hard wood floors had been painted orange in the past. Heavy scratches along the edge wore past the paint. A hallway stretched left and right. A single closed door waited at either end. I started with the one on the right.

The floorboards creaked with every step. The walls were coated in yellow. A heavy smoker had lived here. I watched the gap between the floor and door for shadows. White light lit up the space. Nothing moved. I stopped in front of the door. The knob turned freely. I pushed the door slowly and its hinges creaked low like an old man humming out of tune.

The barren walls were the same yellow-tinged white. The hardwood floor hadn't been painted. There was no furniture or mattress. The room was empty. Not even so much as a scrap of paper littered the floor.

I made my way to the other end of the hall, moving slowly past the stairs and glancing down. I called out to Bear. "Doing all right down there?"

"Yeah, got something to show you."

"Let me clear this other room, then I'm coming down."

The smell intensified with every step. My shirt did nothing to camouflage it now.

I looked down. There was no light in the space between the floor and the door. Had someone put a towel down? Were the windows blacked out? I prepared myself for what might wait in the room. Pictured a body, maybe two. The door was locked. I didn't bother to announce my intentions. There wasn't anything living in there anyway. I kicked the door. It broke at the lock, swung open and slammed into the wall.

I aimed my pistol into the dark. Light slowly flooded the room. In the back corner, I spotted the source of the smell. I leaned back, took a deep breath and held it in. I entered the room and looked for anything that might offer any clues. There was nothing. I closed the door behind me and headed downstairs.

Bear waited in the kitchen. "Well?"

"Found what's causing the smell."

"A body?"

I looked out back, and nodded toward the chains.

"Christ," he said. "The dogs?"

"What'd you find?"

"No basement. No trap doors. Pretty plain house, and I can't imagine that anyone has stayed here long."

"What was it you wanted to show me?"

He laid down a piece of paper on the counter. It was only a few words, but with it we'd leave with more information than what we arrived with.

*Amsterdam. Hotel Grand. Room 815. 11 AM.*

# 15

We were forty miles from Amsterdam. The GPS provided us with the most direct route, and we took it. All the backroads would lead us to the same place, just at a slower pace. Chances of getting stopped were higher in the city anyway. Bear took the wheel. I called Frank.

"Did you get her?" The first words out of his mouth were filled with anticipation. Either he feigned it, or he really had no idea the house was abandoned.

"What kind of surveillance did you do on the place?"

"I just had the coordinates."

"So no drones or monitoring? Frank, don't tell me you didn't at least check satellite images before sending us in there?"

"I can't do that without alerting others." Frank paused for a beat. "Others are a bad thing here, Jack. You know that. I'm as blind as you on this."

"Yeah, well at least you're not out here walking around with your dick in your hand trying to figure out if you're gonna get shot up the moment you step foot out of the car."

Frank exhaled, started to speak, but thought better of it.

"When was the last time she was there?" I said.

"You didn't find her then," Frank said.

"The place was deserted. Nothing there but a couple of dead dogs."

"Dead dogs?" He paused for a few seconds. His breathing was erratic, like he was running down a set of stairs. "How fresh were the bodies?"

"To be honest, I didn't investigate them all that closely. Back to my question, when was the last time she was there?"

"Hang on a sec." The wind howled through his phone. It seemed whatever he had to say, had to be said away from his office.

We hugged the highway onramp as Bear pushed the A6 to its limit. The tires squealed their displeasure. I braced myself against the door.

Frank came back on the line. "I don't have a date. The information came secondhand from a source I've only recently vetted."

"You sent us there with what could have been false intel from some guy you met at the track?"

Bear glanced over at me. I shook my head and waved him off.

"No," Frank said. "He's a solid source. He was a part of her group until recently."

"You better be damn sure he's still not a part of it, Frank. They could be playing us, especially if she knows it was us that executed the original hit."

"Jesus, don't you think I know that? The guy is solid. He knows about the house because he stayed there with her, up until Ahlberg tried to have him killed. He fled and through one contact or another, we found each other."

I glanced over at Bear and tipped the phone. He nodded, indicating he'd heard the important bits of the conversation. I couldn't put it on speaker. Frank would know and he'd clam up.

"Where is this guy now?" I asked.

Frank stammered something indecipherable, then hesitated. "I can't locate him."

"Come on," I said.

"I'm working on it, OK? I got a guy over there who's tracking him. The moment we have his location, I'll pass it along and you can work him up."

"This is bullshit, and you know it, Frank." I stared out the window at the passing landscape. A blur of green streamed by. "What do you expect us to do now?"

"I've got a safe house you can hole up in until I have more information."

"That's not good enough." Last place I wanted to go was somewhere Frank could send a team to watch over us. Things already weren't going according to

Frank's plan. The men we encountered in England. Ahlberg not at the deserted woodlands house. Perhaps he was considering conceding defeat on this one. Admit the error, blame it on us, and accept his slap on the wrist.

"I don't know what you expect me to do," Frank said. "I've got nothing, and apparently you didn't uncover anything while investigating the house. We're stuck until we find our contact, or she slips up and is spotted. I'll text you the location to the safe house."

"No, we're gonna work on our own for a bit," I said. "I'll be in touch."

I hung up on Frank mid-sentence. There was nothing else he could say to convince me to follow his orders right then. I pulled the memory cards and tossed the cell phones out the window, leaving us only with Bear's personal phone. Probably should have gotten rid of that too, but the big man wouldn't give it up. It was his only lifeline to Sasha and Mandy.

"We should ditch the car," Bear said.

I agreed. Maybe Frank hadn't been tracking us with the phones. But any car he provided couldn't be trusted.

We were heading into Amsterdam, which was probably the last place Frank wanted us to go. We'd be on the streets, exposed. One false step and our identities could be uncovered, setting off a diplomatic chain of events that might get us killed, and Frank brought up on charges of espionage and treason.

"What kind of backlash do you expect?" Bear said.

I shrugged. "Nothing we can't handle. And if he doesn't know where we are, he can't send anyone to apprehend us. Not like he has people he can use right now. He can't utilize anyone in his own department, and no other agency is going to go out of their way to help him with this situation looming over his head. Leaves him with contractors or guys like us. And as far as I know, we're the only guys like us left for him to reach out to."

We exited the highway and found a car rental store. Bear dropped the Audi off in a nearby parking lot while I settled for a much lesser vehicle. We were in for a crowded ride the rest of the way to Amsterdam.

Bear met me out front. "You gotta be kidding. How are we gonna fit in that thing?" The look of disgust on his face at the small blue car matched the face he made the first time I introduced him to Frank Skinner.

"We've done worse," I said. "Plus, parking will be a lot easier. You see anywhere we can get a couple phones?"

"Yeah, near where I ditched the car."

The vehicle grumbled under our combined weight. It grated against a speed bump at the edge of the parking lot.

"I don't think this jalopy is getting us to Amsterdam," Bear said as we pulled up to the little store.

Inside we grabbed three phones and several SIM cards. We each took a phone for direct communication and to reach out to any old friends who might be able to provide assistance. The third burner would be used to contact Frank. The extra SIM cards were to keep Frank from tracking us.

Bear grabbed a couple packs of beef jerky. I filled up on coffee. We got back on the road. The little car barely moved past seventy-five kilometers per hour. Still, the drive into the city took less time than I expected. The vehicle weaved through traffic effortlessly. The guy at the counter had said it was better than a Beemer. I wouldn't know. Not my preference.

"How do people read these street names?" Bear said. He navigated from a paper map we picked up at the store. Figured it was better that way from now on. Leave no trail for Frank to follow. "I mean, what the hell is wrong with calling it Main Street?"

"I'm sure they say the same thing in the States, big man."

He managed to wade through the street names and directed us to the hotel. We parked two blocks to the south.

The sun shone down from directly above. The alley smelled of fish. The buildings blocked any semblance of breeze, stifling the smell and effectively raising the temperature. I removed my jacket, draped it over my arm. Bear did the same. The average temperature of the country in the summer was only in the low sixties Fahrenheit. Right now it felt every bit of eighty.

We approached the hotel from the east. The breeze finally found us. The sweat on my forehead evaporated. The hotel looked like it had been built a century or two ago. Its gothic design was unlike the surrounding buildings. A relic, I figured. We approached the entrance. A doorman waited in front. He kept his gloved hand out to the side, ready to open the door for the next patron.

"I'm going straight for the elevator," I said. "Any one tries to stop us, you deal with them."

The rectangular lobby was half as wide as it was long. The place smelled like lemon-scented industrial cleaner. The carpet was red and blue with an elaborate design.

There were employees and travelers scattered about the lobby. They stood behind the counter, fake smiles plastered across their faces. Or they sat in ornate chairs, carrying on conversations about their plans for the day. One of the women behind the counter spoke to us. Bear turned to deal with her as I continued on. The elevator doors parted and waited for me. I got on alone, pressed the button for the eighth floor.

Bear turned away from the counter, gave me a slight nod. I saw him head for the stairwell as the doors slid shut.

The old elevator creaked and groaned up the shaft. It wasn't a smooth ride. Felt like I was moving in six-inch bursts. It was a straight shot to the eighth floor. The doors opened, revealing Victorian-style wallpaper and clashing carpet. It was bad enough to make a drunk man stumble while standing still.

Hell, I was sober and started to get the spins.

I stepped out of the elevator, took note of the room numbers and gathered my bearings. A vacuum ran in one of the rooms. A couple of women spoke in Spanish. I pulled my pistol out and slid my jacket over my hand to conceal it. The room was to the right. I started toward it.

I counted the numbers of the rooms ahead. The one I wanted was halfway down. Right before I reached it the stairwell exit door swung open. I tensed and placed free my hand over the jacket, ready to pull it back and let loose with the pistol.

Bear stepped into the corridor. Judging by the way he held his jacket, he had the same idea as me.

I waited for him to saunter down the hall and we stopped in front of the room together.

"Shit," Bear said, reaching out and pushing open the slightly ajar door.

# 16

Bear signaled with his hand. I waited while he leaned back against the wall, stretched his arm out, and opened the door. Chilled air seeped into the hallway. I silently counted three beats, then whipped around the corner with my pistol extended.

The woman standing there dropped the items she was holding as she threw her hands in the air.

"Don't move," I said, advancing toward her. At the end of the short foyer I stopped and checked around the corner.

"Please," she said with a heavy Spanish accent. "I don't want to die."

"Where is she?" I asked the short woman.

She shook her head. Tears streamed down her cheeks. "Who?"

"The blonde woman." I gestured toward the bathroom. "In there?"

"What?" Her hands were shaking. She shifted from foot to foot as though she had to urinate and was trying to keep it in. Her dark skin dampened with sweat. I thought she might pass out soon. "I'm only the maid. There's no one else here."

"Jesus," Bear said from behind me.

I echoed the sentiment.

"You can put your hands down," I said. "When did she leave?"

"Who?" the woman said, lowering her arms and rubbing her hands and wrists as though I'd cuffed her.

I pulled out the little plastic case I'd stored the memory cards in and inserted one into the burner phone. I found a picture of Katrine and showed it to the maid. She leaned in close, placing her clammy hand on mine. I fought the urge to pull away as I watched her face for signs of recognition. She shook her head, pursed her lips together. There were no tells that made it obvious she knew Ahlberg.

"I don't think I've seen her before," the maid said, looking up at me.

I studied her for a second. She was lying. Her pupils were dilated.

"It's in your best interest to be truthful with me," I said. "We know she was here. We know she stayed in this room. I know you saw her."

She looked away. The steel facade faded by the second. "I can't lose my job. I can't."

"No one's going to lose their job here."

"I will," she said. "I'm not supposed to reveal any information about our guests."

"It's OK," I said. "We're investigators. The woman that was here might be in danger. We need to find her before someone else does. Someone very bad. The kind of person you don't want to run into. Now I need you to tell me when she left."

The maid fell back onto the bed. It squeaked as she sank into the mattress. Her gaze drifted to the window, which offered a view of the side of another building.

"They left yesterday afternoon," she said. "It was well after checkout time, and it didn't appear they were checking out. They, or their stuff, should have been here this morning. But it was all gone. And so were they."

"They?" I said. "Who else was with her? And what time is well after checkout?"

"The other woman," she said. "The dark-haired one. And I guess it was around four in the afternoon."

I stepped into the hallway and spotted cameras at each end of the corridor, as well as positioned in front of the elevators. It had been roughly eighteen hours since Ahlberg left. If the hotel used a modern security system, footage from yesterday might still remain on the hard drive.

"I need your help with something," I said.

"What?" she said.

"I need to get to whatever room they keep the security footage."

She shook her head, again trying to look resolute in her defiance toward me. But the way she rubbed her fingers non-stop gave her feelings away. "I don't know what you're talking about."

I walked up to her and knelt a few feet away, putting us eye to eye. "We've already established that I can tell when you're lying."

She glanced down at the floor, back at me. "I told you, I can't lose my job. I've got three kids and my husband passed away just two months ago. This is all I have. If I lose this, I don't know what will happen to us."

I glanced back and nodded at Bear. He reached into his pocket, pulled out his wallet and produced a thick wad of cash.

"Just give us the key to the security room and tell me where to go," I said. "No one will ever know."

She accepted the money and handed over a key ring that she held by a single key. I had feared that the security footage was in the manager's office behind the main counter. Instead, there was a room in the basement.

I pulled out my phone and snapped a picture of the woman. I kept it up for a few seconds as I acted like I was sending it. "There's two men downstairs. If they see your face, you will not go home to your kids tonight. If they see the front desk take a call that results in them contacting security, you will not go home to your kids tonight."

The tears returned and slipped down her cheeks following the dried pathways from minutes ago.

"Understand?" I said.

She nodded. "I'll keep quiet."

We left the maid behind and took the elevator down to the basement level. In retrospect, we'd have been better off using the stairs.

"Maybe we should ask the people at the counter," Bear said. "They might know where Ahlberg was traveling next."

"They won't say," I said. "And they've got less to lose. Even if they know, they're not going to be as easy to overcome. Not like we can go in there, guns out, demanding they tell us. Let's check out this security system and see what we can find."

The doors opened, but instead of a dim basement, we looked out on the lobby. There was nobody there. They must've grown tired of waiting and took the stairs. The lobby looked exactly as we had left it, except for the two police officers at the counter.

"Dammit," Bear said, shifting toward the front corner of the lift. "We should've brought her with us."

The door remained open for what felt like ten minutes. I homed in on the cops. One held a photo out for the staff behind the counter. It was large enough to make out the image.

"They're not here for us." I put my hand on Bear's back and urged him forward. "Go up there to get us a couple rooms and see what you can figure out."

He stepped out, though he didn't seem to want to. Turning, he said, "Jack?" as the doors closed.

They weren't there for us. No, my gut said they were looking for the same woman we were.

# 17

I STEPPED INTO THE DIMLY-LIT BASEMENT. THE YELLOW HUE CAST FROM THE overhead fluorescents made the walls look as though they were stained with urine. If the hotel wasn't so nice, I'd have been sure of it. My eyes adjusted with every step forward. The marks on the wall were old glue from where wallpaper had once been hung. I wondered if they housed people down here at one point in time.

Unevenly-spaced doors lined the narrow corridor. They were marked sequentially, odds on the right, evens on the left. I kept going until I reached number 12. I slid the key into the lock and turned. The bolt slid with a slight click. I pushed the door open and stepped through. The room hummed with electricity. It was ten degrees hotter, and a hundred times brighter. There were twenty-four monitors on the wall. Two for each floor, and four connected to the cameras located at each corner of the lobby. Each screen displayed a continuous feed. The only thing missing were the elevator cameras, but I figured there had to be a way to manipulate the system so they would display.

My guess that the system was hard drive-based was correct. There wasn't any film to worry about. Our chances of seeing Ahlberg leave the hotel increased.

I pulled the plastic container from my pocket and grabbed the other two memory cards. There were multiple computer systems on and underneath a large desk. A yellow-and-black-handled screwdriver was the only other thing on the surface. I had to find which had the footage for the eighth floor and one of the lobby cameras, preferably the one aimed at the elevator.

I started with the monitors and traced their cables back to individual computers. While doing that, I watched the check-in counter. The two police officers remained in the same spot. Bear stood a few feet away from them. He had the attention of one of the employees, but I knew he was listening in on the cops' conversation as best he could. Problem was, unless he'd taken some courses I didn't know about, Bear did not speak Dutch.

I slipped the memory card into the PC tower connected to the eighth monitor. It took a couple minutes to navigate the file system, which was labeled in English. I copied the contents to the memory card.

Before I could retrieve it, the door opened.

The tall, narrow man said something in Dutch. I couldn't make it out. Had a good idea what he'd asked though.

"I'm a technician," I said. "The security company sent me out. Said you might have a faulty hard drive."

He switched to English. "No one told me about this."

"And you are?" I rose and took two steps toward him. We were about the same height, but I was twice as wide.

He stepped back to the safety of the doorway. "One of the managers here."

"Well, I'm surprised they didn't let you know. They booked me over a week ago. I just flew in from Florida. Came straight here."

"Wait here," he said. "I'll be right back."

The door fell shut. I heard the lock click into place. I pulled the card from the reader and turned back to the monitors. The manager exited the elevator and crossed the lobby. He walked past Bear and stopped next to the cops.

Bear turned toward the elevators, looked up at the camera and made a quick gesture with his head that said "get out."

The footage I'd retrieved from the eighth floor camera would have to suffice. Hopefully the drive was large enough to have all of yesterday's events. We might get lucky and wind up with multiple shots of Ahlberg and the other woman.

I secured the memory card and went to the door. It didn't budge. Worse, the only way to unlock it from the inside was a magnetic card reader mounted to the wall.

I turned toward the monitors. The manager crossed the lobby with the police officers in tow. Bear walked to the middle of the lobby and stopped there. What was he doing? He reached into his pocket, pulled out his phone. A second later, mine rang.

"I see them," I said.

"They're heading down," he said. "They're waiting at the elevator now. Want me to do something?"

"I don't want you getting into trouble over this," I said.

"I'll fake a heart attack," he said.

"You're armed. It won't work."

"Bull." He smiled at me through the camera. "Watch this."

The line went dead. Bear shoved the phone in his front pocket. He balled up his jacket and tossed it behind a potted plant. Then he took a few steps toward the elevator, stopped, grabbed his chest, and appeared to call out. The manager tossed a quick glance back and stepped into the open elevator. The cops, however, turned toward the large man writhing on the floor in agony. The manager stuck one foot out, waved for the officers to join him. They ignored the thin man. Annoyed, the manager exited the elevator and crossed the room to see what the fuss was about. He stood over Bear, wrapped his bony fingers around the back of his head. I couldn't tell what he was saying, but figured it had something to do with me.

"Can't believe you pulled that off," I said to Bear through the monitor.

He'd bought me time. Now I had to find a way out. There was no way the room was closed off completely. I rapped my knuckles against the walls. The thick thud in return told me that the walls were solid. I didn't see a closet. There was no window.

I grabbed the door knob and yanked. It barely budged. I reached for the back of my head and yanked on a fistful of hair. I stared straight up.

"There we have it."

Drop tile ceilings.

I climbed up on the desk near the edge and pushed one of the tiles up and tossed it over. I reached through and found that the wall did not continue past the ceiling. I gripped it and pulled myself up so that I balanced on my waist. The ceiling on the opposite side felt the same. I lifted another panel. The next room over was dark. I used the light on my phone to get a better look at the space. There was an old desk. Nothing else. I aimed the light at the door. There was no card reader mounted to the wall.

I lowered myself into the security room. On the monitor Bear was standing in the middle of the lobby. A crowd gathered around him. The manager and cops were nowhere in sight. Bear grimaced as he watched the elevator doors close. They would be at the door in thirty seconds, tops.

In an ideal scenario, I'd crash their system, erasing the hard drives. I didn't have the time or the know-how to do that. So I unplugged every tower and jammed the screwdriver into the back of each one. I had no idea if that would make a difference.

The room turned a deep blue as feeds cut off and the monitors went to their factory display.

I climbed on top of the desk again and pulled myself up and balanced on the center wall. The space wasn't that high. I replaced the ceiling tile before dropping down into the other room. A few seconds later I heard the manager's voice. The security room door crashed opened. The manager sounded confused. The cops sounded pissed. Why were the screens blank? Where had I gone?

At least I assumed that's what they said.

They spent a couple minutes in the opposite room. I figured the manager was trying to reconnect the systems. He sounded frustrated. Perhaps the screwdriver trick had worked. I felt the tip of the tool dig into my leg, so I reversed it in my pocket. The cops said little. They probably wondered what the hell they were doing down there. I sat with my ear against the wall until the voices silenced and the door opened and clicked shut. I moved to a spot next to the door. If it opened, it would open against me, shielding me from view.

They stood in the hallway, talking. I wished I could understand them. Someone grabbed the knob to my room. Twisted the handle. It clicked repeatedly. The door was locked. One of them pushed against the door. It didn't give.

The manager said something. One of the cops responded. Keys, maybe?

I waited as the voices trailed off. A minute of silence passed. The phone buzzed in my pocket. I answered without saying a word. The sweat beaded on my forehead and matted in my eyebrows slid down the side of my face.

"They're all up here," Bear said. "Where are you?"

"What are they doing?"

"The manager went behind the counter. He's got a cabinet open."

"He's looking for a key." I dragged the pad of my thumb across my forehead, flung the condensation away from me. "The cops are still there?"

"Yeah, both of them. They're waiting by the counter. Man, they look freaking annoyed."

"Do whatever you can to stop them if they head for the elevator. I'm gonna get to the stairwell. Call me when they're coming down."

I already had the door open and was making my way down the hall to the far end. I assumed that the stairs went down this far. I checked each door I passed. All but the last one was locked.

The stairwell was dark, hot and musty. I thought I felt someone's breath on my neck. I didn't care. I called Bear and updated him on my position. He told me the manager was still in the lobby. The cops, too. I climbed the stairs two at a time, skipped the first floor, and exited at the second.

There was a window at the end of the hallway. I slid the lock over and grabbed the lip at the bottom. It felt like the thing hadn't been opened in years. I glanced down at the sill. Two or three layers of paint sealed the window to the frame. I took out the screwdriver I'd found in the security room and used it to cut through fifty years of paint. I tried to lift again. The window grated against its track. And it went up.

I pulled out my phone and called Bear.

"Go to the east end of the hallway. I saw an exit there. I'm getting ready to drop down from the second floor window. Be there."

"You getting old or something, man?" he said.

"What?" I stopped, right leg hanging out, window pressing down against my left shoulder.

"All of a sudden you need a spotter for a one floor drop?"

"Go to hell." I ended the call and stuffed the phone in my pocket. I tossed my jacket out the window then made sure the pistol was secure in my waistband.

The chime above the elevator dinged. The sound echoed down the hall. I looked back. The doors slid open. I eased my torso outside. Pulled my other leg through. A cop stepped out of the elevator. They looked down the hallway, opposite my position. I let my body drop, twisting my wrists to catch the outer sill. I pressed the soles of my shoes against the brick wall. They grated as mortar cracked and rained down on the asphalt below. The door below me opened and Bear stepped out and moved to the side. I let go, bracing for the impact to the ankle I'd injured in Texas. When I hit the ground, I allowed myself to roll back. Bear got a kick out of seeing me take the fall. I didn't care.

"We better get to the car before they come out here," he said, pulling me up by the arm.

# 18

We traveled south out of the city on the A2, past Utrecht on the E25, continuing another ten minutes then exiting the highway. We'd made it out without being noticed. How long until they'd get our identities off the security feed? That wouldn't matter if the screwdriver did the trick.

And it wasn't like the hotel or cops would figure out who we actually were. Though it would've been better had we never been spotted. Things never worked out that way.

It was disappointing not rendezvousing with Katrine Ahlberg. Had she received word that we were coming for her? That might explain the maid's explanation of the woman and her associate leaving after check-out and not coming back. They could have fled the city. Perhaps the country. I pictured them holed up in a safe house we might never find.

"Hungry?" Bear said, taking his eyes off the road long enough to look over for my response. I nodded.

We stopped at a small restaurant and grabbed a bite to eat. The place was deserted. We ate quickly. Neither of us spoke for the duration of the meal.

Back in the car, I said, "Did you reserve a room?"

He nodded. "Two nights."

"Guess they got your ID then."

"One of them." He pulled all corresponding credit cards and photo IDs out and placed them on the dash. He'd come prepared. I would have if Frank had given me the chance. It helped that Bear had more than one identity to use. "They told us everything was expunged, redacted, burned. These governments should have nothing on us."

"Yeah," I said. "That's what they said."

"You believe it?"

I shook my head. "It was a nice gesture, but that's all it was. There's no way that they just hit the delete button. Now, maybe it's at the point where only a handful of people in each country have access, but someone does. You can guarantee that. Not to mention all the countries we weren't exactly on good terms with. Think they're gonna forgive and forget?"

"Right." Bear leaned back and took a deep breath. "I'm wondering how far this'll go."

"I don't know. Don't really care. We'll deal with it when we have to. For now, we need to focus on finding a place to stay for the night, and getting a computer so we can sort through this footage."

"You gonna call Frank?" Bear asked.

"I guess at some point. He's probably itching to send a team after us. Wouldn't doubt that he's got them on standby already. I'd prefer to avoid talking to the guy."

"Who you think he'd send?"

"Someone like us, I suppose."

Bear grimaced as he rubbed the side of his head. "Are there many more left? I mean, that Frank knows."

It was a good question, and one that I'd spent considerable time pondering. The extermination event had wiped the SIS clean. They went after me. I assumed that they had plans to take out the other guys from the past. I thought back to the conversation Frank and I had the other day. He mentioned a few of the guys from the old days. Said they were doing well. Was it bullshit? Or were they really out there?

"There might be a few guys still around," I said. "Would they do a favor for Frank? I know I wouldn't unless he had me dead to rights like in this case. Think about how many laws we broke to pull this hit off originally. Everyone in the group did that kind of crap. Plus, he's heading up the SOG. It might be misappropriation of his resources, but those guys know how to keep quiet."

Bear forced a laugh. "So you're saying we should watch our backs."

"Yeah, that'd be a good start. At least watch mine." I flashed a grin in his direction. "Anyway, no point dwelling on this right now. Let's find a place to stay."

We located a hotel a few miles away. The guy at the counter gave us directions to a store where we could pick up a laptop. After checking into our rooms, we headed out and bought the computer. Less than an hour later we were back in the room with the computer powered on and updated.

Bear took the memory card I'd used in the hotel's security room and inserted it into the system. He navigated through a few menus and opened the file.

"Filled the damn thing up," he said. "Card's only thirty-two gigs. I hope we got enough of the surveillance."

"How much would that hold?" I said.

His forehead wrinkled as he looked up at me while hiking his shoulders a couple inches in the air. "Maybe eight hours for a digital camera. But with this kind of system, I couldn't tell you. Let's see what kind of footage it records."

Some systems only captured events in stills. While others only came on when motion was detected. And others recorded everything.

"It was live action when I was down in the security room," I said.

"Doesn't mean it stores that way." He clicked on the mouse a couple times. The screen went dark for a moment and then came to life with a recorded feed of an empty hallway. "Dammit."

"What?"

"I was hoping it only recorded when there was movement, but it looks like this is going to have everything. Or, I guess I should say lots of nothing."

"Date says it's from yesterday."

"So we might luck out."

We stared at the screen for twenty minutes. Nothing happened. It would've been more exciting to watch flies get it on.

"Any way to speed this up?" I said.

He clicked around the options and increased the feed to four times speed. "That should help."

The time bar on the bottom of the video player flew by. We cut it in half every time someone appeared and watched as they waddled down the hallway.

But for every time the elevator opened or someone stepped out into the hallway, no one went in or out of Ahlberg's room.

Bear grew concerned. We were running out of remaining footage. A knot formed in my stomach as the feeling grew that we weren't going to uncover anything. We'd be left standing at a dead end, surrounded by a ring of fire. We'd have to call Frank.

Bear paused the feed. "Getting hungry?"

It'd only been three hours since we ate. "Let's finish this first."

"Dammit," he said. "All right, man. Let's do it."

I focused as much on the remaining time in the video as I did the footage of the hallway. It whittled down to twenty minutes, fifteen, ten.

"Not looking good," Bear said.

Five minutes were left.

"Put it on regular speed," I said. "Someone's head might pop out of the door and we'll miss it."

"Guess that could've already happened, huh?"

I'd considered that it had. "If we have to take shifts watching this thing at regular speed all night, then we will."

Bear rolled his eyes at the thought of sitting for hours staring at the empty hallway.

There was a minute left. I paced along a four foot track between the bed and Bear. He cleared his throat. The gesture let me know I was bothering him. I counted down the seconds. Fifteen. Ten. Nine. Eight.

Bear looked back. "Stop walking behind me, man."

Five. Four. Three.

"Freeze it!"

The woman stepped out of room 815 and glanced down the hallway toward the camera. Bear did something with the mouse. The video zoomed in on her face. The shot was clear enough, even if a little grainy.

"You sure that's the right room?" he said.

"You can back up and check, but I'm pretty sure that's right."

He zoomed out, and we both confirmed it was the correct room.

"That's not her," Bear said.

"No, it's not," I said.

We weren't looking at Katrine Ahlberg. This woman was a brunette with tanned skin.

"The maid said there were two women in the room, right?" Bear said.

"Yeah, two women." I leaned in closer and pointed to the screen. "Look there, on the door frame. You can see another hand."

He poked the screen with his large index finger. "And some blonde hair. Right there. We got her."

"Now where are they?" I said.

"And who's that woman?" he said.

"Can you turn that into a regular image?"

"Yeah." He looked back. "Why?"

"Because I got someone I think can help us figure out the identity of the brunette."

# 19

Bear zoomed in as far as he could without affecting the integrity of the shot and cut an image of the woman from the footage. He saved a copy of it on each of our memory cards, then left the image open in another program. We both stared at the mystery lady on the screen.

I leaned in closer as though that would reveal her identity. "Who do you suppose she is?"

Bear hiked his shoulders a couple inches. "I don't remember everything about the original assignment, but I remember faces and there's no recollection of her at all."

I thought back to the pictures I saw in Frank's office. "Nothing in the file Frank gave me matches. And we looked at several photos in his office. I can say I haven't seen this woman before."

"Friend?" He held out his hands. "Her lover?"

"Anything's possible, but as far as I know men were her preference."

Bear nodded, said nothing.

"Then there's still the question of what they were doing at the hotel. I'm assuming Katrine met her there. Makes sense given the note we found."

Bear looked over at me. "That note seems odd, right?"

"How so?"

"Like it was planted. I mean, there's no way she was at that house a day ago. Not with the way the place smelled."

"True," I said. "But she could've been there a week ago. Wrote the information down. Took a pic of it. Counted on someone else to dispose of it. Whatever happened there tells me someone got out in a hurry. Perhaps she left first, and her men cleaned up after. Disposed of those poor dogs upstairs."

"Plausible." Bear turned back to the computer. "My guess would be that this brunette is involved in some kind of intelligence community and got wind of Frank's plan. We never asked the maid how long they'd been there. Maybe the two of them were holed up there for a week or so."

"Hiding in plain sight."

Bear nodded. "And when they realized we were in town, they fled."

I thought about what he said for a moment. "The two guys in England who followed us from your town to the marina. The house in the woods. The note. The dogs. What if someone else did that?"

Bear leaned to the side, cocking his head toward me.

"Someone else is after her," I said. "And I'd assume that they know about us."

The big man rose and went to the door. He looked through the peephole, then engaged the safety lock.

"Relax," I said. "One, at this point we're untraceable. Frank doesn't know where we are. They won't either."

"And two?" he said.

"You and I are an unbreakable force when we're working together."

Bear flopped onto the bed like a wrestler dropping off the top rope onto his foe. The frame groaned and bent. I was surprised it didn't snap. He worked a hand behind his head, stared at the ceiling.

"What is it?" I said.

"We're not the same," he said.

"We've never been the same. That's what makes us a great team."

"No, that's not what I meant." He craned his neck forward and met my gaze. "All those years, we only worried about ourselves. You had my back, I had yours, and self-preservation of the team was the name of the game."

"And now?"

"Well, you've got Mia. I've got Mandy."

"And Sasha."

He nodded, let his head fall back, eyes focused on the ceiling. "And Sasha."

"So what's your point?"

"Can we really be one hundred percent effective at our jobs if we have them on our mind? Don't you fear the worry you have over them, returning to them, protecting them, will affect how you do your job?"

"I suppose it could—"

"You suppose, huh?" He laughed. "You're something else, Jack."

"It just doesn't matter. We have to finish this, then it's over. You'll resume the life you're building with Sasha and Mandy. You'll find something you can settle in and do for the rest of your life. Compartmentalize for now."

It's what guys like us had to do. Shove everything that makes you human, wants and desires and needs and love, take all of that and hide it away. Double tape the seams. Whatever had to be done in order to focus on the job.

The ensuing pause and silence that went along with it deafened me.

"What about you?" Bear said. "Is Mia in your future?"

I tried to say yes, but the truth was I had no idea how things would turn out after we finished the job.

"In some ways I think she's better off with Sean and Deb and the kids," I said. "They're a family. I mean, am I gonna settle down all of a sudden? Hell, I don't know if it's possible."

Bear nodded, said nothing. Did he have similar thoughts about his own situation? It seemed he was off to a great start before I showed up.

"And we have to see what happens after this is over," I said. "Is Frank finally going to get off our asses? Can I just become a ghost and try to make a life? Or will I be confined to drifting across the country or the world, never making a home or friends or starting a family?"

Bear sat up, held out his hand. I took it. A smile formed on his face. "This is some deep voodoo, man. We need to be drinking to have this conversation."

I don't know if it was the way he said it, or we just needed relief from the serious conversation, but the both of us burst into laughter.

"Let's go get a drink and some dinner," I said.

He deleted the image of the brunette and the footage from the computer, then started a reinstall of the operating system.

"You want to hit up that contact and send them the pic before we go out?" Bear asked.

"After," I said. "Right now, I don't want to think about Katrine Ahlberg or the mystery woman or Frank or the guys tailing us. I just want a beer and a steak."

We found a small place about ten minutes away. The crowd was local. Always a good sign. The woman that greeted us spoke English the moment we walked in.

"Still stick out, I guess," Bear leaned in and whispered.

The dining room was full. The woman offered us a seat at the bar, noting to the man behind the counter that we were from the States. He had beers in front of us almost before we sat down. Said that these were the American favorites. Bear's presence combined with the atmosphere and the murmur of chatter around us dulled my senses. I felt more relaxed than I'd felt in years by the time my steak had arrived.

And it was one of the best cuts of meat I'd had in years. That was saying something.

Bear agreed. "Damn, this is good."

The guy behind the bar smiled, refilled our mugs and brought a basket of fresh bread. Said they made it there from scratch. Smelled and tasted like it, too. Simpler ingredients were the key. None of that dwarf wheat.

Bear dropped his knife and fork on his plate. I looked over expecting to see the guy patting his stomach. But his plate was half covered with steak. His mouth hung open an inch. His eyes were fixed on the television.

"What is it?" I said.

But I didn't need him to answer.

# 20

I SAW THE IMAGE OF KATRINE AHLBERG ON THE SCREEN. THE STATION USED THE name of her sister, Birgit, on the banner below the picture. The news anchor spoke in Dutch and I couldn't make out any of it. The image shrunk into the corner and gave way to a live shot of a city street littered with an ambulance, police cars, flashing lights, yellow tape, and cops everywhere.

I stood on the stool's footrest and leaned over the bar and got the bartender's attention. "What're they saying?"

He glanced at the screen and his smile faded. He motioned for the others seated at the bar to quiet down. The volume turned up. Everyone directed their attention to the screen.

"Ah," he said. "This is related to… I remember something about this from some years ago."

"What happened?" Bear asked.

"Uh, OK. They say that Birgit Ahlberg, twin sister of Katrine Ahlberg, AKA the Scandinavian Princess — who herself was assassinated ten years ago — was murdered outside of Amsterdam this afternoon in the city of Leiden." He turned toward us, hands extended, palms up. "That's not too far away from here."

"Son of a bitch," Bear muttered.

I leaned in closer to the bartender while keeping my gaze fixed on the television. It was hard to make anything definitive out. They'd covered the body with a white sheet where it fell. The police had done a good job removing civilians from the shot. I wondered if the other woman from the hotel security footage was there. "What else are they saying?"

"Ah, yes, that Birgit had been underground for some time, recently resurfacing at charity events, and that they think it was this appearances that led those who murdered her sister to come after Birgit."

Bear brushed against my shoulder. "We're gonna have to call Frank."

"I'm sure he's already trying to reach us." I tapped the bar top. "We'll take the check now."

The man kept his gaze fixed on us for a few moments. It must've seemed odd how interested we were in the news. But he didn't ask, so we didn't bother coming up with a story. Not like it would matter. We'd never see the man again.

We drove west for thirty minutes. I knew Frank could trace a location from a call. I didn't want to make one anywhere near where we were staying, even with the additional SIM cards available. With Frank's connections now as the head of the CIA's SOG, I had no doubt he could have someone at those coordinates within half an hour if he chose to.

Frank's ragged breath greeted me after the fifth ring. He must've raced out of a meeting to answer the call. "God dammit, that better be you, Jack."

"We saw," I said.

"Saw what?" he said.

"You don't know?"

"Know what?" He exhaled loudly into his mouthpiece. "Quit jerking me off, Jack. You don't know how close I am to sending a team out there to finish you two."

"She's dead."

Silence over took the line. I glanced at the phone's display to make sure we hadn't been disconnected. The seconds counted upward.

"You found her?" he asked.

"Negative," I said. "Someone else got to her. It's all over the news. They're reporting she was murdered on the street."

"I know we weren't the only ones, but I didn't think anyone else had that kind of intelligence on her."

Ahlberg wasn't my only concern. "What about the guys following us? You figure out who else is itching to bat this around?"

"I'm almost positive those guys work for Awad." Katrine and her husband were known terrorist supporters. There were those in my line of work who suspected them of being far more involved than signing checks. "Somehow, someone passed our intel to him. Now, that's my gut talking, so don't go acting on it."

"Are we done now?" I didn't want to remain on the line any longer than necessary. Frank could be tracking us at that very moment. He'd drag out the conversation as long as possible for his men to reach us.

"Hang on, I'm checking on this." He tapped on his keyboard, clicked his mouse, entered a few more strokes. "This is legit. Someone got her. They don't have anyone in custody, and no witnesses have come forward."

"Looked like it was in broad daylight," Bear said.

"It was," Frank said.

"That's almost daring someone to catch you," I said. "Whoever did this has no fear of the law."

"There's nothing else about the crime scene," Frank said.

"Are we done now?" I repeated.

"I'm thinking we need to question whoever did this," Frank said. "But first, I need you guys to verify the body."

"Ah, Christ," Bear said. "Why don't you come over and do it?"

Traveling to a specific location at Frank's request was not high on our to-do list at the moment.

Frank said, "That wouldn't look suspicious at all, would it? Plus they'll have her moved before I get there. This is high profile, and her family is wealthy. I managed to get the morgue location. I don't care what you need to do to get in there. You do it, and make an identification on the corpse. I'll deal with the fallout and clean up any mess."

He gave us the address and disconnected the call. I pulled the sim card from the phone and discarded it like a used cigarette butt.

"Ready?" Bear said.

"One more call," I said.

I dialed a number I'd memorized many years ago. I was the only one who knew the number. And the man who answered would know it was me calling.

"I was wondering when I'd hear from you." He sounded like a fourteen-year-old. Like always.

"Brandon," I said. "Good to hear your voice. Say hello to Logan, too."

"Holy crap," Brandon said. "You got Bear there with you? Must be some serious stuff going down in Amsterdam tonight."

"How'd you know I'd call?" I said.

"Because a week ago someone started diving into databases that no one should be accessing. And they started typing in queries using names that no one should be querying. So, I have to ask, Jack. What the hell was going on in Texas, and does this call have anything to do with that?"

"You know I'm in Amsterdam. That's one of the benefits of this line, right? So why would I call about Texas if I'm five thousand miles away?"

"See, that's what confuses the frick outta me because you appeared to be in a serious mess in Texas."

"Texas is done and I don't want to talk about it. It has no bearing on this other than because of that data breech Frank Skinner found me and brought me to SIS headquarters."

"You mean Langley, right? That's where he works now."

"I'm pretty sure I said what I meant."

"There is no SIS anymore, Jack. You know this."

"Right, which makes this a nasty situation to be in."

Brandon laughed. "When is it ever not with you? Damn, I ain't had to bail anyone else out as much as I have with you. At least you got Bear there with you. I can rest a little easy knowing he'll keep you from screwing things up too much."

Bear laughed.

"Yeah, well, the big guy's gotten soft since you last dealt with him," I said. "Where are you located these days?"

"Fat chance there, hoss."

"Don't say hoss," Bear said. "It doesn't fit your demographic."

Brandon laughed again. "The hell's that supposed to mean?" He took a few deep, wheezy breaths and then changed his tone. "All right, I know you didn't call to turn this into a party line. So what's up?"

"We need a favor," I said.

"That much is obvious," Brandon said. "And it won't be no favor. You're gonna pay for my services."

"Add it to my tab," I said.

"You planning on taking care of that tab anytime soon?" he said.

"Yeah, you know what, add it to Bear's tab. I think his slate is clean."

"All right, all right. I can already tell I'm losing money on this one, so why don't you get to it. What's going on?"

"Kristine Ahlberg." Within a second of speaking her name, I heard Brandon tapping on his keyboard.

"She's dead," he said. "Hell, died a long time ago. And it looks like you already know that."

"We might have been involved. She had a sister, Birgit."

"B-I-R-G-E-T?" Brandon said.

"No E. Two I's."

"She's dead, too. Not so long ago. Today, in fact. And it happened close to where you're calling from."

"We know. Without getting into too much detail, we were sent here to find her but someone beat us to it."

"Probably in a morgue right about now," Brandon said. "Give me a minute and I'll tell you where."

I started to tell him not to bother, but figured having Brandon fact check what Frank had told us wasn't a bad idea. I couldn't put it past Frank to use the incident to set us up. Hell, for all we knew, Frank was the one behind the murder.

Brandon read out the address to the morgue. It matched what Frank had given us.

"Is that all?" he said.

"No," I said. "I'm gonna send you a photo. I need you to find a match and let us know everything you can about the woman."

He gave us instructions on where to upload the file. Bear sent it from his phone to the secure server. Brandon confirmed receipt and told us he'd be in touch within a few hours. We disconnected the call.

I looked over at Bear. "Ready to verify a corpse?"

"Highlight of my day, man. Highlight of my day."

# 21

We drove forty minutes to our destination. Several buildings made up the medical center. At the heart of it was a small emergency room. Two sets of double-wide sliding doors remained open. The temperature that evening was about the same as it had been during the day. Two cops and three nurses stood talking on the walkway leading up to the ER.

We looped around the facility, taking note of security guards and where the police cars were parked. Nobody paid any attention to us. We bypassed the parking garage and parked on a quiet alley a few blocks away.

"Plan?" Bear said on our walk to the morgue.

"No idea what we're going to face in there," I said. "No one's gonna just give us access, so be ready to use some level of coercion."

He looked over at me. "You don't think my smile is charming enough?"

"Only with the ladies, big man."

We clung to the shadows and kept our heads down in an effort to avoid any security cameras.

The unassuming entrance to the morgue was nestled behind a blue and white striped overhang. I expected an access pad or magnetic card reader. Nothing adorned the wall next to the door. I pulled on the handle. It was unlocked.

We stepped into a darkened hallway wide enough for a gurney and people to stand on either side of it. There were two doors along the right wall, and a set of double doors at the end. I figured the morgue was to the left of the corridor.

"Guess it isn't the busiest place at the hospital," Bear said. "This might go easier than we thought."

"Why'd you have to say that?" I said.

Bear laughed. "Getting bored, I guess. Wouldn't mind a little action in here."

It was as if he was begging me to deliver a horrible pun in response. I resisted. It was good to have more of the Bear I knew back, though.

"Let's find the body and do what we gotta do." I took the lead and hustled down the hallway, pistol in hand.

"I gotta feeling we're gonna get *morgue* than we asked for in here."

I looked back at him, shook my head. "You had to go there."

He shrugged. "Delivery made it dead on arrival, huh?"

I took a deep breath. Sighed. "Of corpse, Bear. Of corpse."

"All right, then," he said. "Now we can continue with the job."

We'd dealt with killing and dead bodies and a number of atrocities over the years we'd worked together. But there was something personal about this job. We'd screwed up. An innocent woman lost her life. A not so innocent one had now paid for her crimes. We couldn't atone for the mistake we'd made, but at least we could lay it to rest with the identification of Katrine Ahlberg's corpse. The chapter would then be closed.

I leaned against the right side of the double door and pushed the latch bar with my hip. The room was aglow with fluorescent lights that hung in fixtures lined with dead cockroaches ten feet overhead. There was a good fifteen feet of space in front of me. The room opened to the left and continued around the wall. I leaned into the corner and saw a room enclosed in glass. Two stainless steel tables stood empty in the small room. Presumably that's where they performed the autopsies.

The opposite wall had three rows of six lockers. Had they all been in use at the same time at any point in the morgue's history? I supposed they had to be ready for a catastrophe.

Or overflow from Amsterdam on a rough night.

A man rose high enough to peer at us from over a wide monitor. His face and glasses reflected the red image he had pulled up.

He said something in Dutch.

"You received a body this evening," Bear said.

The man stepped out from behind his desk. He was tall and slim with a matching nose. His lab coat draped over him like a winter jacket and hung loose around his torso. He ran a hand through his thinning hair in an attempt to straighten it. I doubted that he received many visitors in the morgue. Live ones, at least.

"The murdered woman," he said with an accent that sounded more French than Dutch. "Can I ask what this is about?"

"You could," Bear said. "But I'm not at liberty to discuss."

"Then I'm afraid I need you to leave." He pulled a cell phone from his coat pocket. He punched a couple keys, then glanced up at us. "I'm calling security now. You should leave. They are armed and trigger happy, as you say."

"There's no need for that," I said. "I just need your word that if we tell you why we're here, you won't tell anyone else."

He lowered the phone to his side, arched an eyebrow.

"We're with the CIA. We have reason to believe that the woman you took in tonight is a person of interest that we've been searching for. We just need to take a look, ID the body, then we'll be on our way."

"Interesting." He brought his phone and opposite hand together. "I'm afraid your story sounds like bullshit."

"Bear."

The speed at which Bear moved surprised the doctor, as it did most people. The thin man threw his hands up and took a series of short steps backward, nearly tripping over a footstool. Bear closed the gap in an instant and knocked the phone from the man's hand. The cell spun across the floor and ricocheted off the lockers like a hockey puck against the boards. Bear had his paws on the doctor, who found himself twisted like a pretzel before he knew what was going on.

"You assholes," he said. "You know how much trouble you're going to get in?"

Bear torqued the doctor's right arm behind his back. The man screamed in pain.

"That's only the beginning," Bear said. "Now, you sit down and shut up and let my partner and I do what we need to do, and you won't experience anymore pain. But if you get in our way, I will make sure that it's the last thing you do."

The doctor's legs buckled and he went limp. A wet blotch formed on his pants.

"Passed out from fear?" I said. "And pissed himself? Impressive work, Bear."

Bear chuckled. "Dumb son of a bitch. Tell me, how do these guys go through so much schooling, yet have no idea when to back down? They think those fancy degrees will prevent someone like us from attacking them?"

I shrugged. Bear let the guy fall to the floor, then rifled through a couple drawers until he found some medical tape. He began wrapping it around the doctor's wrists, securing them together.

"Think that'll work?" I said.

"If I use enough," he said. "Besides, he ain't gonna do anything once he wakes up."

I turned toward the lockers. Katrine was inside one of them. They weren't marked on the outside. I started on the left and opened each. Three out of the first four I opened were occupied by older folks who had likely passed on from natural causes. The next five were vacant. Hope faded the further I went. What if they'd determined her identity and moved her already? The family was wealthy. They could make things happen quickly.

Bear stood watch as I opened the top locker on the last column.

Empty.

I slid the next open.

Same.

I reached for the final locker.

The double doors banged open.

# 22

THE SECURITY GUARDS BURST INTO THE ROOM WIELDING BATONS AND YELLING IN a threatening tone. Confuse and conquer, I supposed. I rose and stood straight with my back against the cold stainless steel. They barked orders at me.

"Sorry," I said, taking a step forward. The move kept their eyes on me and away from Bear. "I don't understand a word you're saying."

The two men shared a glance. One spoke up. "Get on the ground."

I looked down at the linoleum-tiled floor. "Afraid I can't do that."

The guard sheathed his baton and placed his quivering hand on the butt of his pistol. The department must not have required a lot of drilling, because he hadn't unsnapped his holster.

"Get down," he said with far less conviction in his voice than required. "Now."

The guards hadn't been aware enough to step past the wall. They remained in front of the double doors, oblivious to what went on in half the room.

When Bear jumped out from behind the corner with his pistol drawn, the two rent-a-cops stumbled over themselves in an effort to back away from the big man. The guy on the right regained his balance first. He made the mistake of going after Bear with his baton. The instincts of most men would kick in and they would react by throwing their arm out to protect themselves.

Not Bear.

He lived for the attack.

Bear turned sideways and stepped into the guy, negating the force of the blow. He wrapped his left arm around the guy's right, hooking it under the armpit. He slammed a right uppercut into the guard's stomach. The guy let out a spectral howl as he dropped to the ground like a bag of sand. Bear freed his arm and threw a left cross that caught the other guard on the chin. The man slammed into the wall. He collapsed on the ground before his eyes finished rolling back in his head.

Bear turned toward me. Blood seeped from his middle knuckle. He took a couple deep breaths, said, "Hurry up and get this over with."

"The hell?" I said. "That's a workout for you now?"

"Shut up." He piled the men on top of each other. The first guy finally caught his breath. Bear delivered a kick to his abdomen to remedy that situation. He ripped an electrical cord from the wall and used it to tie their wrists together.

The three live bodies outnumbered the corpses I had seen so far.

I glanced around the room in search of security cameras. There were none. I found it odd, considering the purpose of the place. Then again, by the time the bodies made it to the morgue, they were stripped of all personal effects. Perhaps it was out of respect for the dead they didn't monitor the morgue. Whatever the reason, it worked in our favor tonight.

I pulled the last locker open and removed the sheet that covered Katrine Ahlberg. There were three bullet holes. Two in her chest, and one to the side of her head. All from a high-powered rifle.

Bear walked over and stood on the opposite side of the corpse. We stared down at the woman we thought we had killed a decade prior.

"Guess it's done now," Bear said, wiping blood from his hand on the inside of his shirt. "That's her."

I continued to take in the woman. Like the pictures in Frank's office had indicated, she had aged well despite a decade of stress that went along with living in hiding.

"Why do you think she became so public again?" I said.

Bear thought it over. "Maybe she figured enough time had passed. Hell, the people with the resources to find her could have figured out where she was. It wasn't like it was all that secret to begin with."

A voice poured out of the guards' radios. The request was repeated a couple times. Neither of us understood what was said. The meaning was not lost, though.

"Guess we should get a picture." Bear retrieved his phone and snapped a couple photos of the body. "Let's get out of here, Jack. They're gonna send another team soon to see what's going on."

"*If* there's another team," I said.

"You really want to wait around to find out?" There was a door behind the doctor's desk. Bear walked over and checked it. He opened it a crack. A slight gust blew past, rustling the sheet covering the lower half of Ahlberg. "We'll go out this way."

Shaking my head, I grabbed the end of the locker and began to slide it in, watching as Katrine's body disappeared into the dark.

I took one last look down at the woman.

Then it hit me.

"It's not her."

## 23

Bear was halfway out the door. He stopped, re-entered the room, let the door fall shut. The breeze died. The smell of the alley continued to overtake the sterile environment.

"What?"

I slid the locker out and pulled the sheet all the way, exposing Katrine's full body. "It's not her."

"The hell you talking about, Jack?"

I pulled out my phone and found the pictures I'd taken of Katrine's file. With Bear looking over my shoulder, I opened a photo of Katrine and Birgit. It had been taken the year before the original mission. They stood side-by-side, hip to hip, thigh to thigh in white sand on the edge of an emerald green sea. Waist high waves crashed in the background. I remembered the picture from a decade earlier. The only difference in the women at the time was their hair length. Birgit wore hers much shorter than her sister. This was verified through other surveillance footage that placed Katrine and her waist-long hair with Awad. Birgit's was rarely ever shoulder-length. In the picture on the beach Katrine stood on the right and Birgit on the left.

"Look," I said.

"The hell is this?" Bear said. "Looks just like her. Both of them do."

"There's a difference," I said.

"Which one is Katrine in this shot?"

"Long hair."

He looked at the picture, then the corpse, then back at the picture. It took a few seconds longer than I thought it would take him. He was rusty.

"Jesus," he said. "That's not her."

I zoomed in on the picture, then placed the phone on the corpse's abdomen. The pose the women struck in the photo allowed their matching tattoos — Katrine's on the left, Birgit's on the right — to merge together as one. It was an elaborate piece, colorful, and Norse or Celtic in design. Must've had some meaning to the twins. They each wore half of it. It stretched from above their hips, down their thighs, stopping right above the knee.

The woman lying on the table possessed no such markings.

"Laser removal?" Bear said.

"On a piece that big?" I said.

"It'd leave a scar," he said, nodding and tugging at the hair on his chin.

"There'd be something visible. No plastic surgery would completely eliminate a tattoo like that. Especially with all the color."

I grabbed my phone off Ahlberg's abdomen and took several pictures of the corpse, including a few head shots. Perhaps Brandon could use them. The face appeared to be a match to the eye. Algorithms showed no bias, though. His program could see past the superficial.

"Who you suppose it is?" Bear said.

"Another sister, maybe?" I said. "A cousin? Hell, I don't know. As soon as we're away from here, we need to get Brandon on the phone. He can run these pictures and see if there's a relative that matches."

"What if that doesn't work?" Bear said. "What about Frank?"

I hadn't thought that far ahead. Frank will be expecting an update from us soon. "Let's get out of here before we worry about him."

Bear knelt and checked on the doctor. The man didn't move. "Think he's dead?"

I shrugged. The man meant nothing to me. Bear gave him ample opportunity to sit down.

Bear slapped the doctor's cheek. "Maybe I gave him a heart attack?"

"Doesn't matter," I said. "Check on the guards."

"I don't have a good feeling about this. It reeks of a setup. The guys following us around. The disgusting house in the woods. Our target getting taken out when we're so close. Then this, her turning out to be someone else?"

"I know," I said. "Taken as a whole with how things went down ten years ago, it isn't hard to imagine someone's working against us."

"Frank," Bear said.

"I know that makes sense, but let's not rush to judgment."

"We gotta figure out a way to lure them out."

"Let's start by getting out of here."

We left through the back door. The alley was tight and dark and smelled of ammonia in some spots, urine in others. Perhaps they dumped something back there instead of disposing of it properly. Or maybe a few of the homeless took up back there from time to time.

I checked around the front corner. There was no activity there or anywhere in view. The two guards Bear took out were probably the only ones on patrol, and it might be hours before they were found. I doubted the cops were involved with hospital security. Likely the ones we saw at the ER were passing by and decided to stop and talk with the nurses to kill some time.

The unlit space behind the morgue kept us hidden as we stealthed across the deserted parking lot. A cool breeze swept past. It dried the sweat that lined my forehead and cleared out the lingering smell of the alley. An eighteen-wheeler idled nearby out of view.

When we reached the alley where the car was parked, Bear stopped.

"Let me go alone," he said. "I'll meet you up ahead."

I handed him the keys and walked another couple blocks. The night was still now. I found a large Willow to hide underneath. Slices of orange light covered the area. I watched the apartment building across the street. Most of the windows were darkened. I didn't notice any movement in any of the others.

A car approached. I backed up against the tree. The bark scratched at my back. Bear slowed the vehicle and pulled up to the curb.

"Notice anything?" I asked.

He shook his head. "You standing under a tree?"

"Other than that?"

"Nah, it's pretty quiet out here."

"Ironic, I guess." I rolled down my window and perched my elbow on the sill. "Here we are, trying to figure out what the hell happened, perhaps on the verge of pissing off several foreign intelligence agencies, and the immediate world surrounding us is still and calm."

"Yeah, well, enjoy it." Bear shifted into gear and pulled away from the curb. "I got a feeling things are gonna get pretty damn crazy around here."

The knot in my gut told me he was right.

# 24

We drove southwest to the A58, then went west to Eindhoven. I kept my eyes on the rearview mirror most of the way. I found it difficult to watch for a tail that night. The headlights on the freeway blended into one another after staring at them long enough. Nothing stood out, but that didn't mean anything. Frank knew where we went. He gave us the location. I had no doubt there had been someone nearby watching us. And I was almost certain he told them to follow along. Whoever he sent was a pro. They wouldn't be detectable.

We found a place to eat nearby and parked in an empty corner of the lot. I wanted to head inside to the restroom and scrub the smell off my hands and face. Once that morgue-odor invaded your sinuses, it was near impossible to get rid of.

For five minutes we sat in silence with the windows rolled down. The breeze pushed grill smoke through the car. I barely noticed it.

No one else entered the parking lot. No cars passed on the road leading to it. There were no looming headlights nearby indicating a car idling.

I powered up one of the phones and punched in the number. My finger hovered over the send button.

"You gonna make the call?" Bear said.

I nodded. "Just centering myself."

He laughed. "Gone all yogi on me now?"

I ignored him and sent the call through.

"Jack?" Frank said.

"It's us," I said.

"Why the different number?"

A man stepped out of the restaurant, glanced our way, then back at the door. A long-legged brunette wearing a sparkling green skirt ran up and threw one arm around him.

"Just being safe," I said, watching the couple stroll to their vehicle. "Still spooked by the guys we encountered in England. Figured they must've been tracking me somehow, why not through the phone."

Frank cleared his throat. "Good thinking. All right, so how were things at the morgue?"

"Pretty dead, actually."

Bear chuckled. Frank didn't.

"I don't have time for this, Jack. And neither do you two. If you can't be serious about it I'll send two guys who—"

"Calm down, Frank." I looked over at Bear. He still had a smile on his face. The guy was a sucker for a horrible pun. "It was her. Open and shut case."

"Your word is good enough for me. You know that. But they are gonna want evidence."

"Who's they?"

Bear had his chin tucked to his chest. He shifted his head enough to look at me out of the corner of his eye

"Not now, Jack," Frank said. "Come on."

"We got pictures. I'll upload them after our call."

"Do it now," Frank said. "And call me back in five minutes."

I put the memory card in the phone and sent the photos to Frank. After removing the card, I made sure there were no copies of the pictures remaining. The fewer devices the evidence could be found on the better. And at some point I planned on ditching the cell I'd been using to contact Frank.

Bear patted his stomach. "What now?"

"I'll call back in a few minutes, like he said."

"Hungry, man."

"It wasn't that long ago we ate."

"Yeah, but I had a workout while you stood around playing patty cakes with corpses."

It was as though not a day had passed since we were partners in Iraq, D.C., or New York. We were twenty-somethings again and life was a game. Didn't matter how serious we took our jobs — and we always did — but we knew life was too damn short to take it seriously all the time. Even when we faced a life and death situation, we found ways to lighten it up.

Frank answered immediately when I called back.

"Good work," he said. "I used software to compare it with the photos I had. That's definitely her. A perfect match."

I stared at Bear, nodded slowly. "So we good to come home?"

Frank started and stopped, hesitated a few seconds. I waited for him to proceed. "I need you guys to remain in position a little longer."

"What kind of crap are you pulling?" Bear said.

"Riley," Frank said. It sounded as though he were yelling into the mouthpiece. "I'm not trying to pull anything. I need to get this to the right people. They need to confirm through various channels that the target is neutralized. Like I said, this situation has traveled pretty damn high up the chain. You two have been around long enough to know this won't be cleared up in a couple hours."

"What more do you need?" I said. "You saw the damn pictures. Should we go back, get the body, and overnight it to you? Huh? You prefer DHL or FedEx?"

"Look, I'm on your side," Frank said. "I know it's hard to believe, but you can trust me."

Bear looked at me and made a rude gesture with his hand. Neither of us said anything.

"Here, do this," Frank said. "Ditch your phone. Leave town. Get somewhere you feel safe and lay low for a day or two. Call me at noon your time tomorrow. You can do it from a damn payphone if you want. I'll update you with the current intelligence. All of it. OK?"

I disconnected the call and handed the phone to Bear. He acted as though he were going to dismantle it. I doubted Frank had a way of tracking it without the SIM. Bear pulled the back off, removed the card and tossed it out the window.

"Dammit," he said. "I was looking forward to eating here. And now I have to wait?"

I said nothing.

"So help me, if we run into whoever he has tailing us, they're gonna wish they were escorting some politician's kid to the goddamn Sadie Hawkins dance instead of following us."

We left the parking lot and started making a series of left hand turns. By the last one, it was clear no one was following us. At least not by sight. There were other ways that made more sense. Hell, for all I knew, Frank had a drone perched six miles up watching us.

I called Brandon and updated him on the situation, then sent the morgue photos. While I had him on the line, I asked if he could create another phantom number that would route to Frank's line without giving our location away. I was sick of discarding SIM cards after every call. Brandon hesitated because of Frank's new position. In the end he said he would hook us up with a line that would make it appear we were calling from Tokyo.

"So what now?" Bear asked.

"Drive," I said. "Let's head toward Rotterdam while we wait on Brandon and his software."

The city lights faded to the black of night as we entered the countryside. A random car passing in the opposite direction provided the only light on the barren highway. Every so often another vehicle would merge onto the highway and either race ahead or fall behind.

"We'll need the police report," I said.

"Witnesses?" Bear said.

"A place to start. Someone had to have seen something. It was broad daylight when they executed the hit."

"What if they already got to the witnesses?"

We both knew it was a possibility. There had been times when our missions required us to carry out an assassination in the middle of a busy restaurant, on a sidewalk, and even in the changing room of an upscale men's store. And every time, Frank, Feng, or whoever had issued the command, cleaned up the mess. No one talked.

Ever.

I often imagined Bear would fall into that line of work. Just the sight of the guy would be enough to shut someone up.

"Probably the case," I said. "But worth it still. You and I have a way of convincing people."

Bear laughed. I let him do most of the convincing when he was around.

"Think Brandon can get the file?" he asked.

"More than likely," I said. "I'll check when we hear back."

I settled into my seat. Adjusted the side mirror. Stared at the darkness.

Then it happened.

"Jesus," I said.

"What?" Bear said, glancing between me, the road ahead, and the rearview. He didn't need me to tell him. "Dammit."

Headlights had appeared in the distance a few seconds prior.

Now they were practically up our ass.

# 25

The vehicle behind us swerved to the passenger side. The headlights reflected off the side mirror. I shielded my face and looked away. A bright yellow spot impeded my vision for several seconds. The car drifted a few feet to the side, then closer to center. The bright light faded, but I still couldn't see anything.

"Can you tell how many there are?"

Bear gazed into the rearview. The car was close enough the headlights didn't impede his view. "At least two. Can't make out anything past that."

I shifted the mirror toward me and saw two dark shapes. Without street-lights, there was little chance of identifying features. Was it the men we'd encountered twice in England?

"Tap and hold the brake," I said.

"What?" Bear said.

"Do it and keep your foot on the gas."

The hood of the car behind us lit up red. As did the men inside the vehicle.

"It's them," I said.

"The guys from the marina?"

The view I had wasn't perfect. Within a few seconds the vehicle rapidly dropped back from view. But for those few brief seconds I had a good enough look at the driver to confirm it was the same man I'd seen in town. The same guy who stood at the end of the dock with his pistol extended in our direction.

"It's them," I repeated. "Unless they work for Frank, I don't know how they are tracking us. But they found us."

Bear slapped the steering wheel hard enough that the car lurched onto the rough shoulder. "We switched cars, man. How the hell are they on us?"

"They dropped back fast." I adjusted the mirror so he could see, then turned in my seat. "Dammit, they've stopped."

"Friggin' Frank," he said. "Son of a bitch told them where we were."

"We still don't know that they're Agency men. The body was there at the morgue for anyone to find. They could have been watching for someone like us to come along and then followed once we left."

The other vehicle turned abruptly and crossed the grassy median. A second later, they were heading the other way. The tail lights disappeared long before they should have.

"They cut their lights," I said.

Bear slowed and swerved into the emergency lane. The car vibrated harshly until we stopped. He looked over at me. "Should we go after them?"

"They're gone."

"I can catch them."

"In this piece of crap?" I rolled down my window and the car sucked in the breeze. The air smelled sweet. Fragrant. Lavender, maybe. "We can't risk getting pulled over, man. Not after what happened in the morgue. We can't count on anyone to get us out of jail with an assault charge pending."

He released the steering wheel and looked over at me. "We've got Sasha in our corner."

"You really want to involve her in this?"

"Not if we can help it."

"Right," I said. "So let's keep our asses out of lockup."

He pulled back onto the deserted highway. His eyes flicked to the rearview and stayed there. I wanted to turn around, but we had no way of catching the other car. If anything, we'd put ourselves in a worse situation if they were parked on the side of the road waiting for us.

"My guess is they were watching the morgue," I said. "Whether by Frank's orders, or someone else's. So either they followed us from the moment we stepped outside—"

"—or they got to the car while we were inside and planted a tracking device." Bear took a deep breath and exhaled loudly. "We need a new car."

"And now."

He pulled off at the next exit and located a car rental not too far from the highway. I took care of the current vehicle, ditching it on a residential street. Bear secured a new rental. He pulled up a few minutes later in a 5-series BMW, grinning. I shrugged.

"Not impressed?" he said.

"Not really," I said. "You can drive."

"This thing fits me, it can fit anyone."

"You fit into the last car."

"Barely. And my knees were bumping the dash. You know how hard it was to maneuver in that thing?"

"Whatever."

"Christ, you sound like Mandy."

A few minutes later we were back on the highway, which grew more crowded with every on-ramp we passed. Town grew closer. I stared down each new driver that pulled up alongside us, half-expecting to see the men from the marina staring back at me. There were old men, young ladies, and everything in-between.

Except them.

"Guess we'll know if it was the car soon enough," Bear said.

"Suppose so," I said. "Let's just hope we live through it if it was something else."

He ran his hand over his head and placed it near the base of his neck. Held it there for a few minutes. His face twisted, like he was in pain. I'd seen that look plenty of times. Usually after he'd taken a pipe to the gut, or a bullet to the shoulder. Never from sitting in the car.

"You all right?" I asked.

He nodded, said nothing. Guess the earlier fight had taken more of a toll on him than he thought. He was out of practice and out of shape and it was showing.

"You're not gonna turn into a liability on me, are you?"

He laughed. "I'm already a liability, partner. So you better watch both our backs."

The phone set on the dash vibrated and skirted toward the center.

"Brandon?" Bear asked.

I nodded, answered. "What's up?"

"First, I got you a line to use," Brandon said. "It'll show every call you make coming from a residence on the top floor of a sixty-story building in Hong Kong."

"You said Tokyo before."

"You serious?" he said. "I'll cut that damn line off—"

"Kidding." I said. "It's perfect." He read off the number. I wrote it down. Bear committed it to memory. "Before you keep going, I got one more request."

"I'm billing you by the minute. You know that, right, Jack?"

"Yeah, whatever." I glanced over at a passing Jaguar. British Racing Green. One of my favorite colors. An old lady glanced over. Looked like she smiled, then pulled ahead of us.

"So what do you need?" Brandon asked.

"Police report from the hit. And I suppose any other info you can dig up on what happened today. I need witness names. The officers' names. Anything and everything."

"You got it." He tapped on his computer, starting his search or perhaps making a note to check after the call. "You ready for these results?"

"Lay it on us, my man."

He cleared his throat, then proceeded to tell us something I couldn't believe.

# 26

"OK," Brandon said before clearing his throat. He grunted several times. "Damn cheese puffs, always messing me up. Anyway, onto your corpse. Man, this is some crazy mess here. It's most definitely not your lady. Not sister A. Not sister B. Not some weird mashup of them."

That confirmed what we'd noticed. The thought that the tattoos had been fakes had crossed my mind. After all there was only the single picture taken more than a decade ago with their bodies exposed.

Brandon continued. "Aside from the facial structure, which I'm about to get to, I was able to access some classified docs. Full shots of both women. The tattoos were there from about age eighteen. Now, I don't know if the dudes at Langley, or wherever, are gonna notice this or not, but I'd say you're twelve-to-twenty-four hours ahead of them."

"Any clue if they're sending someone to check out the body?" I said. "Frank's gonna sell them on what we sent. It's possible someone will dig deeper. Want more answers."

Brandon laughed at the suggestion. "You know the only fools that are gonna see those pics are high up enough that they don't do any day-to-day type stuff. No one is gonna compare any more than the face. And on the surface, it passes."

"So how come you're saying it's not her?" Bear said.

"Bear, Bear," Brandon said with a heavy sigh. "I don't stop at the surface."

"Well, then enlighten me, my scrawny friend," Bear said.

"If you hadn't interrupted me, I'd be halfway done explaining it to your thick ass." He coughed a couple times, perhaps because he'd started to laugh. Maybe he inhaled a few more cheese puffs or licked the dust off his fingers. A few seconds later, he continued. "OK, so the pics passed the eye test. Dead blonde girl looks like the living blonde girl, when you account for the pale-gray skin, matted hair, lack of make-up. Oh, and the goddamn bullet hole in her skull."

"Right," I said. "We get it."

"But when I feed them through my software, it's off. I mean, it's close, but not quite right. Follow me?"

"Sure." Following Brandon's chain of thought required an advanced degree.

"So I took the picture from the hotel. Matched it against the corpse. And guess what?" He paused, but wasn't waiting on us to respond. "Partial match."

"What are we thinking here?" I said. "A relative? Both of them are relatives?"

"That crossed my mind, briefly." There were touchtones as he tapped on his screen. My phone buzzed a few seconds later. "Take a look at that."

I downloaded the attachment and opened it. It was a side-by-side shot of the brunette woman from the hotel and the most recent photo of Katrine Ahlberg. There were blue dots spanning each face connected by thin lines. A grid of some sort.

Another message came through.

"Now look at that," Brandon said.

It was a mashup with the photos lined up on top of each other, dots and lines still intact.

"Christ." The grids matched up perfectly on each face. "This mean what I think it does?"

"Yeah," Brandon said.

"The dark-haired woman from the hotel is Katrine?"

"I mean, that's what the pictures say. There's some minor differences, but they can be accounted for with surgery. But the basic outline, so to say, is the same. So unless you can get a better shot of her, maybe in a bikini, I can't say I'm one hundred percent sure. But I trust my software enough to say that I'm ninety-nine-point-nine-nine on it."

"She knew," Bear said. I glanced over at the big man. He was nodding to himself. "Someone tipped her off. But how the hell did she get another person to take a bullet for her?"

"Money?" I said. "Maybe the woman who took the bullet didn't know?"

"More than likely," Brandon said.

"Other thing is," I said, "as far as I know, this just came about on Frank's side. Unless Ahlberg and her body double were perfect matches, the work the other woman had done isn't something that takes place overnight."

"Question is," Brandon said, "who the hell is she?"

"That's what I need you for," I said. "Can you start scanning and matching against the databases?"

"Already working on that." He paused, took a wheezy breath, followed by a puff on his inhaler. After he exhaled, he continued. "But so far it's not returning anything."

"Exhaust every damn source you've got." That was as far as we could get on the corpse's identity, so I switched topics. "What about the police report?"

The key to everything might lie with that report. All we needed was the name of one witness who managed to get a look at the killer, the killer's vehicle, the type of gun they used. With that, we had a chance at figuring out who was behind the hit. Who we were working against. Who was and wasn't on our side.

"I should have it within the hour," Brandon said. "I'll shoot you a secure link when I do."

"All right," I said. "We'll check in with you after we get some sleep. Maybe sooner."

Bear and I sat in silence for five minutes after ending the call. I'm sure our minds chewed on the same questions. Did they arrive at the same possible conclusions?

Katrine had spent a decade pretending to be someone she wasn't. We'd tried to take her life, but false intel led to a massive screw-up and we assassinated her sister, Birgit. What better way to continue on than let the world assume Katrine was dead, and assume the identity of Birgit? Sure, she lost a lot of money by doing so, but it wasn't like her family was poor. As Birgit, she laid low for several years, perhaps operating behind the scenes in the same activities she delved in while living as Katrine. Only when she became more active, perhaps with the thought of more outwardly resuming some of the roles of her previous life, the community noticed her.

Her network had to be strong. There had to be someone from her past who knew she was still alive living under her sister's name. That person had to be well-placed in order to have advance warning of the hit. Access to our intelligence, or someone else's? Determining the "someone else" would go a long way here.

Or maybe Katrine Ahlberg was extremely paranoid and had arranged for a body-double long ago, anticipating the day another attempt on her life would take place.

"I think we should call Sasha," Bear said, breaking the silent lull. I tuned out the hum of the tires on the asphalt in the background. He was running down the same trails as me. We each had a single contact we could trust. For me, Brandon was the man. Bear had Sasha. I felt I could trust her. He knew he could.

"I don't want to get her involved," I said. "Too dangerous, especially when she's got Mandy in her custody. You know Frank is watching."

"Sasha can take care of herself just as well as you and me."

"She's a desk jockey, Bear."

"She wasn't always. And you know they don't work like that. She spends plenty of time in the field. Hell, wasn't that long ago you trusted her with Mia, right?"

He had a point. Around the time I had my last showdown with Frank, Sasha came to help watch Mia while I tied up a few loose ends.

"Let's hold off," I said. "I'm not entirely opposed to bringing her in, but let's see what Brandon comes up with on the police report and the ID of the mystery woman. If there's lingering questions, we go to Sasha."

He nodded tersely, said nothing.

"Remember," I said. "We don't know who's watching who here. It is possible that someone in MI5 or MI6 is working with Frank, or whoever, and watching her. Monitoring her. Keeping tabs on every call she makes and receives."

Bear exhaled loudly, fogging the glass for a few seconds. The street lights turned into large bursts of orange as we passed them. "You're right. Let's find a place to crash."

We exited the highway a mile later and found a small motel. I checked in while Bear parked the car around back. Best to keep it out of sight.

A cool breeze that smelled of jasmine swept across the barren parking lot. Crumpled paper raced through the puddles of dim white light. A couple windows were lit up through drawn curtains, but most of the motel was dark. Didn't seem like the place had a lot of business at the moment.

Bear met me near the stairwell. I led the way up to the second level, down an outdoor walkway, and found our room. The odor of stale cigarettes slapped me in the face. At one point in recent history, I wouldn't have minded. But it had been a while since my last one. Best decision I made in recent years. I could run further and faster than in my late twenties. I figured most rooms here would smell the same, so no point in requesting new accommodations.

I flipped on the light, illuminating the small, dated room. It had green shag carpets and wallpaper from the seventies. There were two twin sized beds. Bear picked his and flopped onto it. The frame groaned and bowed in the middle. His feet hung off the end. His head rubbed against the wall.

"I dunno," he said. "Floor might be better."

I glanced down at the thick carpet and imagined a colony of bedbugs weaving their way through the long threads. "Nah, I think I'm taking my chances with the bed."

I could have slept anywhere at that point. An old, sagging bed might not be the best thing for my back, but chances were I wouldn't notice until I got up.

I fell back onto the bed with the same results as Bear. A few seconds later my eyes were closed. But sleep wasn't forthcoming. My phone buzzed against the nightstand. Had to be Brandon.

"Want to find out?" I said.

Bear grumbled something indecipherable.

"Take that as a yes." I swiped through to the message and downloaded the attachment. "It's the report."

"What's it say?"

I scrolled through, unable to read most of it since it was in Dutch. Brandon had made comments on the important parts, though. In the end I had the names of two cops and one witness. Brandon had made a note alongside the witness' name.

*NOTE: The name was REDACTED on the current file. I had to dig a little deeper for the original. I'll have the address for you by morning your time. Good luck.*

"Coos Joosten," I said.

"That the cop?" Bear said.

"The witness," I said.

He rolled onto his side, propped his head on his hand. "Address?"

"Forthcoming."

He collapsed onto his back. "Looks like we got a lead."

"Sure does."

Only the information would soon be contradicted.

# 27

THE SUNLIGHT CUT THROUGH THE PARTED BLINDS AND SLICED ACROSS MY FACE. The dull ache in my eyes woke me. Bear was already up. He'd showered, left and found some breakfast for us. I found a cooling plate of scrambled eggs and a roll on my nightstand. The plate balanced on my phone, silverware hanging off the edge. Steam from a mug of coffee rose into the air.

Bear sat in the chair across from my bed, an empty plate on his lap. "Eat up. This promises to be a busy day."

I propped myself up, grabbed the plate and inhaled half the eggs in a couple forkfuls. Then I washed it down with the coffee, which turned out to be hotter than the food. I tossed Bear the roll and finished the rest.

"Anyone mess with the car?" We had placed a series of traps on the vehicle to alert us to anyone trying to access it.

"Nah." He rubbed the thick stubble on his cheeks above his beard line. "I think they must've followed us from the morgue by sight or a tracking device on the other car. Either way, they lost us."

"For now, I suppose." I set my plate on the bed. "I still don't get why they turned around."

"Maybe they figured you made them."

"Then why not escalate the issue? There was no way we'd outrun them. They could've taken us right there."

"I guess they could've been called off. Ever consider that we're being played here? Let us do the legwork, then do us in."

"Call me crazy, but right now I'm wishing they would've stuck with us."

"Yeah, I'd like to get my hands on them and find out who the hell they are." He rose and tossed his plate onto the bed next to mine, then pointed at my cell. "Gonna call Frank?"

"Christ, it's too early to deal with him."

"I'd still like to know what he's found."

I nodded, held up my coffee. "Gonna finish this, then I'll call."

Bear stepped outside for a few minutes while I savored the coffee. Not sure where he got it, but it tasted as good as anything I'd had in Europe.

I dialed into the number Brandon had provided for me. Frank answered, sounded a little confused. Probably wondered why the hell I was in Hong Kong.

"It's me," I said.

"Number threw me off," he said.

"I figured. What'd you find out?"

"Nothing from the higher ups. Like I said, it's gonna take some time with them. And I don't know how they're gonna want to proceed. There's already a little talk about having you hang around and try to find who pulled off the hit."

I moved to the windows, peered through the blinds. Bear stood in the middle of the parking lot. Looked like he was in the middle of a yoga routine. He had one leg bent, foot against the other knee. His arms were raised over his head, clasped, index fingers aimed skyward.

"They got people better suited for that," I said. "I'm not an investigator."

"That would involve adding a whole other layer of intelligence to this mess," Frank said. "More agents and agencies and directors and reports. That's not good for anyone, Jack. Especially you and Logan. Both of you have others to think about now, right?"

I pushed aside the anger that welled due to Frank bringing our families into this. At one point, I was off the hook for anything and everything I'd ever done. Both stateside and in any friendly country. Had that changed? Had the events that had transpired between Frank and I changed my status?

"Why especially me?" I asked.

"Some people think you're dead," he said. "Some don't. Some of those who don't would like for your expiration date to arrive. You know as well as I do that I can't just give one part of the story. The whole thing has to be brought to light, start to finish. You were there in the beginning. You're there now. If I'm forced to tell them that, you can guarantee a couple spooks are gonna show up and take you down. Logan, too."

I considered letting Frank in on what had happened last night after we left the morgue. The car on the highway, piloted by the same two men we'd encountered twice before. I still couldn't say for certain they weren't working for Frank. Couldn't say they were, either. But if so, he already knew what had transpired.

"All right," I said. "Lone wolf time I suppose."

"It's how you two work best, right?"

I could see the grin plastered on his face as he regurgitated a line I'd given him dozens of times. He had us exactly where he wanted us, in the middle of his mess. We were the only ones who could clean it up.

"Anything else?" I said.

"Yeah, that police report," he said. "Um, I know you don't want to give your cell number, so I'll upload it to a secure site. You can retrieve it there however you wish."

I wrote down the URL.

"It has a couple witness names," he said. "You might be able to retrieve valuable intel if they haven't been coerced already. You know how these people operate."

"Who's 'these people'?" I said.

"In the general sense," Frank said. "Christ, Jack. Don't you think if I knew that you'd know already? Why dick around with some asshole who happened to watch a woman's head explode in front of him when you can go straight to the source?"

"All right, whatever. I'll get to the report soon and be back in touch in a few hours."

There was no way I was typing that web address in. I forwarded it to Brandon and asked him to retrieve the document. He was the only one I knew who could access the server without revealing his location and passing on a signature Frank could trace. See, a regular proxy that routed traffic through another location wouldn't work. Not with the capabilities Frank had available to him. It took a pro to bypass the Agency's systems. Who better than the guy who designed it for the government?

A few seconds after sending the message, Brandon replied with a *10-4.* A couple minutes later, I received the report in an attachment along with a message that read, "Shady stuff going on here, man."

When I opened the report, I saw why.

# 28

Bear's ass greeted me as I pulled the door open. He was bent at the waist only a few feet away, his hands clasped behind his knees. The guy had always been limber, especially for his size, but I couldn't help but take notice how ridiculous he looked.

"Quit playing with yourself and get in here, man."

He rolled up, laughing.

"The hell you doing, anyway?" I said.

"You should try it," he said. "Great for the mind, body, spirit."

"I thought that was what beer was for."

This elicited another laugh as he walked past me, wiping beads of sweat off his forehead.

"So what's the news?" he said.

"Got the police report from Frank," I said.

"And?"

"Someone's screwing with us."

"How so?"

I pulled up the report on my phone and handed it to him. He tapped the screen with his finger and scrolled through the report. As he neared the witness section, his eyebrow arched high, creating a mess of wrinkles on his forehead.

"Who the hell are Flipse and Rompa?" he said.

I shook my head. "Doesn't match what Brandon sent us, that's for damn sure."

"Son of a bitch." Bear handed my phone back, zoomed in on the officers' names. They had remained the same. "So Frank's setting us up. We go see either of those men, and sure enough one of those bastards is gonna open the door with a Glock aimed at our heads. Won't have time to ask any questions 'cause our brains'll be splattered all over the sidewalk."

"Still can't say it's Frank for sure."

He looked up at me incredulously, shaking his head. "How the hell can you stand up for that asshole, man? After what he did to you? And how he detained you and forced you into this assignment?"

"We screwed up, Bear. It was us that pulled the trigger."

"Based on SIS intel." He stood and walked to the back of the room, leaned against the wall, arms folded across his chest. "He's been screwing us over for years. I think we completed most jobs in spite of him. And once again here we are in the middle of some damn country, with who knows how many spooks on our tail. And Frank's in the middle of it."

"I believe everything you're saying. Trust me, man, I do. But this report could have come from another source and Frank bought into it. If that's the case, then why would he doubt it? What reason would he have to think it's made up? He thinks the right woman was taken out last night."

"We don't know that."

"No, we don't. But that's what I'm assuming. For now at least. You know how I feel."

"Then why are you defending him?"

"Tunnel vision."

He stared me down for a moment, then lowered his arms and tucked his hands into his pockets. He'd been there before. It came with the territory.

"It's dangerous for us to focus in on one person," I said. "Whether that's Frank, or someone else. The moment we do that we're dead men, because if it turns out to be someone else, they'll catch us by surprise and we won't see it coming. Goodbye, Mia. Farewell, Mandy. So long, Sasha. Damn you, cruel world."

"All right, all right. I got it. Christ. Let's get the hell out of this place and go pay a visit to that witness."

Bear left the room first and hopped in the car behind the wheel. We drove a mile or two down the road, made a few turns, then headed back toward the hotel.

No one had followed when he went out for breakfast and no one did so now. No harm in being cautious, though.

Along the way we worked out our plan for speaking with Joosten. One of the reports was false. Chances were it was Frank's, but we couldn't stake our lives on it. So rather than going in guns blazing, we decided to park near the address and wait for the guy to leave. When the opportunity arose, we'd secure him and take him someplace quiet to talk. Where that conversation led would direct how we handled the other witness names on Frank's report. There was no doubt in our minds that they were false. I decided against contacting Brandon. He had backdoor access to various systems and databases, but a search was a search and if someone had flagged these names, they would be watching for anyone trying to gather information on the fake witnesses.

One of the addresses from Frank's report was an apartment located nowhere near the murder. It'd be harder to run surveillance there unless we resorted to technology. So we decided to focus on the other witness from the report.

"Maybe it won't come to that," Bear said. "If this guy we're going after turns out to be the real deal, we'll be done with it."

We stopped before reaching town and loaded up on food, water, and a few supplies for a possible long stakeout. We could luck out and it only would take a few minutes. Or it could be all day. Knowing us, it wouldn't go past that. Either Bear or I would tire of waiting and one of us would go to the door.

We parked next to the curb a block away from the small pale yellow house after driving through the neighborhood three times. It was quiet. Quaint. A couple kids with backpacks strapped on their backs rode past on their bikes. The little girl giggled and waved at Bear. Kind of reminded me of an older subdivision back in the States. The small yards were manicured with fruit trees and newly awakened flowers. The air was still for the first time and smelled crisp. I figured it was around fifty degrees out. Quite a contrast to my recent time in Texas.

"How long should we wait?" Bear said.

"Long as it takes?" I said.

"Not a fan of sitting around, man. How do we know that whoever messed with the original report isn't watching this place?"

I'd considered it and frankly welcomed the possibility. The sooner we were done with the cloak and dagger stuff the better. "Anything's possible I suppose."

"You suppose, huh? They better shoot your side of the car first. Otherwise I'll kill you if this turns out to be a setup."

Thirty minutes passed before the first sign of action. A late-model, mid-sized silver Mercedes pulled up to the house. The door opened, then a pair of slender legs stepped out. Her feet were sheathed in flats. She was tall and thin. A scarf covered her head and most of her face. Couldn't see her hair. She looked around before jogging up to the front door. Someone waited in the car with their arm stretched across the empty seat. Couldn't tell if it was a man or woman. They seemed to keep their focus on the lady at the door.

Bear pulled out a pen and his notebook. He jotted down the license plate, then tucked everything away.

The front door inched open. The woman placed her foot in the opening, her hand against the frame. I could only see her back. The rest was shielded from view. A man stepped into the light.

"Coos, I presume," Bear said.

"You presume, huh?"

"Whatever."

"You hang out with Mandy too much. You know that? Talk like a damn teenager now."

Bear placed his fist over his mouth like he was coughing into it in order to stifle his laugh. Wouldn't be a good idea to alert them to our presence. Hell, we shouldn't have spoken in the first place.

I could hear the man's voice. It was loud and high and a little panicked. The woman took her hand off the door frame and placed it on him. He seemed to settle down. Then her hand disappeared. She was looking down, searching through something in her bag. She handed the guy an envelope. Leaned in. Whispered to him.

As she backed away, he stood there nodding. Bear snapped a couple pictures on his phone. The guy nodded like a child accepting tasks doled out by his mother. The man finally backed away and closed the door. The woman slammed her door after getting into the car. She pulled away from the curb and raced down the street toward one of the two neighborhood exits.

Bear placed his hand on the shifter. "Should we go?"

"You got the plates right?"

He watched the car drive off, nodded.

"We're good, then," I said.

"You get a good look at her?" He was swiping through the photos he'd taken.

"Not really." I leaned over to see the pictures. "How'd they turn out?"

"Grainy from the zoom. Look."

It was impossible to tell anything about the woman, other than she was fair-skinned. The scarf covered her hair, forehead, part of her cheeks. Big sunglasses covered the rest or her face and obviously her eyes. Her lips were bright red. She could have added half an inch to them with the lipstick.

"Doesn't look like we'll be waiting long," Bear said.

I glanced up and saw the man exiting his house. He had on a tan coat zipped halfway and dark blue pants. Keys dangled from his hands. He hopped into the car in the driveway, backed out and started down the street away from us.

Bear shifted into gear and followed. He didn't bother to conceal the fact that we were tailing the man. This wasn't the kind of guy who'd take notice. After a series of turns and a short jaunt on the highway, we pulled into a parking garage. It was like most I'd been in. Smelled of exhaust. Dimly lit in the center. Spaces narrow, some of them numbered.

We drove up three levels to a section where there were few parked vehicles. The man pulled his car into a spot near the stairwell.

Before the guy managed to cut his engine, Bear slowed down enough for me to hop out without falling. I took cover behind a nearby vehicle and waited. He opened his door, but remained seated. He had his phone to his ear. I couldn't make out what he was saying.

A minute later he stepped out and glanced around the garage. The window tint provided plenty of cover. His eyes swept right past. I only waited long enough for him to round his car. Then I raced toward him. The echoes of my steps must not have registered because he didn't turn around until after he'd entered the stairwell. He dropped his bag and stumbled into the wall. Saved me the trouble of tackling him.

I drew my pistol, aimed it at his chest. "Coos Joosten?"

He clutched his stomach, lips working to spit out a response. I thought he might throw up. He managed to stammer out a word. "Yes."

"Come with me."

# 29

Tires squealed as Bear slammed on the brakes in front of the stairwell. I pulled Joosten from the shadows and threw him into the backseat, then climbed in after him. I had little fear of the guy trying something. He didn't look the part. Still, years of experience had taught me to expect the unexpected and to never rely on the sight test when it came to what someone was capable of. I kept as much distance between us as possible, holding the pistol out of his arm's reach.

"What, what, what do you guys w-want?" he stammered.

"Shut up," I said.

Bear glanced at me through the rearview then hit the gas. We sped toward the unmanned exit and merged into stop-and-go traffic.

"Look," the guy said. "If this is about, you know, the thing that happened, I already promised I wasn't going to talk. I swear it on my daughter's life. I won't say anything."

"Why your daughter's life?" I said. "And didn't I tell you to shut up?"

The guy opened his mouth and shut it after I shook my head. Beads of sweat streamed down his forehead, some coming to rest in his bushy eyebrows. Others glided down his nose and side of his face. His hands trembled. His gaze remained steady on the pistol aimed at his chest.

"Get us out of town," I said. "And roll down the window a bit. Coos appears to be a bit overheated."

The cabin sucked in the cool air. The guy took a deep breath, settled back. He dragged his nervous hand across his brow. Wiped it off on his pants leg, leaving behind a wet stain.

"Can you point that somewhere else?" he said, eyes fixed on the gun.

I shook my head.

"Can we talk?" he said.

I shook my head again.

He muttered something in his native tongue, closed his eyes, and lowered his chin to his chest. Perhaps he thought he was going to die.

That's exactly what I wanted him to think.

Twenty minutes later we found ourselves on a deserted dirt road that split a wooded area. The grass track in the middle had spread out, leaving two small brown ruts. The sedan jostled and dipped along the path. Bear slowed to a stop once we were deep enough into the forest that we couldn't see anything through the trees.

The big man left the vehicle idling and stepped outside. He opened Joosten's door and gestured for the guy to step out. I exited simultaneously, keeping my pistol on the guy. Bear had the man in his grasp as soon as the guy stood.

Birds sang all around us. Wind rustled through the trees. The air smelled fresh, clean. A big contrast to the city garage where everything smelled of diesel and gas fumes.

We walked thirty or so feet into the trees. A small animal scampered away nearby. Guess we'd gotten too close for its comfort.

"This should be far enough," I said. "Not like anyone travels this road anymore. Would take years to find a body back here."

"If they found it at all," Bear said. "Scavengers would make quick work of it out here. Scatter the bones around. Could take months to find enough parts to put any semblance of a skeleton back together. Hell, they might never figure out the identity."

The guy's knees went weak. He dropped to the ground. Dead leaves scattered and puffed into the air under the sudden weight. He buried his face in his hands and sobbed. In between his cries, he managed to talk.

"I said... I wouldn't... tell anyone... I haven't... I won't."

"Get ahold of yourself, man," Bear said. "Christ, stand up."

The guy didn't budge.

Bear nudged him in the back with his foot. Perhaps it was more than a nudge, because the guy fell forward and landed face first in a patch of tall grass.

"Goddammit." Bear leaned over, grabbed the guy and yanked him up. The man remained limp. His feet dragged as Bear moved him over to a tree and parked him there.

I stepped in. "The woman who came to visit you. Who was she?"

The guy regained his composure and pressed back against the tree. He wiped his eyes and face. A long strand of snot stuck to his hand and dangled in the air, catching the sunlight. His eyebrow hair stood up and scattered in every direction.

"Well?" I said.

"I don't know," he said. "I'd never seen her before this morning."

"What'd she say?"

He scratched the back of his head against the tree bark for a second or two, looked up into the foliage. "She reiterated what the men had said to me."

"Which was?"

"You don't know?"

"Would I be asking if I did?"

He furrowed his messy brow at me. "I suppose you might if you were testing me to see if I'd spoken to anyone."

Bear coughed. Guess he was impressed at the guy. Or getting pissed at me for not getting the information.

"You see that man there," I said, jutting my chin toward Bear. "If you don't tell me what I want to know, then he's gonna extract it from you. You want that?"

Joosten glanced at Bear and shuddered. He shook his head while casting his gaze downward. Perhaps he felt ashamed at cracking so easily.

"All right, then," I said. "What did she say to you?"

"Keep my mouth shut. That's it."

"We watched the whole thing go down." I leaned into the guy. All the sweat had left a residual stink on him that I associated with fear. "What was in the envelope she handed you?"

His eyes glossed over as he glanced around.

"There's no escape," I said. "You can run, but you won't get far. Tell me what was in the envelope. Answer a few more questions. Then we'll take you back to your car."

"A, uh, down payment," he said.

I waited for him to continue and said nothing.

He lowered his voice as though the trees were recording his words. "For keeping quiet about what I saw."

"What'd you see?" I said.

"Do you work for them?"

"I don't work for anyone."

"Then why do you care?"

"I have a personal interest in what happened to that woman. Problem is that no one knows anything. Except for you. So why not tell me what you know?"

He glanced around again while biting his bottom lip.

"There's no one out here," I said.

He shifted from foot to foot for a few seconds, then recounted what had happened. "There were two of them. They confronted her."

"Men? Women?"

"Men," he said.

"What'd they look like?"

"Uh, I dunno. Locals, I guess."

"You guess? How could you tell?"

"Nothing stood out about them. They were average guys to me. I really wasn't paying attention. I was sitting there, having a coffee. It's the kind of area where people are walking about, shopping, stopping, talking. You know. So seeing these women stopped by these men was nothing that got my attention."

"Women," I said. "Can you describe the other?"

The description he gave of her matched the woman from the hotel. I pulled the picture up and showed it to him.

"Yes," he said. "That's her.

"But that's not the woman who came to your house this morning."

He shook his head.

"OK," I said. "Go on."

"The men, they turned to her, the brunette, and pushed her out of the way. See, this is what I remember more than anything. They knocked her into the, uh, how you say, railing. I caught it all out of the side of my eye, then I heard the noise of the metal grating against the concrete walk. Oh, how it sounded like a car wreck. The woman, she grunted as she hit it full force with her stomach. And when she tried to stand, the guy shoved her so hard, she flipped over the railing. I guess she had enough of the beating by then because she crawled into the café, leaving her friend alone with the men."

"Didn't come back out?"

"I don't know." He leaned back against the tree and stared up again. His demeanor was more relaxed as he recounted the events. Didn't know if that meant he trusted us now, or if it was due to his brain focusing on a problem.

"Either she did or she didn't," I said.

"It's not that simple."

"Elaborate."

"After she went in, the first and second gunshot rang out and the other woman fell to the ground. It was chaos after that."

"Which of the men shot her? And where first?"

"Neither. It came from somewhere else. The red bloom filled her chest, so I assume that's where the bullets hit. Right? Anyhow, the men seemed as surprised by the shots as I was. I distinctly remember locking stares with one of them. He looked frightened, as though the next bullet was meant for him. Perhaps the first, too."

"What'd they do?"

"They took cover for a few seconds. They ran after the third shot. I think it was then that they ran. You'll have to excuse me, everything but a few memories is now a blur after watching that woman die like that, choking on her own blood before that final shot caused her head to jerk violently."

His words painted a picture that played on repeat in my mind.

"Anything else you can remember?" I said. "Maybe someone coming up to the body, checking it, and then running off? The other woman coming back out? Seeing a shooter on a roof? Anything like that?"

"No," he said. "Really, everything is so jumbled together I couldn't tell you if the tomatoes I smelled were from the cafe or at home later that night."

I glanced over at Bear to gauge his feelings on the story. He stood with his arms loose, leaned back and nodded slightly, indicating he bought the man's story. I did, too. Aside for the occasional glance up to recall a memory, there was nothing he did that could be taken as a sign of deception. And the guy obviously had not been trained to conceal lies. He'd opened up and recounted every memory he had about the murder.

"The woman who came to your house," I said. "Did you recognize her?"

"Hard to see her face the way she was dressed," he said. "But, no, I didn't recognize what I saw or her voice."

"OK. Wait here."

I walked with Bear to the car. The idling engine would help to muffle our voices as we discussed what the man had said. We had to determine if there was any benefit to keeping him around for a while. Perhaps he'd open up further, tell us a few more details that he held back whether consciously or not.

We never got that far.

# 30

THE SHOT SOUNDED LIKE A CANNON ERUPTING AMID THE TRANQUILITY OF THE forest. Birds scattered, squawking their warnings to all nearby to get the hell away. Bear and I drew our weapons. The line between training and instinct at this point in our careers was blended. Both had been counted on enough that they were ingrained as the same reaction. One or the other or both took over and we aimed our pistols in the same direction.

Bear fired off three rounds into the green veil. The chances of hitting anyone were low, but the move bought us some cover and a little time to gather our bearings.

Using the trees as shields, I made my way toward Joosten. He writhed on the ground, clutching his chest. Blood spilled from the gaping hole he tried to plug with his fingers. A crimson stream trickled from his mouth. He coughed a couple times while trying to speak, sending a cloud of blood-laden saliva into the air. The muscles in his cheeks spasmed. His near lifeless eyes stared at me, begging for help.

The risk of moving closer was too great. I wanted to help him and put him out of his misery, but he'd been exposed to the shooter where he had stood. If I went to that same spot, I'd be dead, too. In the grand scheme of things another thirty seconds wouldn't make too much difference to Joosten. He was beyond saving.

So I waited, listened, watched. Bear did the same a dozen yards from me. Leaves crunched under heavy footsteps. Someone whistled, an obvious sign there were at least two of them and they were working together. Were they coming for the body? Or us? If they wanted Joosten's corpse, they were welcome to it.

I started a slow retreat to the car, remaining low to the ground and darting between trees, using them as cover. At the same time I kept an eye out for movement in the woods. Things had settled somewhat. The sound of their approach had dimmed to nothing. The animals had not returned. The area took on an eerie silence.

Bear met me about two-thirds of the way. It would have taken maybe ten seconds had I been walking. But maneuvering in a way to remain unseen had left me feeling that the journey had taken an hour.

"Make a run for the car?" Bear whispered.

"They could be watching it."

"We just gonna stay here all night? I mean, they know we're here. Probably got another team en route to block us in."

"Then I guess we should get moving."

Bear lunged through the gap between where we stood and the next tree over. The second he cleared it, the bark near his face exploded into hundreds of shards. The shooter was a half-second off.

And he'd pay for it.

I stepped to the right with my pistol raised, located the man. He was a good fifty feet away. Plenty close enough for me. One shot. Dead center. The guy dropped where he stood.

His partner yelled out. I saw him cutting through the woods like he was going to assist the fallen man. He must've wised up because in my anticipation of his destination, I lost him.

"He's running." Bear didn't wait for me to respond. He took off in the direction of the man, hurdling the guy I'd killed and dodging low hanging branches.

"Christ," I muttered, taking off after him. I stopped and looked down at the corpse. Didn't recognize the guy. A quick search of his clothing turned up no wallet, no cell phone. They'd ditched before coming out, perhaps in their vehicle.

I heard Bear off in the distance. "Who the hell are you?"

His large hands wrapped around the man's neck, pinning the guy to a tree with his feet a foot off the ground. The guy kicked against Bear and the tree. It had no impact on the situation.

"Who are you?" Bear repeated. His nostrils flared, cheeks twitched, and his eyes looked as though they were going to shoot fire at the man. The guy's twisted mouth tried to spit out words, but his crushed larynx prevented it.

"Let him down if you want him to talk," I said.

Bear raised the man higher. The guy's eyes rolled back and he wet himself.

"Goddammit," Bear said as he let go and stepped back.

The man fell into his own puddle of piss. He grabbed his throat. His face turned from blue to deep red. He looked up at me, then Bear. Perhaps out of instinct he reached for his pistol, which had fallen nearby. He almost got to it. Bear lunged forward, drove his knee into the guy's arm, smashing it against the tree with a snap. He let out a gargled scream. Bear reached down, yanked the guy up, tossed him into another tree.

"Who are you?"

The man was on his knees and one hand. The other hung at an odd angle. Strands of blood seeped from his mouth and cuts on his face. I stepped closer to him. He looked up, made eye contact. He smiled, revealing several broken or missing teeth in his mouth. The guy managed to make it to his knees, wobbling the higher his torso went. Slowly, he lifted his hand to his face to wipe the blood away.

Or so I thought.

I took a step back, raised my sidearm at his chest.

He shoved something in his mouth, then clenched his jaw tight. By the time I reached him it was too late. Thick white foam poured through the gaps in his teeth. His eyes rolled back, and his body convulsed several times before falling over.

"What the hell?" Bear said.

"Poisoned himself," I said, kicking the opened tin into the space between us. "Cyanide would be my guess."

"We dealing with the KGB now?"

I shrugged. Anything was possible at this point. I looked up at Bear. "Someone who didn't want to be caught."

# 31

We were both on edge as we walked back to the car. Bear spun toward every noise with his pistol extended. I almost shot a squirrel that ran out from under a pile of brown leaves. Were there more men out there? Did someone have us in their crosshairs at that very moment?

Continuing to use the trees as cover, we moved toward Joosten, stopping to snap pictures of the slain assailants. Poor bastard had expired. His dull eyes stared up at the green canopy. Nasty way for a guy like that to go. Probably had never even been in a fistfight in his life. Then he had the misfortune of being in the wrong place at the wrong time and became witness to a brutal execution.

I assumed that the two men we killed were the ones Joosten had seen confront the woman at the murder scene. He had mentioned that the guys seemed startled by the gunshots. That was part of the act. They were on the ground to control the situation. Isolate the target by moving everyone else away. In this case, they caused a scene that made normal people nervous. Most men and women won't confront a hostile individual, let alone two of them. They'd rather turn a blind eye and cross over to the other side of the street than get involved.

Joosten had hinted that he had been visited by these very same men. They had told him to keep his mouth shut. And then they had continued to monitor him. Perhaps by his car. Or maybe one of them had bugged an item the guy used every day. His phone or wallet, something like that. As soon as his daily pattern deviated from what they considered his normal routine, they went on the offensive. Must've been close, too, because we weren't in the woods for that long. They saw him with the two of us and figured the best course of action was to eliminate the threat.

They should have aimed for me or Bear.

Collateral damage.

That was what they settled for instead.

We made it to the relative safety of the BMW. Bear took the wheel again, navigating the rutted dirt road. The tires crunched on the ground. A cloud of brown followed in our wake. We were silent, both of us scanning as deep as we could into the trees. When we reached the clearing I spotted their vehicle parked a hundred yards or so away.

"Let's check it out," I said.

Bear had already started turning the other direction. He threw it in reverse and whipped the BMW around. We approached the parked vehicle slowly and cautiously. I had my window down, arm resting on the sill, pistol sweeping the woods. If there had been a third, we would have seen him by now if he intended to exact revenge for his fallen partners.

Bear pulled up alongside the car. The late model sedan still ticked and banged. I hopped out. Heat radiated off the hood. I checked the driver's door and found it unlocked. The car was empty except for a messenger bag on the backseat and a handheld device facedown on the dash. I assumed they used the unit to track Joosten.

Bear opened the backdoor and grabbed the bag. He yanked on the seats, and pushed on the floor. I did the same. Neither of us found any hidden compartments inside. I popped the trunk and the hood. Up front, we checked behind the grill. They could have used it to wire something they wanted to remain hidden. There was nothing there. The trunk also was empty. Bear pulled up the spare tire cover, removed the tire and tools and checked for a compartment underneath.

"Nada," he said.

"Check the wheel wells," I said.

He took one side, and I the other. Neither of us found a damn thing.

"What's in the bag?" I said.

He opened it, pulled out a couple pieces of paper. "Pictures of the guy."

"Take them and leave the bag."

"What about that device on the dash?"

"I'm tempted. Maybe Brandon can use it. Only concern is someone could be monitoring it."

"We can hide it down the road." Bear leaned in and grabbed the unit. "Call Brandon on the way."

I wasn't sure where we were going at this point. Joosten had been our only lead other than the officers on the report and the two false names Frank had supplied on his version of the report. If we were going to talk to anyone else, it was between those four.

We returned to the BMW and sped away from the scene. The area seemed deserted, but we couldn't trust looks. After all, we had thought the woods would be a sanctuary where we could question the witness. For all we knew there could be a housing development a quarter-mile away. None of the weapons were silenced. Anyone outside would have heard everything. Presumably sirens would be blaring if they had.

I called Brandon and updated him on the situation. Told him about the dead guys and uploaded the pictures we took so Brandon could ID them for us. I told him about the device we took from the car. He had me read some codes on the label fixed to the bottom of the unit.

He entered several strokes on his keyboard. A moment later he stopped humming a song I couldn't place.

"Get rid of it as fast as you freakin' can, man," Brandon said. "That thing is tracking your ass right now and whoever is on the other end is heading toward you fast. Damn, they're really moving!"

The road was empty. Bear pulled over. I got out and chucked it like a last ditch effort to win the game from beyond mid-field. It sailed sixty yards or so through the air, bouncing off trees as it landed somewhere in the woods.

"That'll keep whoever comes looking searching for the bodies a little longer," I said.

"I got some more news for you," Brandon said.

"Christ, what now?" Bear said.

"You're gonna like this," Brandon said. I could see his smile in my head. He might've been bound to a wheelchair, but the guy could light up a room with his toothy grin. "You ready?"

"Lay it on us," I said.

"I know the identity of the corpse."

# 32

THE WHISTLING SOUND APPROACHED FAST FROM THE SOUTH. I CAUGHT THE TRAIL of smoke a second before the woods erupted into a ball of flame. The explosion rocked the car. Chunks of wood rained down around us.

Bear took his foot off the gas. Must've taken his hands off the wheel for a few seconds, too, because the car coasted off the road and almost landed in the ditch. I reached over, righted it.

"Bear, you with me?"

The big man shook his head, knocked my hand out of the way and pressed the gas pedal to the floor. I was slammed back into my seat. My head rapped on the door frame. We raced out of the fallout zone. I glanced back and saw black smoke rising high over the orange flames.

I searched for the phone. Found it on the floor.

"The hell was that?" Brandon said.

"A rocket hit near where I tossed that tracking unit."

"That's why they were coming so fast," Brandon said. He tapped furiously on his keyboard. "Goddamn drone, man. Holy hell, get out of there now and call me back. I'll try to figure out who this thing is registered to."

We'd been waiting to see what Brandon came up with. Wondering who the dead woman had been, and why she looked so much like Ahlberg, but obviously wasn't. That would have to wait a few minutes though. We had to get moving, maybe even ditch the car. I kept my lookout over the sky while Bear navigated the roads.

I expected another strike to land near or on us, but it never happened.

On the highway, firetrucks and ambulances and police cars raced past us.

I pulled out my phone and started dialing.

"Who are you calling?" Bear said.

"Frank," I said.

"Wait."

"For what?"

"You dialing the right number?"

I glanced down at the screen. I was calling the man on his direct line, which would provide him with our exact location. If he was in charge of the drone, we wouldn't stand a chance.

Bear continued. "And all he's gotta do is look at his activity feed and he'll know where we are."

He was right. As much as I wanted to confront Frank on the explosion, I had to wait a couple hours. Give us time to put some distance between us and the attack site. I put the phone away.

"It was him," Bear said. "We need to start thinking of how to get out of this mess."

I nodded, unable to think of anyone else connected with access to a drone capable of launching a rocket to a precise coordinate. The phone buzzed against my leg. It was Brandon. I answered and confirmed the rocket strike. We turned the conversation back to the corpse.

"Is it a family member?" I said.

"Nope," Brandon said.

"Is it Katrine?" Bear said.

We'd been down that path. Despite the obvious missing tattoos and markings indicating they'd been removed, it still remained a possibility. Perhaps because we wanted it to be the most logical choice in spite of the evidence. Wishing didn't make it so.

"Nah," Brandon said. "I told you that already. Don't you listen?"

I put my arm out to stop Bear from responding. Years ago he would have slapped my hand away, leaving a big paw mark on me. Not today. He slammed his mouth shut like a guppy that inhaled a mouthful of water after being in the open air too long.

"In light of recent events, I don't think either of us can handle the suspense any longer," I said.

"First, let me tell you what it took to get this information," he said.

Brandon was reveling in this. Most of the tasks he performed for agencies and friends — the few that there were anymore — left him bored out of his mind. He spent his days inventing new software to speed up his job. Some programs he sold to the government. Usually the U.S. There were a handful of countries he'd work with, all of whom were friendly. He had a strict code that he wouldn't work with terrorists or governments that sponsored them. Some might say that's a blurry line. And Brandon agreed, but it didn't stop him.

The gig financed his life. Allowed him to help people like me free of charge. And despite his joke about my open tab, I'd always paid him, and planned on doing so for his help with the Ahlberg situation.

"OK," Brandon said. "I went through every single government agency database. I knew there was a good chance I wouldn't find anything in the States, but I did it anyway."

"Did you come up with a match there?" Bear asked.

"Hell no, man. Waste of time. I used some of my older systems to do that in the background while I searched the EU DBs."

"What'd you find there?" I said.

"More on your Ahlberg girl," he said. "That's one thing I wanted to tell you about. The French government knows something is going on. It doesn't appear they had quite figured it out."

Bear turned toward me. We used to have a couple contacts with French DSGE, but both had recently been lost.

"You think that was who followed us in the U.K.?" Bear asked.

"Might've been. I'll see what I can find there."

"Careful you don't dig too deep," I said. "Don't want to alert anyone."

Brandon laughed. "Trust me, people are alerted. I'm seeing more sniffing around my gear than I'm comfortable with. You know how it is, a whisper might as well be someone yelling in the Grand Canyon. Those echoes travel a long way."

"Back to the dead girl," Bear said. "Who is she?"

"Right," Brandon said. "So I get through the main EU databases and find nothing. Tried a few other sources and got lucky."

"Who'd you hack into?" I said.

"No hacking required," Brandon said. "At least, not what I consider hacking."

"So what was it?"

"Social media. Facebook."

"You found her there?"

"Yeah," he said. "And in a German newspaper's obituary section from last year."

# 33

WHAT THE HELL WERE WE DOING AT THE MORGUE? ACCORDING TO BRANDON the woman we saw in that locker had died twelve months ago. And somehow between then and now she had taken over Ahlberg's life. Since when did people start rising from the dead and taking up careers in espionage?

"Did I hear you right?" Bear said.

"Yup," Brandon said. "She's been dead for some time."

"What's the obituary say?" I said.

Brandon read through the first couple sentences in German, then went silent for a few seconds.

"Doesn't really say how she passed," he said. "Name's Martina Kohl. Left behind a husband, Bernd Kohl, two children, her parents, siblings, you know how it goes."

"And this is from a year ago?" Bear said.

"You think I don't know how to read, man?" Brandon muttered something indecipherable under his breath. "She passed a year ago. Almost to the damn day."

"Get me the address of her husband," I said. "I'm gonna start there."

"Already got it, and it's on its way to you. But you got a problem."

As if we didn't have enough already. The whole assignment had been nothing but a headache years in the making.

"What is it?" I said.

"She's from Germany."

"We're in the Schengen zone. No docs required. Shouldn't be a problem crossing over by car."

"They do targeted stops if intelligence dictates," Brandon said. "I've been monitoring for mention of either of your names."

"And?" I said.

"So far, nothing. But whatever passport Frank gave you might be compromised. Just keep that in mind should you get pulled over soon after entering."

We ended the call and drove another twenty miles before exiting into a small town I didn't catch the name of. Bear pulled into a deserted parking lot and cut the engine. The windows were down but the air was still. It smelled bland, as though it'd been neutralized in a large filter.

"What do you make of all this?" Bear asked.

"I've had a couple thoughts, but I don't want to assume anything and start running with the wrong idea."

He leaned his seat back and stared up at the sky through the open moonroof. "The death a year ago had to have been faked."

"Or Brandon got a bad match."

"Yeah, I guess. But assuming he didn't."

"Assuming," I said. "Exactly the thing I don't want to do."

"Assumptions are all we have to go on right now." He grabbed the steering wheel and pulled himself forward, pivoted in the seat and faced me. "Woman fakes her death only to die a year later while pretending to be someone else."

"Sums it up." I had nothing further. It stopped there. The how and why of it all was a puzzle, and I needed a few more pieces to put it together. I saw where he was going. Hell, I wanted to join him for the ride. But it'd be a mistake that could lead to us missing something obvious.

"I can see why someone would do it, is all I'm saying," he said. "There could be things, I don't know, maybe she was dying already."

"I want you to get ahold of Sasha," I said.

"You wanna loop her in?"

"Not exactly." I watched a truck pull into the lot. They parked on the opposite side. Two women stepped out. "I think you need a couple days away from this. Go home, if it's possible. She can probably figure out a way to get you back into the country unnoticed. Or maybe she can come over here and meet you somewhere."

"I'm not bailing on this. We're too far in for me to quit."

"I'm not asking you to quit. I just have no idea what else you'll do while I'm in Germany."

"While you're there?" He shook his head. "Think you're going alone?"

I knew he'd hate the idea. In a situation as screwed up as this one, splitting up could be a death sentence. We wouldn't be there to watch each other's backs. We'd lose the team aspect of working together, which always benefited us.

"I think it's best," I said. "Neither of us knows what I'm going to find at that address. Maybe it's legit. Maybe it's all a setup. If so, then I should be the one to deal with it. Not you."

Bear sat there for a minute, staring down his torso. He took a couple deep breaths as he thought it over. "Maybe I could check up on—"

"No. No checking up. No running down leads. Take a couple days off. I got this, Bear."

He nodded slowly, his chin resting against his chest. Neither of us had to mention out loud all that was at stake. He understood my reasoning even if he didn't agree with it.

"Let's head into town and make sure there's a place for me to stay," he said.

We switched positions in the car. I drove us through the town so Bear could make note of the hotels, restaurants, and so on. The plan was to meet back here in forty-eight hours. Any attempts at communicating would take place through Brandon, who had created a dial around for Bear.

"You get a lead, you move," he said, exiting the BMW. "Don't worry about getting back to me."

"Likewise," I said.

I pulled away as Bear headed off into the center of town. It was odd parting. We'd reached a point where we had no longer been working together. Hell, neither of us was working in that field any longer. All I wanted was to disappear and find a way to raise Mia in a normal fashion. And Bear hoped to provide a life for Mandy that'd give her a shot at normalcy. Adding Sasha to that mix only furthered the cause. The fact that we were in a foreign country fixing what amounted to a now-defunct SIS problem was bullshit.

But we were stuck in the middle of it nonetheless.

I glanced up at the rearview one last time before turning right to leave town. Bear had already assimilated into the crowd and was nowhere to be seen. In a way, I hoped the conversation we'd had moments ago would be our last one for quite some time.

Soon I was back on the highway, with my sights set on Leipzig, Germany.

# 34

A DRAB YELLOW CARPET LINED THE FLOOR OF THE NARROW HALLWAY. I couldn't tell if the salami smell came from someone's apartment or the floor. Through one door I heard a television. Sounded like cartoons. The next was silent. The one after that, a man and woman argued. Couldn't tell what about.

When I reached the apartment number Brandon had sent me, I paused. I couldn't shake the thought that the entire thing was a setup. But why send me all the way to Leipzig, Germany? They could kill me anywhere. Hell, they could've done it down in Texas. No one was around. And in the span of a few days there had already been enough death to go around that small town for a couple years. Why waste any more money ferrying me around if that was the plan all along?

At some point I had to accept the feeling was a malfunction in my intuition and simply proceed with the job.

I reached around my back, placed my hand on the butt of the pistol secured there. A door opened down the hall to my left. I glanced over and saw a young woman carrying a baby. I smiled, nodded. She returned the gesture then went back inside. Guess she thought I looked untrustworthy. She was probably right.

For several seconds, I stood there, frozen. What was I waiting for? Someone to burst through the door? Ahlberg to show up? Frank to somehow call or get a message to me telling me to leave? I hoped he had no idea where I was.

Fact was that no one could communicate with me at that moment. I had one phone on me, and not a single person knew the details. I was untraceable, location unknown. For all intents and purposes, I was a ghost.

Not for the first time either. It had played to my benefit in the past.

The hallway fell silent. No televisions playing cartoons, no couples arguing, no women with babies observing and judging me.

I dialed in to the task ahead. Prepared myself for any and every situation that might occur the moment the door opened.

I knocked on the door, gripping the pistol tight in anticipation. I had to fight the urge to draw it prematurely.

The man that opened the door looked to be in his late thirties with slivers of gray throughout his thick head of hair. The scruff on his unshaven face was even worse. He wore grey sweatpants and a stained white t-shirt. Wine, perhaps. It looked like he had recently woken up. He was a couple inches shorter than me, and considerably slighter. I probably had sixty pounds on him.

His gaze swept up and down. "Yes?"

He'd pegged me for American.

"Sorry to bother you so early," I said. "But I need to ask you a couple questions."

He closed the door a few inches as he stepped back. I stuck my foot against the frame to keep him from shutting it.

His eyes narrowed, and his gaze fell upon my hidden arm. "Who are you?"

"My name is Jack. I'm from the U.S. I need to talk to you about your dead wife."

His face went slack and his hand fell from the door, letting it swing open. The man made no effort to stop me as I stepped inside.

The apartment was small. I only saw two doors. One to a bedroom, the other to a bathroom, I presumed. Seated at a small kitchen table were two girls. Looked to be around ten or eleven. A couch was pulled out into a bed. The sheets were tangled up. There were two pillows, one for each girl, both wrapped with pink cases.

The man said something in German to his daughters. They rose, leaving their breakfast on the table, and went into the bedroom. The latch made a loud click as the door shut.

"My wife died a year ago," the man said. He had his hands on his hips and stood unnaturally straight. "End of story."

I pulled a chair away from the table and motioned for him to sit down with his back to the door. He hesitated a few seconds. I reached behind my back. He put his hands up in front of him and sat. I wondered if this was the first such visit he had received with the way he responded to the anticipated threat.

I stood across from him so I could see the door and most of the apartment. With him secure, I took a look around the place. Dirty dishes were piled next to the sink. At least three days' worth. The carpet was cluttered with clothes and toys and DVD cases. Looked as though it hadn't been vacuumed in a month. A layer of dust coated the coffee table and television stand. The girls had looked taken care of, though. They weren't malnourished. Their clothes fit and looked new. And the man himself looked to be in decent shape.

Was the condition of the place a reflection of the man's mental state?

I wondered what their life was like when he and his wife were together. Did they live here? Had they been better off than he was now?

"Well?" the guy said.

I took in the rest of the apartment then settled my gaze on him.

He crossed his left arm over his right. His watch slid down his forearm an inch. I hadn't noticed it before now. He wore an Omega Planet Ocean with an orange bezel. The model was easily worth over five thousand dollars. The cost of one brand new could probably cover rent in this place for six months, maybe more.

"We have things to do," the guy said. "My girls need to go to school. I have work."

"I won't take much more of your time," I said. "I just need you to tell me the truth about your wife."

# 35

He inched his head backward until he stared up at the ceiling. Was he choosing his words or coming up with a story? He filled his lungs with a deep breath, leaned forward over the table, and exhaled, letting his lips flap together. He looked up at me, held my gaze for several seconds.

"Can I have a cup of coffee?" he said then he started laughing while shaking his head. "Christ, I'm asking for coffee in my own house. What the hell?"

I saw the fire in his eyes. This man was not used to being in a subservient position. He gave the orders. I wondered how difficult the internal struggle in him was at that moment. Did he want to strike out? If his daughters weren't present, would he have already? I gave him a second to settle down, then moved toward the counter where the coffeemaker was perched.

The dark brew smelled fresh, so I poured a mug for both of us, then took a seat opposite him at the table.

"Ready?" I said.

He nodded then started his story. "My wife was diagnosed with liver cancer three years ago, uh, and two months now. The prognosis was grim. They said she likely had a year to live."

"These doctors," I said. "They were good? Or were you stuck with whatever insurance told you to do?"

"No, they were good. We had our pick, and I researched the hell out of them.

We even took her for a, um, second opinion in Berlin. They gave her the same prognosis. Lucky to live a year, they said."

"So what'd you do?"

He blew the steam off the top of his coffee and took a sip. He savored it for a few seconds before swallowing. "She followed the treatment course, which seemed to help for a little while. You know, it's hard to tell if it was the cancer or the treatment that made her feel and look so dragged out."

I followed his gaze over to the bookshelf where a picture of his wife was perched.

"That was her before she became sick," he said.

I stood, walked over to the bookshelf. "May I?"

He extended his hand, palm up. "Sure."

The resemblance between Martina Kohl and the Ahlberg twins was remarkable. She could have passed for a sister or cousin.

"You said she died a year ago," I said, still staring at the ghost in the frame. "But that she fell sick over three years ago with twelve months to live. What happened after she beat the original time frame the doctors gave her?"

He puffed out a laugh. "She said, 'Screw those ignorant bastards.'"

"The doctors?" I glanced up at him.

He nodded. "They gave her a year, and she beat it. So she decided to tackle the cancer on her own."

"But she beat it with their help, right?"

"No, she only did one round of treatment. Said it felt like that was going to kill her faster than the cancer." He shook his head, smiling to himself. "You believe that?"

I said nothing. Couldn't tell if the statement was one of anger or incredulousness.

"She still saw them," he said. "But she wouldn't let them do anything to her."

"Over the next year or so did she improve? Get worse?" I played into what he'd said earlier. "Obviously she passed, but was it sudden or did it drag for a long time?"

He sat there for a few moments, thinking it over. Then he leaned back and looked toward the bedroom.

"Everything OK?" I said.

"Sorry," he said. "My girls."

"You can check on them in a few. Tell me what happened with your wife."

"In those months she seemed to get better and was back to herself, taking care of the girls, and me." He smiled momentarily, perhaps recounting a memory of his wife fixing his tie or making sure he had his lunch before heading off to work, maybe even getting frisky under the sheets. "She resumed the things she loved doing."

"Such as?"

"Running was a big one," he said. "Especially on trails. She would take off for a day and night every few weeks to camp and hike and run trails. Frankly, I never saw much point to it. I guess if a bear or something was chasing me, I'd run. But why else?"

I shrugged, said nothing.

"My wife seemed healthy again." He spread out his arms and let his hands fall on the table.

"Was the cancer in remission at that time?"

Staring down at the table, he shook his head. "One can suppose, but she stopped going to the doctor. Stopped getting X-rays. It was as if she was acting on blind faith. My priest actually said that he believes she had enough faith that doing it her own way would work she had tricked her body into thinking she was OK. And perhaps that's why it happened so fast. The cancer was there, eating away at her all that time and she did nothing to combat it."

The bedroom door cracked open and one of the girls poked her head out. She said something in German.

Her father waved her back in the room without saying anything. His face and ears had turned red. At first I thought it was in response to his daughter trying to leave the room early. I soon realized it was for another reason.

"It was selfish, what my wife did. She thought nothing of the girls, her daughters. Nothing of me."

"Maybe it's selfish of you to assume that," I said. "She was the one dying. Inside, she might've felt that she lived her life more fully during that year than at any other time. Perhaps she loved you and the girls more than ever in that year. Your own blindness to the situation caused you to not see it. Maybe she felt that a year living the way she wanted was better than the treatment and feeling, not simply knowing, that she was dying."

"She was dying." His hands balled into tight fists. He lifted them but stopped short of slamming them down on the table.

"There's a difference between knowing you're dying and feeling every moment of it happening."

He sat motionless for a minute, then started shaking his head.

"No," he said. "It was all because of that damn woman."

# 36

A SWATH OF DEEP RED COATED HIS FACE. HE DRUMMED HIS FINGERTIPS violently on the table. I imagined it wasn't easy to relive what had happened to his wife. Especially when he was forced to tell a stranger every detail. I'd lost people too soon and understood the emotions that went with it. So I let him take his time. He'd held nothing back thus far. At least it seemed that way.

After a moment of silence, I pressed for more. "What woman?"

"She went by some made-up name." He shook his head. "I won't even repeat it, it's so ridiculous."

"It'd help if you would," I said.

"Veronica Ingersleben. That helpful?"

I wanted to say no but refrained and nodded instead.

"I only met her a few times," he said. "She was a natural or alternative healer. I still don't quite understand how my wife found her. The internet, I guess. She'd started spending so much time on the computer after the diagnosis, looking for alternative methods to fight the cancer."

"What did this woman look like?"

"I always thought she resembled Martina." He stared past me, his eyes fixed on some spot above my head. "She had dark hair, but it looked unnatural. Like she'd dyed it. And her skin always looked tan, but you could tell it was from an oil or cream. A bronzer, I think you call it?"

I nodded.

He continued. "She saw this healer quite a few times. Weekly, actually. The woman made my wife drink foul smelling green drinks, eat raw meat, and consume all kinds of herbs and other oddities. She provided her with oil to consume, too, from the cannabis plant."

"But it helped, right? You said she resumed the activities she enjoyed, but it sounds like you were against her working with this healer." I had to keep him talking, answering questions, that way if I asked anything point blank he'd be more likely to respond.

"Yeah, it helped for a while. But in the end, the result was death." He placed his elbows on the table, lowered his head into his open palms. His eyes misted over. "If it were up to me, she never would have seen that healer-woman. She would have kept battling the traditional way, and she might be alive right now. It would be her at the table with me, not you. My girls and I wouldn't be left in this state of utter confusion on what to do next with our lives."

"You keep living," I said.

He shrugged.

"Is that everything?" I asked.

He looked up at me with a penetrating gaze. His face set in stone. He said nothing. Was it the trauma of reliving the loss of his wife?

I felt for the guy, and at the same time, I had to remain focused on the alternative healer. That was the link to Ahlberg. I pulled out a recent photo of Katrine and placed it on the table in front of the man.

"Who's this?" he asked.

I studied his face, watching for any sign of recognition or concealment. I saw neither.

"Have you ever seen that woman?" I said.

"Would I ask who it was if I had?" he said.

"Possibly." I placed another photo on the table. "If you wanted to hide something."

He straightened and, biting his bottom lip, glanced toward the bedroom where his daughters waited.

"If there's something you're not telling me," I said, "it's best you come out with it now. Last thing you want is the guys above me visiting you after it's been determined you withheld information."

He became flushed, and his forehead dampened with sweat. He recognized Ahlberg in the second photo, and that set off a chain reaction of what-ifs in his mind. He pushed his chair back, walked to the sink. Water spilled over his turned-up palms. He doused his face, turned back to me, his shirt and hair each half-soaked.

I stood and repositioned myself to block him from any attempt at leaving. With his behavior, I couldn't discount he might try to jump out the windows lining the opposite wall.

The guy mumbled something to himself. I couldn't tell if it was in German or English. Either way, it was indistinguishable.

"What's going on?" I asked.

He grabbed the back of his head, pulled, stared upward.

"Tell me," I said. "It may seem insignificant, but I can use any information you have."

"That woman," he said. "She looks like the healer. Not one hundred percent, but close enough. I guess the hair could be the difference. The healer was always coated in makeup in addition to the tanning lotion. Heavily, I might add. Her lips were always so red, and she tried to make them look fuller than they were."

"Do you know where she is?" I said.

He meshed his fingers together and cracked his knuckles, then stuffed his hands in his pocket.

"My wife is dead," he said.

"Yes, died a year ago," I said.

He nodded, said nothing.

"Unless she didn't?" I said it to gauge his reaction.

He fell back a step, colliding with the counter and using one hand to stop him from falling. His face paled and sweat beaded on his forehead and began streaming down his cheeks.

"Tell me about her final moments," I said.

"I...," he dropped to his knees. "I can't."

"Too painful?" I said. "Or just plain bullshit?"

Fear replaced the pained look on his face.

"How long did you think you could get away with this?" I said. "What was the plan? You'd meet up in a year or two someplace remote and resume your life together?"

His mouth hung open. "What?"

I pulled my pistol and aimed it at him. He spread his arms out, clenched his eyelids.

I raised my voice a notch. "Did you really think you could get away with this?"

"It's in the freezer, wrapped in a bag to protect it." He squinted his eyes closed, and held his hands out in front as he scooted his feet underneath him. "I never cashed it in. She told me to wait, so I waited."

I kept my pistol trained on him as I tried to figure out what the hell he was talking about. What was in the freezer? I gestured with my head for him to rise and go to the fridge.

"Get it out," I said. "Put it on the table. Then step back."

He pulled the freezer door open. Cold air escaped and formed a wispy cloud around his head. I repositioned myself to see what he was doing inside. I had to be prepared in the event he pulled a weapon out. He pushed aside ice cream, frozen meat and other food, and leaned far enough in that his shoulders were past the opening. When he turned, he held a bag. I couldn't tell the contents through the hazy plastic. He tossed the package on the table and walked back to the sink.

"I knew something was wrong from the beginning," he said. "That's why I never claimed the money. A ten million dollar policy? I think I would have noticed a monthly payment for that amount of coverage." He looked up from the cloudy bag on the table. "Understand? Something was wrong. And I figured one day the insurance agency would send someone like you to take the money back. Much easier if I haven't cashed it in, right?"

Insurance? He thought I was there over a damn insurance policy?

"Where is she?" I said. "And don't lie to me. You know how serious fraud is, right?"

"She's dead," he yelled.

I yelled back louder and raised the pistol for additional effect. "Then why are you afraid to claim the money?"

"I told you, I never knew she had a policy to begin with. It just didn't seem right."

I waited for him to continue. He required prompting. "And?"

He took a deep breath and steadied his trembling hands before walking to the curio. He rose up on the tips of his toes and reached for the back of the top shelf. A cookbook fell to the floor, opened to a minced meat recipe. Several printouts of recipes had spilled onto the floor. When he turned toward me, he held a simple white urn that had turned grey with dust on the lid. I'd lost many close friends and family over the years. Once they were gone, they were gone, save for a select few. I imagined that's how he felt as he held the urn, caressing it as though he were touching his wife's face once again.

He set it on the table, lifted the lid, and knocked the urn over. Ash spilled out, cascading over the edge of the table and onto the floor. Air from a nearby vent sent a cloud of his wife's remains floating off. Bernd Kohl looked up at me with dead eyes.

"I never saw the body."

# 37

He scooped up a handful of the ash, parted his fingers slightly, let the remains slip through. They drifted and formed a small pile. His breathing was labored. His focus turned to the pistol. I presumed he feared what would happen next.

"You weren't there when she died," I said, confirming the facts as he'd laid them out.

He nodded, said nothing, looked away.

"And you never saw the body, only the cremated remains?"

He nodded again refusing to make eye contact.

"When did you get the insurance check?" I said

"The day she brought me the urn," he said.

There were only two 'she's' mentioned in this conversation. "You mean the healer? The one that resembles that woman in the photo on the table." The picture was covered with his wife's remains now.

He glanced at the pistol, then at me. A half-dozen wrinkles sliced his forehead into sections. "Yes, the healer. Only she was different this time. Gone was the ruse of one who could cure disease. She looked hardened and cold and pale. More than capable of killing me."

"She threatened you."

He took a long moment before responding. "She told me to wait before cashing it."

"And if you didn't?"

"She'd take the girls. Someone like you would show up at my door, and I'd lose everything. My kids, the money." He clawed another scoop of ash, and clenched his fist. A tight line of remains cascaded to the table. "And my life."

I studied him, wondering if that was all. What kind of timeframe had she given him? Was he supposed to receive a call from her when he was allowed to deposit the check?

"So we moved," he said. "To this shitty apartment to wait it out. She told me that I'd know when the time was right to claim the money. And then, well, then I was to leave the country. Go someplace remote and start a new life. But that's not going to happen now, is it?"

I stared him down, said nothing.

"Answer me, you prick!" He slashed his arm across the table, clearing it of the urn and most of the cremated remains. "Kill me now if you're going to do it. Or are you too much of a pussy to shoot me with the kids in here?"

I'm not sure when he grew a backbone, but his tirade had zero chance of working. "You're not in a position to make demands. And I have a couple more questions for you."

He drew in a deep breath and sighed, dejected. "What? I've told you everything."

"You sure?"

"Everything I can remember."

"Did she give you anything else? A forwarding address or phone number?"

He shook his head.

I rose and rounded the table, keeping the pistol aimed at him. He started sobbing when I disappeared from his field of vision. This could go one of two ways. Either he'd told me the truth as he knew it, and no threat existed by letting him live. Or, he lied, was in on it from the beginning, and the first thing he'd do after I left was make a phone call reporting my presence. For all I knew, the guy had one of those security cameras hidden in a teddy bear recording the whole thing.

His sobs trailed off. Had he accepted his fate? Maybe he figured if I hadn't done anything yet, I didn't plan on it.

"Call your girls out," I said.

"Oh, Jesus, no," he said.

"Now."

He wiped the tears and snot and ash from his face with his sleeve, called his daughters by name. A moment later the bedroom door opened and the young girls stepped out. I tucked my pistol away before they noticed it. It might've taken a while considering the condition of the kitchen. They stared at their father and the mess of what had been their mother's remains. The oldest said something to her father in German. Tears streamed down her face. He reached out, pulled both girls to him and hugged and shushed them. I couldn't understand what else he said to them but they both turned their attention to me and nodded.

"It's OK," I said. "Those aren't her ashes."

He floated his gaze toward me, confusion on his face. He ushered the girls back to the bedroom. "What do you mean?"

I raised the pistol and aimed it at his chest. "They stay, for now."

"Girls," he said. "Stop."

They turned and saw me aiming a weapon at their father. I expected screams and tears. Neither child blinked.

"She's dead, Bernd," I said. "You can cash the check."

He looked back at the table, then under, and around at the floor.

"Looking for this?" I held the freezer bag up, pinned between my pinky and palm. In the same hand, I fingered a lighter.

His face went slack. Soon he'd tell the truth.

"Go back to the bedroom, girls," I said.

The room fell silent except for the air pushing through the vents. Sounded like a beach on the gulf with small waves breaking on the shore.

"Is she really dead?" he asked.

"You knew she wasn't when you received this, didn't you?"

He opened his mouth to speak, stopped, licked his bottom lip. Working up a story, I supposed. He held out a hand. "Listen, sometimes things are so bleak, and you are so without hope, you agree to do something that makes no sense. Because only in that state can you possibly find a rational explanation for the crazy."

I didn't care to listen to his garbage. "What was the plan?"

He glanced around the room. "I don't know all of it."

I lit the lighter, angled the flame toward the bag.

"Please," he said, throwing up both hands. "That is my daughters' futures. It's all they have left of their mother."

"How much is it really?" I knew it wasn't ten million. With that kind of scratch, he could've found a way to hide. If he had wanted to.

"A million. Enough, I suppose, to get us away and start a new life."

"All right," I said. "If you want it, you need to tell me everything."

He stumbled onto a chair and slumped back as though what he was about to say would drain him of all his energy and he had to be prepared.

"She was sick the entire time," he said. "She had improvements here and there, but nothing much. In the end, the diagnosis never changed. It was a matter of months that she would live. We knew that any kind of treatment was going to drain us of everything we had. She told me that Veronica could make her comfortable. Give her a little less pain for the remainder of her life."

Had his wife sold him a line? After all, a year had passed since she left and was murdered.

He sighed. "And then there was the offer."

I shook the bag. He nodded.

"Yes," he said. "They arranged for that so once she passed, the kids would be taken care of. It was the only way. She convinced me of it. So she left, and I never saw her again. That woman arrived with the urn and the check and told me not to cash it in yet."

"And you knew she wasn't dead yet."

He held steady for a moment, then lifted his head and let it drop down again. "Yes."

"How?"

"She told me."

I couldn't imagine that Ahlberg had let Martina keep in touch with her husband. "In secret?"

He nodded. "She'd manage to get a phone and call or message a couple times."

"When's the last time you heard from her?"

"Two weeks ago." He drew a circle in the remaining ash on the table, then a line dividing it in half. "That was the last time I heard from her."

"What'd she tell you?"

"She never went into too much detail. Just that she was getting treatment and being taken care of."

"She send pictures during this time?"

He frowned, shook his head. "Unfortunately, no."

I didn't bother to tell him that his wife had undergone slight plastic surgery in order to look like Ahlberg. I also failed to mention that she had overcome the cancer. It grew more apparent in my mind that the ongoing sickness had been a ruse for the sake of the plan. For whatever reason, Martina decided that money for her daughters was better than them having her in their lives.

"Is she really dead?" he asked.

I nodded.

Tears filled his eyes, spilling over and running down his cheeks. There were no sobs to accompany them. He'd lived this moment so many times and likely awaited the ending so that he could move on.

"Anything else?" I said, half-extending the freezer bag.

He shook his head. I tossed the bag to him, turned toward the door.

"What if she comes back?" he said.

"Your wife? This ain't the movies, man. She's not rising from the dead."

"No, that woman."

I wanted to tell him what he could expect if she did. Because maybe that was Ahlberg's plan. Set all this up in order to get the money she promised to Martina Kohl to give up her family, her life.

I opened the door, leaned out into the hall, then looked back at the guy.

"She's not coming back."

# 38

THE BRIGHT BLUE LIGHTING OF THE DUNGEON ENTRANCE COATED BRANDON'S desktop and washed out the backlighting on his keyboard. He glanced at the bag of cheese puffs that were just out of arm's reach.

"Ahem," the soft voice boomed through his speakers.

Brandon glanced up at the chat box on the upper right portion of his main screen. Kimberlee stared back at him, an eyebrow arched and her lips pursed.

"Keep your hands off those manufactured fat sticks," she said. "You've got a month until our visit and I want you in to be in proper shape for it."

Brandon sighed as he looked at his protruding belly. "I don't know, babe. I think round is a nice shape."

She rolled her eyes.

For a man in his condition, he'd stayed in relatively good shape for most of his life. The spare tire around his mid-section was a recent development. He tried to tell himself it was because he was a year closer to forty — too close in fact — and that he would soon resume the workouts his doctor had recommended to him years ago. Soon routinely waited for tomorrow to arrive. He'd only fallen out of the habit in the last two years. But now he had a reason to get fit and continue to beat the odds that said he should have died over twenty years ago.

Kimberlee's scowl shifted to a wry smile. She adjusted her camera and zoomed out, revealing the low-cut top that barely covered her nipples. Brandon leaned forward, thought he could make out the edge of her right areola. The camera quickly zoomed in on her face.

"Hey," he said. "I was searching for something there."

"Lean back again," she said. He did as instructed and once again, she zoomed out. Brandon leaned forward. Kimberlee repeated the process a few more times. "See, this is how we begin your workouts. Feel that burn in your abs?" She scrunched up her face like some crazed fitness trainer.

Brandon's laughter was interrupted by the sound of an attack. He shifted gears. They would not be defeated by trash mobs. He reached for his mouse and knocked it off the desk. His eyes were glued to the simulated violence on his monitor.

"Christ, Kimberlee, heal me before that damn mob kills me." He reached for his grabber tool with one hand and secured the mouse. With his other hand he entered several strokes on his keyboard. A series of special attacks were carried out by his virtual avatar.

After the carnage had subsided, Kimberlee said, "Maybe you're too distracted right now to play."

Brandon shifted his gaze to her video feed and noticed her right index finger hooked in her bra. She tugged on it, stretching it outward, but not down like he hoped she would. He marveled at the beautiful woman who was ten years younger. Why the hell was she with him? Outside of a few awkward relationships in college, Brandon had avoided the traps of commitment.

Of course, he convinced himself of that because he was unable to find a woman willing to be with him. He tried to blame his condition. Being a wheelchair-bound cripple had its drawbacks. But he knew that wasn't it. He never made the effort, never left the house, never attempted to meet someone he could be interested in.

The job kept him busy and fulfilled his need to be a productive person. In the early years, he worked for the Agency. The man who was now the director of operations had recruited him after Brandon had fallen into a little trouble for playing around. That's what he called it at least. The Feds had another name for what he'd done.

Hacking.

But the guy had had enough clout to get Brandon out of trouble so long as he used his powers for the Agency and their purpose.

These days Brandon contracted with several intelligence outfits, domestic and foreign, government and private sector. He worked with independents, too. People like Jack Noble, who he had known for years, were always calling him to help straighten out their messes. Brandon smiled as he recalled a time when Jack and his partner Bear had saved Brandon's life. Had it not been for the duo, Brandon wouldn't be staring at Kimberlee's ample cleavage right now.

Outside of the job, he made no attempts to meet people. Isolation was his preferred state of being. Food and medical supplies were brought to him through a service that also provided cleaning and took care of the maintenance of his house. They were never allowed in his office, the room he now occupied and which he lovingly referred to as *The Cave*.

Three thirty-four-inch monitors adorned his desk. Four more were mounted to the wall above. He had sixty-inch plasma displays on the other three walls, all constantly displaying intelligence feeds and financial data from around the globe. Brandon knew before most of the world's leaders when something was about to go down. He'd predicted terrorist attacks with accuracy. Sometimes those in charge listened to him and the threat was thwarted. Other times, they brushed him off and innocent people paid with their lives.

It was easy for him to access the classified data he relied on to earn his living. He'd engineered the majority of the systems. And the ones he hadn't designed he had managed to crack relatively easily and, more importantly, without anyone noticing.

At any given time if you walked into The Cave you would find Brandon constantly engaged and monitoring the various feeds while performing whatever task the Agency, NSA, FBI, or a host of other acronyms had asked of him.

But today wasn't like that.

He focused on Kimberlee's smile and occasionally her breasts.

He'd met the woman through a mutual acquaintance. The ATF agent had told Brandon that his cousin was quick-witted, hot-tempered, and shared a similar background. She wasn't a hacker or computer whiz, though.

She was a paraplegic.

Thrown from a horse at the age of eight, her spinal cord had been severed between her L3 and L4.

But where Brandon isolated himself, Kimberlee feared nothing. She set out to conquer the world. And now she seemed focused on conquering him. She knew exactly what he did for a living and she didn't care. He supposed she found it exciting. She was dating a spy, albeit one that did his work from behind a network of computers and monitors. But the intelligence he provided was as important as the work the men in the field performed.

They were less than one month away from meeting. Twenty-nine days to be precise. He had the date marked everywhere he looked. If all went well, they'd soon be together full-time. She might be the first to ever enter *The Cave*.

"Are you there?" Kimberlee said.

Brandon shook his head and cleared out the thoughts of the future and instead focused on the semi-nude woman smiling at him. He returned the smile and leaned forward.

"That's better," she said. "Now, just how much gold are you willing to send over to me if I reveal a bit more to you?"

"That depends—" Brandon noticed the screen on the wall to the right flickering. He pushed away from the desk and spun his chair around. "What the hell?"

"Brandon?" Kimberlee said. "What's going on?"

"I'm gonna have to get back with you in a minute, babe." He pressed a button on his screen and the video game and chat window disappeared.

In front of him the plasma screen seemed possessed. Lines of code were flying past at well over a thousand rows a minute. Brandon could speed read with the best of them, but this was beyond his abilities.

He pulled the keyboard from his desk and issued a command that switched control to the television. Once connected, he could do nothing to stop it from the apparent dump it was performing. His mind raced to recall everything he had on that system. There were years worth of financial records for politicians, governments, terrorists and their supporters. He'd been careful not to link his own records to that computer.

The speakers on his desk rang out with a quick *boop-boop* sound. Kimberlee was attempting to reach him again. He'd ended their call without much warning. Maybe he should give her an update. He turned his chair toward the desk, dragging his keyboard shelf along.

"Holy hell."

If he hadn't been strapped in, Brandon might've fallen out of his chair. The three monitors on his desk looked like the plasma on the wall. Line after line of white text against a dark gray background raced past. He switched his keyboard to control his main system. Every command he issued failed to respond.

"The hell is going on?" He slammed his fists against the surface of his desk. Pain rode through his arms up to his elbows. He grunted against the shock, fearing he'd broken something. Brandon clenched and unclenched his fist and fingers. Everything worked. His brittle bones had remained intact.

The plasma to his left was out of his control, as was the matching screen on the back wall. He didn't bother to attempt to override them. Whatever was happening was taking place beyond those four walls.

He turned and glanced up. Two of the four wall-mounted thirty-four-inch monitors were still under his control. Both screens were linked to the same PC. He adjusted his keyboard and mouse and entered the system.

Without thinking, Brandon issued command after command in an effort to regain control of his office. He thought about bringing up his security feeds but put it off for the moment. The overhead light cut off. The ceiling fan stopped circulating. The screens cast a dark glow over the space. The whirr of his computers that weren't running on a water-cooled system overtook the room with rhythmic bursts of air. He wondered if that's what it sounded like inside a jet in the middle of the night. Despite experience controlling drones flying thousands of miles away, he'd never been inside a plane.

One of the systems blinked off. Was it his doing? He thought about the command he'd issued moments before and realized that nothing he'd done would have powered down the unit.

"Son of a bitch."

It felt as though he raced against the clock. What were they doing with the data? How long until they took control of this system?

He decided it was in the best interest of the country that he run a self-destruct directive. The computer contained all his personal files on the men he had worked with directly. Not the pencil pushers and geeks who hid behind their computers when they had working legs and able bodies. But the men out in the field.

Brandon glanced at his phone and thought about a recent conversation. The thought led him to Jack Noble, just one of the many operators Brandon had complete files on.

A blinking cursor sat at the end of the waiting command. All he had to was slap the enter key and the system would dismantle itself one byte at a time.

Brandon froze. Years of work was locked up in that system. As solid as his memory was, there were things he could not recall. Information that a simple keystroke would reveal to him.

He tried to think of a plan. Brandon had a row of servers in a clandestine data warehouse available to him. The reason his most confidential information was not already stored there was because he could not control access to the rack. The right team of agents and analysts could breach his files.

That didn't matter now.

His mind raced to recall the details in order to start transferring the information. The system in question was large, but his internet connection was basically a wall of fiber optic cables with triple redundancy built in. He could utilize all of it at once and transfer the data in a matter of two seconds.

An image of Kimberlee formed in his mind as he put together the string of letters, numbers and symbols required. She was smiling, tugging on the lacy edge of her bra.

"Not now!" Brandon shouted, breaking free from the temptation.

Stroke by stroke he entered everything he needed to encrypt the drive and send the contents to rack one, server a, console four.

The progress bar moved slower than that damn strip of grass on the *Plants vs. Zombies* game. Brandon tapped on his desk. Perhaps too loudly. It caused him to miss something.

The screen going blank was not lost on him, though.

"No, no, no," he said. "The hell is going on here?"

His fingers danced on the keyboard. They worked faster than his conscious mind could think. It didn't matter. He'd lost control.

The screen brightened and he watched as someone else controlled the cursor. It was as though the sons of bitches knew exactly where to look, too. They accessed his files containing details on independent operators. There was a series of right clicks followed by the files disappearing, obviously being cut out and pasted somewhere off screen.

Several names remained. One in particular.

Jack Noble's folder highlighted blue. Brandon expected it to disappear. Instead they opened the folder. A program must have taken over because every subfolder and file popped open individually and at a speed beyond what a human was capable of.

Brandon tried once more to regain control. Hell, he didn't even need full control. They could have all the data on the past missions. That wasn't what was important to them.

And then he had it. He was able to pull up the same folder on the adjacent screen. Brandon typed fast and furious and navigated through the file tree. He was in search of something buried deep and password protected.

The system couldn't keep up with him, not with the load it was currently under. Brandon opened up a file and created a simple bash program that would disrupt the other user. Eight lines of code. That was all it took. He read over it three times, then executed the program.

His illuminated keyboard brightened, then went dead. His mouse no longer controlled the cursor. The monitor he was working on went blank.

They had executed the kill shot first.

On the other screen the chaos of thousands of files opening in rapid-fire succession stopped at once. A person was at the controls again and they worked their way through a maze of folders until they came to the one Brandon so desperately wanted to destroy.

They now had Jack's phone records in their possession.

# 39

I LEFT WITH MORE INFORMATION THAN I HAD ARRIVED KNOWING. THE IDENTITY of the dead woman and her past were confirmed. But I had no idea where to go next. No clues or leads, and nothing obvious jumped out at me. As much as I didn't want to, I would have to lean on Frank soon.

Bernd Kohl broke down on my way out of the small apartment. I didn't stop or look back or attempt to offer any words of condolence to the guy. What could I say? His wife and possibly he himself had made a deal and now he had to live with the consequences. I did find myself hoping that he'd be smart, cash the check, and get the hell out of town without leaving too much of a trail behind for the sake of his girls.

Any concern I had over it disappeared as the door slammed shut behind me. The sounds of his sobs faded and had disappeared by the time I reached the elevator. I considered that Ahlberg had someone watching the apartment. Was her network large enough after spending so many years in isolation? Did she still maintain the support of Awad?

I walked past the elevator and headed down the hallway toward the stairwell. The building lacked security. I hadn't spotted hall cameras, not that I was too concerned about being spotted. Bernd wasn't about to reach out and report my presence. Unless he'd put on a performance back there that fooled me, the guy was in way over his head and probably figured any attempts he made to reach out might result in him losing the funds.

I descended the stairs, leaping the final three. An exit to the outside was placed inside the stairwell on the first floor. I took a moment to scan the surroundings through the narrow slit of a window. The barren alley offered little in the way of hiding places. Brick and asphalt were all I saw fifty feet in either direction.

Warm air carrying the noise of chatter and traffic rushed inside the building as I pushed the door open. I had parked the car a few blocks away and decided to take a winding route back to it, filled with false steps to determine if I was being tailed.

The road in front of the apartment was busy with both pedestrians and vehicles. I merged into the flow of foot traffic and followed the herd.

There was plenty to take away from my conversation with Bernd Kohl. His wife looked enough like the Ahlberg twins that she was a natural choice to serve as a body double. She might've had a procedure or two done, but only surface-level stuff. It took a program like the one Brandon had used to notice the true differences between the Ahlbergs and Martina Kohl.

The question was why she did it. I wasn't sure I bought the cancer diagnosis. That seemed like something the women had cooked up to create an agreeable mindset in Bernd. There had to be more to her story. Things the husband didn't know, or didn't want to admit. Perhaps she had a debt they could not repay. Ahlberg offered to take care of it.

How had they come to know each other? And when did they meet? With the internet the possibilities were endless, though I tended to think it was much simpler. As my mind wandered, I envisioned a scenario where the women found each other and hatched the plan. I wanted to revisit Bernd and ask about their finances before his wife told him she was sick. I decided against it, figuring that Brandon could provide a window into their lives by accessing banking and credit records.

With that I put my presumptions on hold.

A door opened ahead, flooding the area with the smell of dark roast. I worked my way across the crowded sidewalk and headed into the cafe. It was a small room with only a few tables and a counter. Everything looked sleek and modern. The barista stared at me expectantly without comment. I ordered a triple espresso. While waiting for my drink, my phone buzzed. I answered the call.

"Brandon?"

There was no response. I checked the screen to make sure I had answered. It didn't even sound like we were connected. Usually there was a hint of fuzz. The line was silent. I looked around the room, wondering if the excessive use of steel had somehow affected the signal.

"I'll be right back," I said to the man behind the counter. He nodded without looking up while marking a cup with a fat black marker. I stepped around the short line behind me and went outside. The call had by now disconnected. I dialed into Brandon's line and waited. It rang twice, then disconnected. I stared over at the roofline of the building across the street wondering what in the hell was going on.

I told myself to relax. It was easy to get worked up over little things while in the midst of a job. Calls failed all the time. I was in the middle of Leipzig, Germany, dialing into a Hong Kong number that'd route to the States, while using a market store grade SIM card. There were bound to be fluctuations and disruptions in service.

Back inside my drink waited on the counter. Bear had pulled some cash out prior to leaving and spotted me a few hundred Euros so I wouldn't be forced to announce my presence with the use of credit cards. I handed the guy a ten for my six Euro drink. He didn't bother to make change. I decided then and there I'd never visit this cafe again even if the Pope himself were serving.

Another block further I stopped in a clothing store. After wearing the same outfit for over twenty-four hours I was ready for a change. Frank hadn't left me with many options. I picked out a pair of tan chinos, a blue oxford, and a pair of leather hiking boots. The ones on my feet clung to the smell of that disgusting house in the woods. I paid for the clothes, then put them on before leaving the store. I used the shopping bag to discard my old gear into a dumpster in the back alley.

The espresso had kicked in by the time I reached the BMW. My heart rate had climbed ten beats per minute. I considered walking another mile to slow it down. After all, I didn't have a clue which direction to go in and Germany wasn't a country where I had many contacts. Hell, come to think of it, I had none.

I considered traveling into France, but my DSGE contacts were no longer breathing. Outside of Pierre and Laure Desault, who were both deceased, no one in the country would provide me with assistance.

My phone buzzed again as I reached for the door handle. I checked the number and answered.

"Brandon? Can you hear me?"

The line was full of static. "Jack?" He mumbled something indecipherable. "Jack can you—"

A heavy burst of grating static overtook the call for several seconds. Brandon came back on the line.

"Jack, listen—" there were a few moments of dead air, "—get out—"

After that I couldn't understand anything he said. A few seconds later the call died. I tried calling him back, but all I received was dead air. The signal hadn't made it past Hong Kong.

I sat inside the car and rolled down the windows to take advantage of the breeze.

I glanced at the cell. It was easy to interpret the tone of Brandon's voice as desperate. The man didn't get worked up in that way. He might crack a joke, and in the process raise the pitch of his voice, but he never yelled. And the quality of our calls was never that piss poor. I started to fear the worst for the guy. He always assured me that his current location was as secure as a nuclear bunker.

Impenetrable.

I debated for several moments whether to call Frank. He didn't know Brandon's location, but he might have an idea what had spooked the computer genius. I held off on reaching out. I had no desire to reveal my location quite yet.

I heard squealing tires and looked to my right. A black Mercedes S550 raced toward me.

It looked as though my location had already been compromised.

# 40

Sasha attempted to conceal her tears from Bear. She tucked her chin, turned her head, closed her eyes. He'd only seen her cry once, and it was at a television commercial where a daughter left home for college and the father wasn't ready to let go. She told Bear never to mention the incident and he wasn't about to cross her. Sasha was an MI6 veteran of more than fifteen years. She could handle herself, and him, if need be.

In her hand she held the test results. The envelope had arrived the day Bear and Jack left. Sasha had kept them in the knife drawer until he returned. He had no desire to look at the doctor's report, though. They'd all been negative from the first time he stepped foot in the guy's office.

He thought it was symbolic — or was it symbiotic — how the horrible headaches had started around the time of Mandy's fight with amnesia.

"Do you want to know?" Sasha dragged the back of her hand across her face and rid herself of the tears and stared him in the eye. All evidence she had been crying was now eradicated.

Bear walked to the fridge. He stood with the French doors open. The cool air enveloped him, filled his nose with the smell of tomatoes. A chill raced down his spine. It wasn't from the refrigerated air. It was probably the contents of the paper Sasha held.

He grabbed a beer and popped the cap on the bear's head bottle opener.

Mandy had given it to him and told him it was a Father's Day present. She had carved the four inch figurine herself, designed so that the fangs caught the cap and pried it right off with a single pull like any other bottle opener. He had proudly mounted it where all could see it in the kitchen. It was obvious by the look in Sasha's eyes she did not approve of the location. She kept those thoughts to herself and smiled as she looked on at the pride Bear displayed after he finished securing the bottle opener.

Bear wished Mandy were there at the house. He felt her absence every time he took a breath. His heart ached. Sasha had wisely whisked the girl to a colleague's aunt's house in Iceland. She showed him pictures of the place. It was remote and quiet. The kind of location Bear saw himself heading to someday soon if Sasha would go along with him.

Bear turned his attention to the English IPA. It wasn't as bitter as its American counterparts, which he appreciated. The brews could be overly hoppy stateside. He considered that a beer snob would refer to the Jenny Greenfinch as a more sophisticated and subtle IPA. To him it just tasted good.

"Are you planning on burying your concerns in beer tonight?" Sasha's words penetrated like a lance.

In fact, he had. "I've got too much going on to even think about what some quack job thinks about my headaches, Sasha."

"It's not what he thinks, you damn fool." Her voice raised, and he wondered if this was the tone she took when one of her people had screwed up at work. "Those tests aren't shaded by someone's thoughts. They are black and white. Plain and simple, what you see is what you get."

Bear held back the words on the tip of his tongue, knowing that dragging this out into a full-blown fight would serve neither of them well.

Sasha took a deep breath and proceeded calmly. "Don't you think it's better you walk out that door knowing what you are facing rather than it being a question always in the back of your mind, causing you worry and frustration?"

Bear no longer wanted to discuss it. "Ever heard of Katrine Ahlberg?"

Sasha seemed taken aback by the change of topic. She narrowed her eyes and shook her head a few times. "What?"

"Katrine Ahlberg," Bear said. "Ring any bells? Think back a decade ago, back when you were still wet behind the ears."

"I was made for intelligence work," she said with a wink. "And I do recall that name. The Scandinavian Princess, I believe they called her. She was married to that terrorist, Christ, what's his name?"

Bear waited a beat to see if she'd remember.

She did. "Awad. That son of a bitch. How he's eluded us all these years…"

"Probably has to do with his relation to the Crown Prince."

"Right, one of his two thousand cousins. Please, if the right people pushed on the Crown Prince and threatened to cut off a few business relationships, Awad would be plucked off the street in broad daylight. In fact, they'd broadcast his torture nightly if it were demanded."

"Is he someone you've been watching?"

Sasha bit her bottom lip. Bear sensed that she realized she could go no further with the conversation. "Look, I know you won't say anything, but I still have rules I have to adhere to regarding specific intelligence. Let's get back to Ahlberg, though. Why did you bring up a woman who was killed ten years ago?"

"Because she's still alive."

"What?"

"The wrong woman was killed."

"How do you know that?"

"Because I was there when it happened."

Sasha stumbled back into the island. She knew the kind of work Bear and Jack performed in those days. It wasn't a mystery. Perhaps the association with names she knew made it real though. She gripped the countertop and steadied herself.

"Then who was it that you assassinated?"

Bear leaned back against the refrigerator. The stainless steel surface felt cool against his back even through his shirt. He took in a deep breath while considering how to phrase it. These weren't conversations he liked to have with anyone. In the end, simple won out.

"Her twin sister."

He could see Sasha searching her mental storehouse, trying to recount everything she could about Katrine Ahlberg. It had been so long ago that Sasha had likely dumped all information she had on the woman. Why keep tabs on a ghost? Turns out someone should have.

"We were duped," Bear said. "I don't know by who, or how they did it, but the intelligence was tampered with and we were led to Birgit instead. We were brought back in to rectify the situation. The man who issued the command both then and now is now in charge of the Agency's SOG."

"Jesus." Sasha reached for Bear's beer bottle and took a long drink. "Frank Skinner?"

Bear nodded as he took back his beer and wiped her lipstick off the top. "He's not the guy you want to screw with right now. Believe me, if I had the option of doing this or wringing his neck, he'd be dead right now. But I can't do that, so we're gonna finish this and then I'm done. I don't care where I have to go in order to be far enough away that they never find me again. I'll go there." He glanced away for a second then re-established eye contact. "And I hope that you'll come with me."

Sasha glanced at the test results face down on the counter next to her. She winced involuntarily. "If Ahlberg hasn't been a problem for the past decade, then why all of a sudden does this need to be rectified? And why can't Skinner use one of his SOG teams? Christ, this is what they excel at."

Bear shrugged the question off like it was a bad pitch on a 2-0 count. "I don't have the clout to question that anymore."

"Where's Jack now?"

Bear filled Sasha in on what had happened since he and Jack left the house up to the scene in the morgue and the duo splitting up.

"A body double?" Sasha said. "And willing to take a bullet like that? This is absurd. Someone's tipped off Katrine. That's the only logical explanation. And this operation has been in development for longer than a few weeks, I'll tell you that much." She paused a beat. "Jack hasn't been in contact yet then?"

Bear shook his head. "Haven't heard anything."

Sasha left the room. Bear pulled another beer from the fridge, thought of Mandy as he popped the cap inside the bear's mouth. He hoped the girl was managing OK in Iceland and not spending her hours worrying about him.

"Let's see what I can find out." Sasha placed her laptop on the counter. It was an extremely thin device and barely weighed a pound. The first time Bear had picked it up, he nearly launched it into the ceiling. That was the last time Sasha allowed him to handle the computer.

"I don't want you getting in trouble," he said.

She waved him off. "I've got ways to access my systems that will not alert anyone." She glanced up at him and picked up on his disapproval. "We may have intelligence that has not made its way to you. Or perhaps it has and Skinner is holding back on you. Wouldn't you like to know?"

Bear didn't doubt that. There wasn't a time in history when he fully trusted Frank. Not even during the days when Jack vouched for the guy.

Sasha had slipped into analyst mode and worked too quickly for Bear to keep up with her. She entered data on several screens. Row after row of database entries flew past in the background.

"I'm not finding a whole lot," Sasha said, looking up at Bear. The soft light from the laptop screen bathed her face in light blue.

"Try searching for her sister, Birgit. Hell, while you're at it, let's see what Awad is up to today."

Sasha nodded and shifted her gaze back to her work.

Bear heard his phone ringing from the other room. He walked over to it and snatched it up before it would have diverted to a voicemail box that he had no plans on ever accessing. The number on the screen didn't register, and he didn't think it belonged to Frank. Only a few people had access to the line. Perhaps Jack had fallen into trouble and was calling from a different phone.

"Yeah?" Bear said.

"Riley?" The man's voice was distorted by static.

"Who is this?"

"Riley, if you can hear me, get the hell out of there now."

# 41

The black luxury sedan raced toward me. Sunlight reflected off the windshield, making it impossible for me to get a look at the driver and whether there were passengers. I took a deep breath in an effort to calm myself. There were more than a dozen possible reasons for someone to haul ass down a narrow back alley in a hundred thousand dollar Mercedes.

I couldn't think of one at that moment, though.

I slammed my door shut and started the BMW, threw the shifter into reverse and spun the wheel so I would wind up face-to-face with the S550. Never made it that far, though. The driver of the other vehicle slammed on his brakes. The sound of his tires grating against the asphalt penetrated the cabin of the BMW. I glanced through the passenger window and saw the Mercedes' front doors whip open.

I never saw or heard the vehicle that crashed into the back of mine. The impact shoved me toward the center console where my hip and side took the brunt of the impact. A moment later I was slingshotted in the other direction. My head cracked against the driver's window. The shattered glass sprinkled the pavement outside. The cooled steering wheel made a good resting spot for my forehead as I grimaced against the throbbing pain that stretched from my temple to the base of my skull.

Outside there were at least two men yelling at each other from either side of the BMW. They weren't shouts of anger. One was giving directions, the other confirming.

The driver's side door groaned as someone tried to pull it open. When they hit the BMW I assumed the intent was to spin the vehicle, leaving me disoriented while they flooded me with chaos. Instead the driver had hit too close to the center, leaving the frame bent and the door stuck.

The guy reached in and grabbed hold of me. I worked my hand to the seat belt release and pushed the button. The metal buckle made a decent weapon. Whipped my arm and flung the buckle in this direction. It wouldn't have done much if it hit him, but his instincts took over anyway and he flinched back. During the reprieve I managed to pull my pistol free. He saw the weapon come over the door ledge and dove to the ground.

Glass imploded from the passenger side of the vehicle and bounced off me. I ducked forward, brought my face around to catch a glimpse of what had happened. Someone had shot the window at an angle. Not only was the side window shattered, a chunk of the windshield was as well, and the area surrounding it fractured in a spider web pattern.

I aimed in the direction of the shot, but could not pinpoint the location of the shooter.

"We've got you surrounded," the guy outside my door said. I tried to place his accent. It made my head hurt worse.

I grabbed the handle, pulled, and drove my shoulder against the door. It didn't budge.

The rear window exploded. The bullet whizzed past close enough I swear I saw it spinning. It buried in the dash. These bastards were crazy. They had to know that once the bullet hit the first surface anything could happen. After the first impact, the trajectory of the bullet would be unknown.

"The next one might split your skull," the guy said. Where the hell was he from? It wasn't German or Dutch. "Throw your weapon out the window. We just want to talk to you."

Yeah, that was likely. I'd used that line and then shot a man in the back of the head before.

The rear window made a sound like dull wind chimes as someone quickly broke away the remaining glass. I angled my arm backward and shot full well knowing by looking at the rearview there wasn't a target in sight.

"That's going to get you killed," the man yelled.

I stuck the pistol out of the window and pointed it down and fired.

The man scurried to his feet. The soles of his shoes dug in and scattered the gravel as he sprinted away. Shots rang out like firecrackers on the Fourth of July. Each tire was shot out, as were the remaining windows. Bullets slammed into the side of the car, each one slapping it with a sickening thud. I covered my head and waited for the burn, but was never hit.

At least not by a round.

The fist that slammed into the side of my head was gloved. The loose, rough stitching cut into my cheek. Warm blood seeped out of the wound. The assailant took another swing, hitting me in roughly the same spot as where I'd slammed into the glass that used to adorn the driver's side window.

For a moment everything went black and I felt my body slumping. Then I was rising. Tiny shards of glass cut my back, buttocks, and thighs as they dragged me out of the BMW. They could've used the passenger door since the driver's didn't work. Guess that would've been too easy. And less painful. Considering the volley of fire they sent my way, I figured I must have managed to piss them off.

But I was still alive.

There had to be a reason for that.

By the time they dropped me on the ground, I had recovered enough that only the edges of my vision were dimmed. I groaned for their benefit as I pulled my elbows tight. There were four boots. Two black, two brown. They would've been better off using them against my head than planting them flatfooted on the ground.

Summoning every ounce of fight I had in me, I launched myself headfirst like a reckless defensive tackle into the guy directly in front of me. The top of my skull slammed into his groin. He half-screamed, half-cried a second after impact. I figured by that time his nuts were considerably closer to his throat than they had been since birth. I pushed through until I was on my feet and he was on the ground. His handgun fell and skated across the asphalt out of reach.

I moved for the weapon.

The other guy jumped on my back and we both went down. I managed to get my right arm under my face before it hit the street. The ground shredded my new shirt. And my wrist. The man flung his arm around me and tried to wrap it around my throat. I tucked my chin to my chest, rose up, then pitched forward quickly while reaching back and grabbing hold of anything I could grasp. The man flew over my shoulder, headfirst into the street. I crawled on top of him. He flung his elbows back but only managed to connect with my upper arms. I worked my right arm under his chin and around his head. He started to buck against me. I flattened out and secured the chokehold with my left arm, pushing against the back of his head.

Perhaps it was the repeated blows to my head, but I found myself locked in tunnel vision. I only cared about this guy, forgetting that there were others out there. I forced myself to focus on the surrounding area, heard the voices of a man and a woman. Footsteps pounded the ground. Gravel skated along the asphalt. I let go of my man and hopped off his back.

When they struck it wasn't violent or even all that hard of a blow. It didn't have to be if the assailant knew what he or she was doing.

The man came up behind me and delivered a strike to my kidney. I bent to the side with plans to roll through and deliver an upper cut to his chin. All I did was play right into his plan. One which required no counterstrike. He had his hand around my head in no time and I sucked in the chemical-laden white cloth.

Fire ripped through my mouth, nostrils and throat. The world turned into a fishbowl. My eyes focused and unfocused as things grew nearer and then fled away from me.

The guy let me go. No surprise. It wasn't like I was going to get far.

*Run*, I commanded my legs. They defied me.

I thought I heard sirens, but my assailants made no mention of them. The men I'd beaten rose. I tried to walk away from them. In reality, I stumbled forward then sideways a couple steps and dropped to a knee. My other knee hit the ground. I managed a few more inches on my knees before I fell forward.

At one time I was practically immune to the drug and others like it. We drilled regularly, seeing how long we could go before the effects would take us down. In the end we all went down, but the longer it took for the chemicals to work their magic, the more damage we could do. In simulation and real life practice I had managed to defeat my would-be-captors every time.

But that was a long time ago. Now I was closer to mortal than I'd ever been. Partly age. Partly my desire to leave a life that refused to release me.

If I made it through this, I decided, I would flip the leaf back over and return to my old ways.

Someone grabbed hold of me, hoisted me up and dropped me on my back. I stared up at a slender pair of long legs clad in a skirt. Peeking out of the bottom of the blue fabric was half of a tattoo that I instantly recognized. Before my vision failed me, I glanced up and saw her dark mane tussling about in the breeze.

"Ahlberg," I mouthed.

"Sleep well, Mr. Noble," she said.

# 42

"Now, Riley," Brandon yelled into the phone. "Get out of there now!"

There was no answer from the man on the other end of the line. He thought he heard Bear say something at one point, but the connection sounded like it was dead from the moment he pressed send.

Brandon's entire office was offline. The manufacturer names bounced across the screens of the monitors and televisions.

The footsteps upstairs came and went. It was impossible to tell how many there were, but so far the access door had not been breached.

Brandon cursed himself for acting in such a sloppy manner. Why have a state of the art security system installed if he wasn't even going to bother monitoring the feeds? At least he would have had warning that the men had arrived. It might not have spared him, but he could have triggered the systems to back up all data and then destroy themselves. The list of those who would benefit from access to his files was sizable. From terrorist cells to foreign governments to corporations, analysts would have a field day with all the data Brandon had collected over the years.

But it wasn't a terrorist or secret agent from China or North Korea in his house. This threat was homegrown.

Who was leading it?

The stomps simmered to a shuffle directly overhead. Brandon closed his eyes and honed in on the sounds around him. Without the whirring of the computer fans he was able to hear the muffled voices. The floor was too thick to decipher their words, though.

He grabbed his cell phone and dialed Jack's number again. "Come on, man," he whispered into the mouthpiece. The line rang repeatedly but Noble never answered. Brandon hung up and dialed Bear. The result was same.

What else could he do?

Brandon backed his chair up, spun, and went to the bookcase positioned underneath the television on the rear wall. He pulled out a thick volume with a barely-legible title on a worn red spine. He flipped the book upside down and placed his thumb on the biometric scanner. The lock clicked, allowing Brandon to open it and retrieve the Springfield Armory XD-S pistol. His hand shook as he practiced taking aim at his reflection in the plasma. Beads of sweat coated his forehead. He brushed aside his nervousness, telling himself that it didn't matter how steady his shot was. If they made it through the door, he'd unload all but one bullet from the nine-round magazine.

All the intelligence in the world did them no good if they couldn't decipher it. That last bullet would protect the information by destroying the cipher.

Brandon turned the pistol on himself and imagined what it would be like in the moment he pulled the trigger.

A thought occurred to him at that second. He had provided Jack with a dial around number to reach Frank Skinner.

What the hell was the number?

Brandon spun one hundred eighty degrees in his chair and faced the rounded entryway into his office. A pair of boots pounded against the floor above, walking four or five feet in one direction, then going back the other way. Each step was deliberate. The person paced non-stop. There was no talking now. At least not loud enough for Brandon to hear.

He held the phone in front of him and tried recalling the sequence of digits he had provided to Jack. Two deep breaths steadied his rapid heart rate. One at a time he punched in the numbers. He placed the phone to his ear and heard the distinct international ring tone.

The footsteps above him stopped. The call was answered. The voice above spoke, muffled.

But Brandon heard it clear in his ear.

"Jack?" the man said. "Where the hell are you?"

Brandon ended the call amid a flurry of activity in the room above him. He had a hunch that the men at his house were from the Agency, but he sure as hell didn't expect it to be Frank Skinner and his SOG guys who had hacked into his system.

What if it wasn't Frank who had done it, though?

Scenarios raced through his mind. Perhaps Skinner got wind of what was going down and managed to arrive at Brandon's house first to protect him. After all, a talented enough hacker could have performed all the computer tasks from a shack in rural China. They didn't have to be outside his northern Virginia home for the takedown.

Brandon was an asset to the Agency. There was no way anyone had green-lighted his termination.

Of course, Frank Skinner never worked within the framework of the rules.

Brandon rubbed his eyes and thought of Kimberlee. When she brought up the idea of them getting together, her idea was for them to travel to the Virgin Islands. The trip would have been this week. But he had insisted that they wait another month. It'd be easier to travel then, considering they were both wheel-chair bound. The fewer tourists, the better. And the height of hurricane season was best for island travel. At least he'd read online that was the case.

Brandon punched in her number and stared at the ten digits. The hell would he tell her? He brought the phone up to his mouth and whispered I love you to the contact picture that had popped up. Then he hit the home key, clearing her number off his screen.

He could only imagine what had made the scraping sound outside his office. Possibly a battering ram. The door banged and crunched and bent and bowed. It was ten inches thick and they were dismantling it like it was made of construction paper. The hinges busted off and skated across the floor. The door pushed in six inches or so. He saw black-gloved hands sticking through the crevice. The room went dark. Red emergency lighting clicked on followed by soft whites along the edge of the floor and under his desk.

A head clad in a ski-mask and goggles poked through. Looked like an old G.I. Joe figure. The hell was his name?

Snakeeyes.

*Fucking Snakeeyes is gonna take me out.*

Brandon's lungs spasmed. He was beyond controlling his breath at this point. Air rushed in through his mouth and nose and was lost. He managed to spit some out. Drew a little more in. It was pointless. Snakeeyes shouted and the door fell forward, clipping his desk and sending his three main monitors crashing over, screens shattered. They were over a thousand dollars each.

*Assholes.*

Brandon lifted his arm and took aim at the door, unleashing a volley of 9mm ammunition at the men standing there. Two fell back into the arms of the others. The men repositioned out of sight. Brandon continued shooting until all that happened when he squeezed the trigger was an audible click.

*Shit.*

He'd forgotten to save one bullet for himself.

Three men entered the room with their HK-7s in the ready position. One took aim at Brandon while the other two rounded his desk and called out in turn that the room was clear. The guy in the middle stepped aside and Brandon saw a man he never thought he'd meet in person.

"Skinner."

## 43

The line went dead and Bear set the phone down and glanced around the room. The static on the line had made it difficult to determine who had been on the other end, but if he had to put money on it, it was Brandon. And that was enough reason to send him into a hyper-alert state.

"Where are you going?" Sasha asked.

Bear said nothing in return as he left the room and headed down the corridor that led to the front entryway. He took up next to a window and scanned the driveway leading to the house. There was no one out front. The surrounding yard was green and lush and deserted except for a few birds and rabbits feasting on the grass.

"I think I've found something on Ahlberg," Sasha called out.

He turned from the door to make his way back to the kitchen. A burst of light in his peripheral beyond the front gate gave him reason to pause. Had he really seen it? The doctors had said he might encounter such things as a result of his headaches. Then again, it could have been a chrome side mirror on an approaching vehicle. Another glance through the window revealed nothing new.

"Riley, you have to come see this," she said. "Apparently Awad has been moving a lot of money around and selling off some of his assets."

Bear lingered at the window for a few seconds more, allowing his unfocused gaze to stretch out over the yard. The edges of his vision wavered. He'd been told that wasn't a good thing and it, too, was related. But his vision had been like that for years, so he paid no attention to it.

"Bloody hell," Sasha said. "Birgit Ahlberg liquidated all of her assets three weeks ago. Everything." And a few seconds later. "Where the hell are you?"

He returned to the kitchen and flipped his phone over and glanced at the cracked screen. No new calls.

"Did you hear me?" she said.

He nodded. "Yeah, that's great."

"No, it's not great. Something major is about to happen. These two are financing what could amount to yet another crippling attack. I have to notify a whole host of people to this information." She paused a beat, trying to get in front of Bear's shifting gaze. "Are you listening to me? What is so important in the backyard that you can't appreciate the fact you've uncovered evidence that a terrorist attack is in the works and it's related to what you've been doing with Jack?"

Bear glanced at Sasha then back to the yard. Had he seen something?

"Do whatever you gotta do to notify them right now," he tapped the counter, "then pack it up."

"What?" She straightened, slipped off her stool, and went to the back door. "What's going—"

Sasha dove to the floor as the glass above her head shattered. Two more rounds burst through the pane, clearing all but the most stubborn parts of the window. The jagged remains hung there, reflecting the light.

She crawled on her belly until she was out of view and next to Bear. He had reached for the laptop before dropping for cover behind the island. He handed it to Sasha and armed himself.

"Who is out there?" she said, flinching at the next burst of gunshots. More glass scattered across the floor. Splinters raced through the air.

"I got a call that I believe came from Brandon a couple minutes ago. He said, 'Get out now.' I got a feeling we're surrounded."

Sasha flipped the laptop open and hammered on the keyboard.

"Now's not the time," Bear said. "We gotta get you into the bunker."

She didn't look up from the screen. "I want to see who's doing this."

Bear peered around the island, pistol extended, ready to fire. "You think they sent you a damn instant message ahead of time?"

She glared up at him. "Let me do my goddamn job, Bear."

He liked it when she used his nickname, though now wasn't the time to think about such things. Bear grabbed the laptop and slammed the lid shut. Sasha protested as he grabbed her under the arm and dragged her through the hallway into the windowless waiting room. Sasha protested the entire way, demanding he return the laptop.

Bear pulled the pocket door closed and secured it. Behind him Sasha shifted several books out of the way on the third shelf of the bookcase. Once a large enough section had been revealed, she pulled off the thin paneling. The dull blue glow from the access screen brightened the hidden compartment. She entered the eight-digit security code.

"We really should update this to a biometric system," she said.

Bear put his finger to his mouth as he crossed the small room. Together they pulled the right side of the bookcase away from the wall. Sasha slipped into the darkness. The opening was hardly wide enough for Bear to squeeze through, but he'd done it before and that was when he weighed ten pounds more.

Bear managed to make it into the tunnel. After ten feet, he stopped. "Take your computer."

Sasha turned and retrieved the device. Her footsteps echoed after she disappeared into the dimly-lit tunnel. The only lights were fixed where the wall met the floor, and they served to brighten the immediate area. They were not strong enough for someone at the entrance to discern a target even thirty feet away.

"Are you coming?" she called out.

"I'll be down there in a minute. Need to make sure this is secure. Get in the room and lock it down until I'm there."

But he only went as far as the armory. The cutout was six-wide by six-high and two feet deep. If you didn't know it was there you'd never spot it. Bear had memorized the exact amount of steps it took him to reach it should something like the current event — or a zombie outbreak — ever occured.

He grabbed an HK MP-5 and a backup Beretta 92FS 9mm pistol and strapped a tactical knife around his lower leg. Was it enough? He tried to guess how many men were out there. An exercise in futility. All he could figure was that it had to be a significant force for Brandon to have picked up on it. Whoever it was wasn't afraid of a mid-day showdown either. The unsuppressed reports from the shootout in the backyard would have been heard all around them. These bastards planned on hitting hard and hitting quick and knew exactly what they wanted to take from the estate.

The soft thud coming from the dark end of the tunnel confirmed that Sasha had made it down the fully-extended fourteen-foot ladder and had secured herself in the safe room. It had been built in the forties and reinforced several times since then as the potential threats dictated. The hidden chamber was loaded with supplies, including additional arms and ammunition and enough food to last six months. What it lacked was reliable communications equipment. It was something Sasha said she had meant to take care of — like the biometric readers — but had failed to do so.

Maybe tomorrow.

And that was why instead of waiting for backup in the form of police or MI6, Bear moved quickly and quietly down the corridor toward the bookcase.

He would face the threat head on.

# 44

I gulped at the air that flooded my face like a Great Egret emerging from the water after escaping the fishing net that had trapped it while it dove and struck its prey.

There was a constant whoosh of wind surrounding me, drowning out all other noise. My ears rang. My mouth tasted like metal. My eyes burned. Blackness engulfed my sight. Was I blind? Or blindfolded? I reached for my face but my arms wouldn't move. Were they bound or did I lack the ability? I couldn't feel my wrists or hands. Come to think of it, I had no sensation other than the feeling of the wind splashing my face.

Panic raced through my veins as I tried to recall what had happened. I took a slow, deep breath and relaxed my mind. There had been an accident. Someone slammed into the driver's side of the BMW, and I felt a subsequent flash of pain in my head. Had I broken my neck?

No, it wasn't my neck. I remember moving after the accident and being outside the vehicle.

I willed my fingers to move even the slightest amount but nothing happened.

"He's moving," the guy said. I remembered the voice. Still couldn't place the accent.

I felt a sharp pain, like a pinch, on my arm. A minute later my heart pounded against my chest wall so fast and hard it ached. I couldn't tell if I was breathing anymore. The blackness burst into bright white and I was out again.

~

I CAME to feeling as though I was on a vibration plate that occasionally jostled me against a hard surface. I had the distinct feeling of sitting upright. My head rested against something solid and cool. Occasionally I banged against it.

I no longer felt the breeze, but the air around me was cool. It smelled fresh, like being on the porch after a spring rain. But it wasn't that nice. Something chemical about it. I still couldn't see anything, though I sensed others around me. I reached for my eyes. My arms didn't move. Restraints bit into my wrists. I was happy for a second that the feeling in my hands had returned. At least then I knew for sure that I hadn't snapped my neck.

Of course it also meant someone held me captive.

"He's up again," a different man said in heavily accented English.

I felt a pinch on my arm, presumably a needle. The liquid entered cold. Heated up after a few seconds of making its way through my circulatory system. This felt different. I guessed that my previous tolerances remained, albeit a fraction of what they used to be. They couldn't control me with one drug so they were using multiple. The sensation spread and by the time it reached my chest, I was out.

"Sleep well, Mr. Noble," a woman said. It was the last thing I heard.

~

WE WERE no longer moving when I awoke. The air smelled salty. A flock of seagulls carried on a cackling conversation nearby. I recalled taking aim at them with a .22 when I was about eleven years old. Dad didn't like that. He knocked the rifle out of my hand and threatened that I wouldn't use it again until I was eighteen. That was the last time I thought about killing a bird.

I expected darkness when I opened my eyes. I was half-right. The light faded to the east. Out over the ocean the sunset turned the sky into a panoramic painting of purple and pink and dark orange. My vision blurred the longer I focused on one thing, so I swung my head the other way. The muscles in my neck ached. I stared at the occupied seat next to me.

The slender legs were barely covered. The right was adorned with an intricate tattoo. I recognized it instantly.

Lifting my gaze, I came face to face with Katrine Ahlberg, the woman I'd been sent to kill a decade earlier who had somehow managed to evade my bullet and spent the next ten years evading detection while assuming the quiet life of her sister Birgit.

She glared at me through narrowed eyes. Her dyed brunette hair was pulled back into a high pony tail. I couldn't deny that she was a gorgeous woman.

"Mr. Noble."

"Katrine."

She smiled, uncrossed her legs, supposedly in an attempt to lure me in. Her gaze dropped to the needle filled with red liquid in her hand.

The hangover hit with full force. What the hell were they drugging me with? And why? The easy answer was that someone had sold me out. So why go through the trouble of taking me along for the ride? Kill me and be done with it. I swept my gaze around the vehicle. We were alone. Just the two of us parked alongside a quiet beachfront road. Through the windshield I saw lightning in the dark storm clouds bunched together to the south.

"We gonna do this here?" I shifted in the seat, bringing my left ankle under my right knee. I was surprised I could do it. I turned my torso toward her. My fingers grazed the door handle behind me. Ahlberg sat stone-faced without any reaction to any of my movements. She was either the most unaware person I'd ever met — and considering how she'd spent the last ten years I doubted that — or someone was watching us.

I decided I'd take that chance.

I grabbed the handle and pulled it while throwing my weight back to expedite the process of opening the door and rolling out.

Only I didn't roll.

My skull banged against the window, sending a flood of fresh pain around the front of my head and circling my eyes.

The door didn't budge.

Laughing, she brought the needle up and plunged it into my thigh. I'd made it easy for her to do it, too.

"Child locks, Noble." She retrieved the now empty needle and lifted it up for me to see. "Christ, some top assassin you are."

I faded away again.

# 45

"Brandon, I presume." Frank Skinner appeared relaxed as he took in the sights of the small room. He lifted his phone. "We get it all?" He waited a beat, nodded. "Need him brought in?" Another few seconds passed. Frank looked down at Brandon and smiled.

Brandon found it hard to breathe at that moment. He tried to convince himself that he'd heard incorrectly. If they got the data, they *needed* him. Frank wouldn't smile about that, though.

It felt as though an elephant sat on his chest. He wanted to lift his arms and surrender, throw the gun on the floor, anything to let Frank Skinner know that Brandon was not a threat. But he couldn't move. The edges of his vision darkened. It felt a lot like the time he was five years old and his brother's friends tossed him into the deep end of the pool. Toughening him up, they had said. Survival of the fittest, they had said. He almost drowned that day had it not been for the cleaning lady diving in after he'd been face down for three minutes.

But this was a different feeling.

Why was his chest so heavy?

He gulped air like a guppy out of water as Frank lifted his Sig and aimed it at Brandon.

"Guess before you go," Frank said, shaking his pistol so the red dot circled

Brandon's heart, "I should let you know your friends aren't gonna be around much longer. But I do have to thank you."

More men entered the room and dismantled the computers and carried them out.

The wheezing sound coming from Brandon's throat was uncontrollable now.

"You really helped Noble and his stooge sidekick figure things out. In fact, they've done enough that I really don't need you around here anymore." Frank squeezed the trigger, unloading a single round.

Brandon felt the burn and pain radiating. He expected it to be much worse. Was that because he was already dying from the heart attack?

"Oh, one more thing," Frank said, leaning forward with his hands planted on the desk. "We're gonna have to take in that girl you've been seeing and bring her to the Farm for a couple weeks." His lips thinned and he sucked in air, making a whistling sound. "It's doubtful she'll make it out alive."

Brandon looked down at the crimson bloom spreading out from the hole in his chest. There was no pain anymore. It was like he was looking down on the situation from above. His body went numb. He could no longer detect his heart pumping.

One of Snakeeye's partners kicked Brandon and his wheelchair over sideways. He landed with his head near the wall, leaving him with a view of the men filing out of his office. They had left him there to die.

Brandon felt his strength fade quickly. He tried to hold in the blood seeping from the wound on his chest, but it did little good. It poured through the tiny cracks between his fingers. However, in the process he managed to trigger the switch on his medical alert necklace, the one he had hidden inside his shirt because he was too embarrassed to let Kimberlee see it when they video chatted.

# 46

The chemically-created fog inundated the hallway, providing cover and concealment for a team of operators who had entered the house through the back. The front door remained intact and unlocked. The time spent in the tunnel had left Bear under-prepared for the situation. How many men had penetrated the house? Who were they? What were their capabilities?

They knew how to throw a smoker, he knew that much.

They had started the assault by shooting out the window near where Sasha had stood. Did they miss her on purpose? Were they warning shots? Perhaps they had orders not to take the woman out due to her position within British Intelligence. Or maybe they were a ragtag team of misfits who had no business running a takedown.

Bear missed the feeling of holding an HK MP-5. The powerfulness, preciseness in a closed combat situation such as the one he faced.

One at a time, he ascended the stairs to the second floor, keeping his footfalls and his shoulder against the wall to his right. He imagined a cat prowling.

While Bear was unsure of the overall size of the team, he was confident they had split into smaller units. He would find at least two at the top of the stairs.

At the first landing this was confirmed.

He heard one of the men issue a whispered command. It turned out to be a fatal mistake.

Bear stopped on the last step. He steadied his breath and tuned into his sense of hearing. Skills erode over time, but he refused to believe that so many days had passed for him to have lost more than a small fraction of a step.

The creaking floorboard in the middle of the hall had been a giveaway on a number of nights when he had snuck downstairs for a late-night snack. Sasha had heard him leaving or returning and either chastised him or disrupted his plans.

On this afternoon it was the man clad in black tactical gear who found himself giving his position away by stepping on the loose piece of wood.

Bear eased himself to the corner, MP-5 at the ready. He swung around and knew exactly where to shoot. He squeezed the trigger for a half second and three rounds exploded from the barrel and hit the man in rapid succession. The first landed dead center, but the guy's vest stopped the bullet. The next two found their way into his neck, tearing through flesh and destroying the important network of arteries and nerves that resided there. The guy went down without so much as raising his weapon. The shots had achieved both intended effects as the man's partner emerged from the bedroom on the right. The guy never looked at his fallen comrade. He kept his sights on Bear.

Another squeeze of the trigger. Three more rounds left the MP-5. The cluster of shots hit the guy in the upper right arm and shoulder, spinning him around but not doing enough damage to take him down. His wounded shoulder smashed against the wall. A patch of blood trailed across and dripped down the wall as the man recovered and turned with his sidearm raised in his left hand. He fired wildly. Must've been a righty who never drilled with both hands. Plaster erupted from the walls and ceiling a few feet from Bear. The dust coated his face.

He took an extra second to aim and fire the next three-round burst. They hit the guy in a tight line starting between his eyes and stopping an inch above his brow. The man jerked back and fell at his partner's feet, his left hand still clutching his Sig.

Bear searched the bodies and came away with an MP-7 equipped with a suppressor, an extra magazine, the second man's SIG, and a handheld radio. He nearly chucked the unit into the bedroom when it came to life with a burst of static.

The gunfight had drawn some interest.

"Blue, report." The voice was grainy but Bear easily discerned the southern-

American accent. He pegged the attackers for a team of Mercs. Former soldiers hell bent on making the most they could before their skills eroded. He couldn't blame them for trying. Too bad this would be their last op.

"Report, Blue. Report."

Seconds passed and then Bear heard pounding on the steps. He smiled and armed himself with the MP-7. He hovered in the bedroom doorway where he could duck for cover if necessary.

With his sights five feet above the floor, he nailed the first guy up. He only had to adjust his aim a fraction of an inch. The first shot destroyed the man's cheek bone. The next two went in near the temple. The man hadn't bothered to pause at the top of the steps. He came around the corner, eyes cast downward at one of his partners. Now he joined him dead on the ground. Someone reached out, grabbed the guy by his feet and started pulling. At the same time Bear saw a third arm, smoker in hand — there was no way they were going with a live grenade in the house. Bear fired a shot that nearly severed the limb at the elbow. The smoker fell to the floor. The pin remained around the guy's index finger.

Fog filled the hallway quicker than Bear had anticipated. He wasn't sure whether to move forward, hold his position, or retreat into the bedroom.

Two voices called out.

Bear dropped to the floor. The visibility was better. The first man cleared the stairs and entered the hallway. The red laser from his sight cut through the smoke a good five feet above Bear's prone position. Bear followed the line to the source and squeezed the MP-7's trigger. The laser spun circles through the fog and settled on the ceiling.

Bear didn't wait to determine center mass on the next guy. Instead, he aimed at the man's ankle and let loose three straight three-round bursts, planting the rounds in the guy's shin, the bottom of his foot, and in his groin. The man writhed in pain, yelling out while bleeding out.

Bear didn't stop to aim as he passed the man. He dropped his arm and squeezed the trigger, starting at the navel and not relenting until the weapon stopped spitting out ammunition. He dropped it and scooped up a new MP-7 from one of the freshly fallen men. Wasn't like the guy needed it anymore.

Heading down the stairs, he held his MP-5 in one hand and the new HK in the other. Their positions were offset, allowing him to cover the maximum amount of ground. Did they only send four mercs? He stopped his mind from wondering who "they" were and continued down the steps with his back against the wall while focusing on his immediate environment and listening for movement beyond the limits of his sight.

The quickly repeating tinny sound didn't immediately register as gunshots until one slammed into his shoulder. Bear dropped and rolled through the remaining stairs, fighting back the pain. His arm stood up to the test, though, and he managed to hang onto both weapons.

The man dressed in black gear seemed surprised to see Bear dive across the hallway. His inaccurate shot slammed into the three-hundred year old oak door, spraying tiny slivers of wood into the foyer.

Bear unloaded with both weapons, catching the guy in the thigh and stomach. There was no time to investigate whether the wound was fatal. Another man had entered the hallway from near the kitchen and opened fire.

Bear slammed through the pocket door that shielded the windowless room from view. He scrambled to the adjoining wall, closed his eyes and breathed deep and waited. He knew in this spot that the floorboard would move slightly when someone stood directly opposite the wall. Amazing the things he picked up in the place playing hide and seek with Sasha's nieces and nephews. And if a forty pound five-year-old could give her position away, there was no doubt that a grown man could.

He placed the hand of his wounded arm on the ground. The quiet amplified the ringing in his ears. He glanced at his shoulder, surveying the damage. The bullet had grazed him. Didn't appear to be any muscular or bone damage. He might need Sasha to stitch it up, though.

The floorboard rose. Bear pressed both weapons against the plaster wall and squeezed the triggers. White dust exploded out and coated his face. He adjusted each weapon about six inches and fired again. And then repeated the process twice more. Each time the man on the opposite side of the wall grunted until the moment when his lifeless body collapsed.

Bear dropped to the floor and wiped the plaster off his face and blinked his eyes to flush the debris. The burning would take a few seconds to pass.

On his feet again, he left the windowless room and checked the bodies in the hallway. Both were dead. As expected, neither offered clues as to the men's identities.

Leaving the corpses behind, Bear swept the rest of the house and scanned the backyard. There was no one else.

He tucked one of the weapons away and pulled out his cell phone. His first call went unanswered. *Where the hell are you, Jack?* He had been unable to reach the man and hadn't heard a word from him. After what had just happened in Sasha's house, Bear was concerned a similar fate awaited Noble.

Bear then decided to place a call to a man he detested. They'd skirted the rules Frank Skinner had wanted them to play by, but it was time to bring him up to date on the situation. He punched in the number Brandon had provided to Jack and waited while his call routed through the Far East.

Frank answered on the second ring amid a bustle of chatter in the background. "Jack? What's going on?" The other voices faded away.

"It ain't Jack," Bear said.

"Logan? That you?"

"Yeah."

"What is going on? Why haven't you guys reported until now?"

"You tell me what's going on, Frank."

There was a pause of several seconds. Frank cleared his throat. "I don't have time for these games. Every second we piss away is more time for Ahlberg to get away from us."

"Let me be more specific then." Bear tended to his wound, wiping blood away with a dish towel soaked in peroxide. "I'm with Sasha right now—"

"God dammit, man. I told you not to bring her in."

"I didn't bring her in, *man*. Me and Jack split up."

"You did what?" Frank's breathing grew loud and fast and ragged.

"He had to run down a lead. I needed a day to take care of something. Came back here."

Frank muttered something that Bear couldn't pick up.

"Anyway, we were just attacked by six dudes dressed head to toe in black tactical gear. I only heard one of them, but the son of a bitch was from the States. Alabama if I had to pinpoint where he grew up. So I'll ask you again, what the hell is going on?"

"Son of a bitch," Frank said. "They must know and they tracked you back there." The phone muffled for a few seconds and Bear picked out two distinct voices, though he was unsure what they were saying. Sounded like they were underwater. "Look, I need you to stay put for just a couple minutes. I'm gonna make a call."

Bear hung up and tucked the phone way. "Stay put my ass."

A trickle of blood seeped from his shoulder. He pulled the severed skin apart and gauged the depth of the wound. On second glance it might not need stitches. He'd ask Sasha soon enough.

Perhaps sooner than he thought.

"Get off me." The scream came from the tunnel inside the windowless room. No doubt the voice was Sasha's.

Bear raced from the kitchen into the hallway and past the open pocket door. The bookcase was cracked open two feet. Had he closed it when he exited the tunnel? He couldn't recall anything from his last visit in the room other than shooting the wall. He took two steps toward the entrance then froze in place upon seeing the blonde-haired woman's reflection in the mirror standing in the spot he had occupied minutes earlier. She had him covered with her weapon, and he doubted she'd miss from this distance.

"That's it," she said. "Don't move."

# 47

Frank Skinner stared at the pile of intelligence they'd printed so far. It had come from a tiny fraction of Brandon's files, but Frank couldn't get too excited over what they'd found despite the fact that it all but served his ultimate target up on a platter.

"What's going on, boss?" Rugg asked. The thirty-three-year-old ex-Ranger had been Frank's top operator since he had taken over the SOG.

He looked up from the papers and stared at his man for a moment. He filled his lungs, blew out forcefully. "We lost the entire team."

Rugg's eyes widened. He stepped closer so the men were face to face. "All six men? What the hell were they up against?"

"One pissed off mountain of a man." Frank noticed that all eyes in the room had fallen on him. The men who worked for him would undertake any mission he asked of them, and all knew the possibility of death surrounded them, but when an entire team was wiped out in an afternoon, they all felt it. "I gotta step outside for a minute."

He exited through the backdoor and took a short walk across the yard and into the woods. Twenty feet into the leafy canopy his phone rang again. He answered expecting to hear Logan's voice.

"You lost a lot of men here today," the woman said.

"Yeah, where the hell were you?" he said.

"Outside," she said. "Where it was safe."

"Where are you now?"

"Inside, where it's safe." She paused a beat and said something to someone present with her. "We have the large man and his wife. We'll see you at the pre-arranged location soon?"

Frank grunted his confirmation, hung up and then called in to have the Gulfstream V ready for takeoff within the hour.

# 48

It wasn't safe to remain in Sasha's house following the small war that had taken place within its walls. The blonde-haired woman who looked like Ahlberg and the Middle Eastern looking man with salt-and-pepper hair bound and gagged Sasha. They secured Bear's wrists with flex-cuffs and wrapped his legs with rope. His refusal to go willingly had been met with a strike to the head with a metal club. The blow didn't take Bear down, so the guy hit him again. This time Bear dropped to a knee. The third strike sent him to the ground amid Sasha's pleading for them to stop hitting him over the head.

Anywhere but the head.

When Bear came to, he was being dragged through the house by the man. The guy was a hell of a lot stronger than he looked. Bear thrashed and nearly knocked the guy over. The man dropped Bear's bound feet and retrieved his sidearm.

"There's a chance you will survive this if you stop acting like an idiot," the man said. He sounded like a Saudi. Bear had an idea as to his identity. "We have no fight with the woman or her organization. We do not want to deal with them, but we will if necessary. So take this as your final warning. Cooperate or your wife will be shot in the head and dumped in the river."

Bear looked beyond the man and saw that Ahlberg had Sasha secured. Next to them on the wall was a portrait of Mandy. Ahlberg shoved Sasha against the wall, knocking the framed picture off its hook.

*God, don't let them notice the girl.*

He reminded himself that the girl was safe. They'd have to torture the both of them to get her location, and so far, they had no reason to pursue that course of action.

*Play along, Bear.*

The woman aimed her pistol at the back of Sasha's head.

Not much time had passed since Ahlberg had left the hotel and her body double was murdered. Perhaps fearing she had been filmed she had decided to dye her hair back to avoid detection. Or maybe she just didn't care anymore.

"Understand?" the man yelled. His voice was gruff and heavily accented. The shout roped Bear back into the current situation.

Bear could withstand any torture or punishment they doled out for him. But he couldn't watch Sasha be subjected to it because of his refusal to comply. He'd have to see where this led. He nodded and raised his hands, which were still conjoined via a pair of rubber flex-cuffs. He knew from experience that it would be near impossible for him to escape from them. He'd rather have chains draped around his wrists. At least he could use those as weapons against his captors.

The Saudi leaned over and cut the rope that bound Bear's legs. "Don't get any ideas. This is not so you can attempt an escape. We have to move quickly in the event that someone overheard the shootout and the police are en route."

Bear rose to his feet, said nothing. He contemplated taking the man on, but even if he reached the guy, there was nothing he could do to stop Ahlberg from shooting Sasha. Hell, she'd sold her twin sister out. The woman's heart was made of ice.

The guy looked back at the women and nodded. Ahlberg led Sasha through the door. A moment later the four of them stood at the edge of the rectangular green lawn. Bear didn't hear the helicopter until it appeared over the woods behind the house. It was an executive model, built for passengers and speed.

The helicopter touched down in the middle of the yard. The grass bent flat in swirling patterns under the heavy gusts produced by the rotors. The pilot must have been previously instructed to keep the bird ready to fly.

The doors swung open and a man dressed similar to the six Bear had disposed of hopped to the ground. Bear spotted another man dressed the same waiting inside the craft. They ordered him inside first. He soon after found himself covered by three armed men who watched him even after he fell back in his seat. The pilot got in on the action, too. Ahlberg had done her homework on Bear. Or someone had filled her in recently.

They placed Sasha next to Bear only after securing his legs together again. They strapped his torso to the seat. She received the same treatment. Her hair brushed his face as she rested her head against his shoulder while the Saudi, Ahlberg, and one of their black tactical gear-clad guards discussed their next move with the pilot.

Bear considered their current location and distances to mainland Europe. It was possible that the helicopter held enough fuel to make the crossing. The weather was fair and there would be little risk traveling over the channel. If they were going to cross to the Netherlands, it was about a hundred miles over water.

"Where do you think they're taking us?" Sasha's breath felt hot against his already-burning ear.

He shook his head slowly, keeping his eye on the group outside the helicopter.

She leaned in even closer. Her lips grazed his earlobe. "I tripped the switch."

Inside the hidden section of the bookcase was a small lever that once flipped would alert her boss at MI6 that something had happened at the estate. She had a similar device in her flat in London. They were coded separately, and her boss would know exactly where to send the security team. The problem was that the bookcase was meant to be closed and not reopened — and especially not left open after one member of the team had left the passageway. Knowing that the odds of reaching Sasha were slim, the tactical team would attempt to secure the house before entering the windowless room, where they would find the smashed pocket door, the opened bookcase, and soon after realize that Sasha and Bear were not present.

Also troubling was the fact that the team would have to come up from London. Even driving recklessly after making it out of London traffic, it would take them ninety minutes.

Minimum.

"When?" Bear asked, turning his head slightly toward her.

Her head rolled off his shoulder, she scratched at where his beard had tickled her face. She glanced up at him. "When that asshole led me out."

Bear took a deep breath and held it in despite the burn in his chest. He calculated how much time had passed. Not enough. A moment later he expelled the air. "They're over an hour away."

Presumably Sasha was already aware of this. She leaned in close again and whispered. "They'll see what happened, and they'll find us. Trust me."

Although trust never came easy for Bear, he had welcomed Sasha into his life and accepted her words and actions without question. This, however, was too much for him to take on a leap of faith.

"Appreciate the optimism," he said. "But we're screwed."

Ahlberg, the Middle Eastern man and the security detail piled into the bird. They were in the air, flying low, eastbound into the darkening sky, and soon after, out over the sea.

# 49

After their initial evaluation, neither of the highly skilled George Washington University Hospital trauma surgeons currently operating on the frail man thought he would survive the single gunshot wound to the chest.

In fact, he had already died once after arriving. The ER staff had managed to revive him. Had it been a few minutes prior to the helicopter landing, they might've left him dead on the stretcher.

His only chance at survival was the emergency surgery necessary to repair the network of arteries, blood vessels, organs, bones, and muscular tissue that had been destroyed by the bullet.

As they closed the surgical incision after spending the previous eight hours doing all they could to fix the man, they shared a knowing look that it had all been in vain.

Brandon Cunningham, they feared, would be dead by morning's first light.

# 50

THE SOFT GLOW FROM LIGHTS MOUNTED HIGH ON THE WAREHOUSE WALLS CAST the open space in a dim yellow wash. The room smelled like a fishing pier at the close of business on a good day. Water lapped against the wooden sides of the empty boat slip inside the structure. The lane of water took up a quarter of the room. The exterior wall extended below the surface, perhaps all the way to the ground to prevent anyone from swimming under to get inside.

They'd restrained my feet to the legs of the chair, my arms behind my back, my chest to the seat back. And they used a device that forced my chin to my chest and held my head in place. I still managed to turn it enough to the side to get a good look at the place in my peripheral vision.

I'd started coming to about an hour ago. It was a slow process full of wondering what the hell had happened since I was chemically knocked out again. No one had entered the room except for a family of rats as large as Chihuahuas. The biggest of them walked across my foot and for a moment I expected him to make a meal out of my big toe. After wiggling my feet for several seconds, avoiding his teeth in the process, he gave up and ran off to join the others.

I attempted to create a timeline of the events in an effort to determine my present location and the current time of day. My last conscious moments were on the coast. I looked out over the water as the sun descended into the Atlantic. That was at approximately seven p.m.

Presumably we were in France at that time based on the position of the setting sun directly to the west. The mental map in my head said we could've been in a few spots in Belgium, and possibly the Netherlands, but given the time of day and how long it would have taken to reach the coast from Leipzig, the northern coast of France made the most sense.

At one point during the ride from Germany to the coast I had awoken in a lucid haze. Memories from that moment were fleeting. They administered another dose of the chemical before I had a chance to gather my bearings. Hell, were we even in a car at that point? Perhaps we'd flown out of Germany. There were plenty of private airstrips where no one would have taken notice of them carrying my unconscious body from a car to a plane.

Taking those data points, I figured the drug they used on me lasted anywhere from four to six hours, which meant it was currently closing in on midnight. We could be anywhere along the coast of France. It's possible they reversed course and traveled back north to the Netherlands, but I didn't think so. For starters, it was warm. And humid.

The warehouse had windows ten to fifteen feet up and they were open. The breeze rarely made it down to me. Sweat coated my body from sitting there fighting the restraints.

My best guess was that we'd gone south of the Bordeaux region near the border of Spain, possibly even crossing over into the country.

Soft footfalls descended from the only place I hadn't managed a visual yet. Behind me. Ahlberg appeared to my right. She walked along the vertical strip of flooring at the edge of the boat slip. Halfway to the wall she turned toward me and approached. Her dark hair was draped over her shoulders. She had on a pair of short black athletic shorts and a plain white tank top.

She strode directly up to me, standing tall with her shoulders pulled back. Full of confidence and without a hint of fear on her face. She jammed her thumb into my eye and forced my upper eyelid open. With her other hand she shone a bright light in my left eye, then repeated the process on my right. Her Moroccan-oil-scented hair spilled out and brushed against my lips, cheeks and neck. The sensation was not lost on me even in my current predicament.

Her hands grazed my back. The restraint on my head loosened. It hurt to straighten my stiff neck, but I forced it up and back and dropped my head to the edge of the chair back. I was temporarily blinded by the pen light but felt the slight vibrations under my feet as she stepped back. I blinked away the lingering starburst and found that she had moved out of my line of sight.

The restraint around my chest fell to my waist. My wrists were freed. The only thing holding me down was gravity. But the thing keeping me in place was the wires that bound my ankles to the chair. I figured I could break those or the chair easily enough.

"Stand if you wish to stretch out," she said. She stood in front of me again with her hands at her side and in full view. There was no needle, unless she had it tucked in her waistband or inside the pink bra that peeked out from the edge of her shirt.

I tightened my core and rose. My knees nearly locked as I straightened my leg. I almost forgot they'd been bent for at least twelve hours now. It became even clearer that I could easily snap the legs away from the chair. Ahlberg knew it, too, which was why she had retreated a few steps back. Her glance rose over my head and then she nodded at some unseen man. I looked back, but the man had concealed himself well enough that I couldn't locate him.

Glancing down, I saw the tattoo in its near entirety. Only the very top of the piece was hidden by her shorts. They didn't conceal much else, either. She moved toward me. Close enough that I could have reached out and strangled her. She figured I wouldn't with the threat of an unseen person waiting in the shadows to neutralize me. I only had to give them a reason. I told myself not to do that.

"I'm going to ask you a series of questions and you only get one shot at answering them." She stared me in the eye. Her gaze was unwavering. Her eyes were like cold, lifeless steel. "If you lie to me you're going under again and I can't promise that you will come back from the drug-induced sleep this time. And if that possibility doesn't scare you because you think you can lie convincingly, consider the fact that I probably know most if not all of the answers already."

I clasped my hands behind my back and arched in a quick stretch then rolled my head to the right and left. The combination of the accident, the fight with her men, the car ride, and being bound with my chin locked to my chest had left my spine and every supporting muscle stiffened.

"Do you understand?" she said.

I looked her up and down. A tinge of doubt entered my mind. Something was off and I didn't know if there was any way for me to survive the interrogation. A purposeful glance around the room revealed no instruments of torture, so she clearly was going to rely on the threat of the drug and what I assumed was drowning following it.

"Yeah, I got you."

"Where were you last week?" she asked.

"The USA."

"Be more specific."

I played along. "Texas."

"Why?"

"Why does anyone go to Texas?"

She glanced over my shoulder. I resisted the urge to look back.

"Did you think I was kidding?" She snapped her finger and I heard the man ready his weapon. The threat had elevated. How much did she know?

"My Jeep broke down. The rest was coincidence."

"The rest?" She leaned her head to the right. "What else happened while you were there?"

I didn't answer.

"I said what else happened when you were in Texline?"

She'd slipped up. Someone had fed her intelligence, and as far as I knew only two people knew of my location last week, and Brandon wasn't about to sell me out.

"Get to the point," I said. "Texas has nothing to do with any of this. How'd you find me? Who turned you onto me?"

Her smile was even colder than her stare. She leaned in close to me. "That part was easy. You're a sloppy operator these days, Noble."

"Yeah, well, that's probably because I should have retired three years ago."

Her breath was hot on my face. "Why didn't you?"

I shrugged. "Trouble just happens to find me."

She walked past me, shoving her shoulder into my chest as she passed. "As it does to me."

A stream of cool air enveloped me from behind. I turned in time to see a cone of orange light on the floor fading away as the door fell shut. I hadn't heard her open it.

Minutes passed. I stood there looking around the room, watching shadows waver, wondering who, if anyone, was in there with me. The smell of her hair faded and the dead fish returned. The water continued to lap against the edges of the boat slip. The room was quiet otherwise.

I felt the breeze hit my back again. Looking over my shoulder, I saw Ahlberg's slender silhouette followed by a man about the same height and three times wider than her. The area went dark as the door fell shut. Ahlberg approached. The man remained behind.

She kept a safe distance from me this time. That confirmed that I had been alone. If someone was in there watching me they would have let her know whether I had attempted to arm myself in some way. All I had to do was break off a piece of the chair and I'd have a club and possibly a stabbing weapon.

Standing in front of me, she gave nothing away. "Why are you here?"

I'd give her what she was after. "To fix a mistake."

She arched her right eyebrow. The smooth skin on her forehead wrinkled. Looked more like what I expected in a forty-year-old. "What mistake?"

"I killed the wrong person ten years ago."

"Who were you to kill?"

"You."

She crossed her arms tight over her chest. Her breasts swelled over the lacy edge of her bra and the tank top. "On whose orders?"

I said nothing.

She dropped her arms and stepped up to me. "You think your government gives a damn about you now, Noble? That the man who issued the command cares what happens to you after this? Any idea what he's been up to today?"

"You already know the goddamn answer, lady." We were chin to nose. Her hot breath intertwined with mine. I fought the urge to strangle her there and be done with it. My strength hadn't returned and I might not kill her by the time the guy lingering in the shadows got to me.

She didn't back down. "So who did you kill?"

"Birgit," I said pushing my face forward. "And you damn well know it because you provided the false intelligence to the turncoat. You set your sister up to take that bullet and now you're going to receive yours."

She took a few steps back, held her arms out, smiled, and glanced down at her outstretched leg. "Are you as good as I've heard, Noble?"

I followed her gaze to the tattoo adorning her skin. It really was an impressive piece.

And on the wrong leg.

I wasn't looking at Katrine Ahlberg.

# 51

COMPLETE DARKNESS HAD OVERTAKEN THE SKY BY THE TIME THE BIRD TOUCHED down on a remote airfield. Given the direct southeast heading of the flight, Bear assumed they were somewhere near the French-Belgium border, approximately fifty miles from the coast. Woodlands surrounded the location. A small one-lane road weaved through the landscape and emerged from the forest just a few feet from the tall chainlink entrance gate. A large rusted chain wrapped around two thick steel rails. The entire strip was enclosed with eight foot high fencing topped with barbwire. This wasn't the kind of place that was open to the public.

Everyone had exited the helicopter except Sasha and Bear. The men in black gear stood watch outside with the door closed. Occasionally Bear would see the woman passing. Her hair glowed in the moonlight.

The whomping of the rotors and whine of the turbine faded, leaving them in silence. The couple decided against engaging in conversation. No one had remained inside with them but that did not mean they were not listening. Anything they had to say to each other could wait. There had to have been a reason why they were brought here. As far as Bear was concerned it would have been easier to kill him back at the house than put him on a helicopter and cross the channel with him on board.

*What did they want?*

His thoughts turned as dark as the slice of sky he saw through the window.

What if Ahlberg knew that Bear was activated to kill her? And perhaps, instead of preemptively killing him, she instead had decided it would be better to torture him first. He swallowed hard at the thought of enduring having his head dunked in tubs of water, his fingernails pulled from their beds, the non-stop beatings. Any of it. All of it. Depended on how far and hard each party was willing to go.

Bear refused to be soft because screw them that's why.

"What're you thinking about?" Sasha whispered.

"Mandy graduating from college and then going to law school." There was no reason to let her into his dark world.

She squeezed his forearm. "Must have been a grueling ceremony. Your muscles are tensed. Hard as a rock."

He dropped his chin to his chest and sighed. "We should keep quiet."

Several minutes later they heard the first faint buzz of an approaching craft. Bear leaned toward the window and scanned the sky. He saw the lights coming at them from the southwest.

*Friend or foe?*

"You have some way for your boss to track you?" He glanced at Sasha.

Sasha shook her head as she squeezed his wrist. "Nothing on me at this time."

He doubted the savior option held much water at this point. The craft passed close enough that Bear could tell it was a small jet. It circled overhead a couple times after reducing speed, finally coming in for a landing starting at the opposite end of the rural airstrip. The Gulfstream stopped close enough that Bear read the tail numbers out loud to Sasha.

"That sounds familiar," she said.

"It should," he said, nodding. "It's CIA owned. I've been on that jet before."

She leaned over him, planting her hand on this thigh. "Who do you suppose?"

He brushed her hair away from his face and pulled strands out of his beard. "I don't suppose. I know exactly who's on that plane."

As if on cue, the door opened, stairs dropped down and two men emerged dressed eerily similar to the security detail who had occupied the helicopter during the crossing. To make matters worse, the tactical teams met in the middle and exchanged greetings.

Frank Skinner weaseled through the opening carrying a small duffel bag in one hand and his pistol in the other. Hunched over, he descended the narrow steps quickly and ran past the four operators standing out in the open. Frank looked back and said something to the men. They all nodded and simultaneously slipped from sight.

Bear and Sasha leaned toward the opposite window to see if Frank had continued past the helicopter. Ahlberg stood with the Saudi near a waiting sedan. Bear noted that he had not seen or heard the vehicle approach. They must have come in without their headlights on. Why? Who would be watching out here? Maybe the French DSGE, but they would've needed advance warning. He considered that maybe the vehicle was already here.

Frank embraced the blonde in a quick hug and shook the Saudi's hand. They exchanged smiles as though the three went back some years.

*A decade, maybe?*

Bear had dozens of questions and had yet been afforded an opportunity to ask a single one of them. As long as Sasha's life was threatened, he found himself at odds over what to do. Exercising restraint was not in his usual bag of tricks. He wished Jack was there. Not that either of the men were on the cerebral level of Einstein. They often preferred to use strength in such a situation, but Jack was the tactician of the duo and would be plotting thirteen steps ahead opposed to Bear's six.

"What is the head of the CIA's SOG doing meeting with a known terrorist supporter?" Sasha said.

Bear looked around.

"Right there." She pointed at the Saudi. "That's Khalid Awad."

Perhaps it was the repeated blows to his head, filing a job well done away in his mental cabinet, the way the Saudi had aged in the past decade, or a combination of it all, but Bear hadn't put it together. It made sense. The first thing Katrine Ahlberg would do is reunite with her husband upon making a break. Had he been in on the switch ten years ago?

"If you know that he's funneling money to those assholes, why haven't you done anything?"

"Because of his family relations. My hands have been tied." She turned to him, brow furrowed, fire in her eyes. Bear knew the look and it was not meant to invoke positive feelings. "And your excuse?"

He pulled away from her. "I don't make policy. Only follow orders."

"Coward." She shifted in her seat to stare him down. In the dark he noticed the glimmer of the sweat on her brow. "What kind of excuse is that? You had the opportunity to kill him ten years ago, did you not?"

He said nothing.

"Yet you didn't, correct?"

He refused to answer her when she talked to him like a new hire at *Legoland.*

She continued her tirade. "Maybe we wouldn't be in this goddamn position right now if you had aimed the gun at the right person when you pulled the trigger."

"Sasha, I'm only gonna say this one time." Bear took a breath deep enough that it hurt his chest. "When the situation dictates it, I operate outside of the rules established for me. The Ahlberg hit was by the book. Executed perfectly. Perhaps too much so, now that I look back and understand some of the dynamics here. But we had no way of knowing who and what, and we were told under no uncertain circumstances that Awad was to survive."

Several seconds passed. The tension on Sasha's face abated. "I'm sorry. This is slightly stressful for me. I know you're used to busting out of situations like this, but I've been relegated to a desk with minimal recess time for too long now."

He squeezed her hand. "We're a team. In more ways than one. We'll get through this."

The door whipped open. The Gulfstream's engines wound down to a low drone. Two black-clad operators stood in front of them.

"Who's getting it first?"

# 52

Frank avoided the piercing stare of the woman he might've been in love with ten years ago. He wasn't one to mix his feelings. Hell, his own ex-wife doubted Frank's intentions toward her on their wedding night. When it came to Katrine, things were different. *Had been different.* They'd seen each other in secret for five years prior to him finding out that someone in the Pentagon had an issue with the woman and wanted her eliminated. If anyone knew how he felt about Katrine Ahlberg, they might have questioned how he could jump at the opportunity for the SIS and himself personally to spearhead the mission to assassinate her.

He lifted his gaze up to hers. She smiled softly. The gesture looked foreign on her cold face. And it was then that he recalled the thoughts that raced through his head as he sat in on the private committee's meeting and heard the words, "Ahlberg has to be eradicated before she spurs Awad into action." The old farts all shot Frank an odd look when he immediately offered to take the job. It wasn't typical of the SIS to run such a mission, though they often were part of the team for foreign assassinations.

Frank smiled at Katrine, recalling the real reason he acted so quickly in that meeting.

He did it so that he could keep her alive. And at the same time, it would break her and Awad apart. Or so he thought. Their relationship apparently had survived Katrine's ten year journey of living life as her sister.

Frank had prided himself on the setup and how he'd passed off the falsified documents as the real thing. The intelligence flew up and down the chain and the assassination plan was approved. If things went wrong, it would have been Noble who took the fall. Frank would have immediately pointed to the fail-safes he placed within each piece of evidence he submitted that would then illustrate how Jack had gone rogue. He even had a plan worked out that would point to Noble working in secret with Awad. This might have been enough to get the order to remove Awad as well. And it would have been the last Frank ever heard from Noble.

Things didn't work out that way, but the end result was acceptable. They passed off the murder of Birgit Ahlberg as the assassination of her twin sister Katrine. Frank buried the case afterward, and it hadn't been reopened until Jack was brought to the old SIS building a few days prior due to some rookie in Langley noticing some chatter that should not have been present. Frank managed to keep the guy quiet and he started digging.

And as to Katrine, Frank hadn't seen her since. There was no goodbye between them. There couldn't be, and he wondered how in the hell she and Awad had pulled off keeping their relationship intact.

Frank thought he might never see the woman again. And then two things happened.

The real Birgit resurfaced in Amsterdam. It was a miracle that anyone noticed. And an even bigger one that Frank was the guy who had. If anyone else had learned of her existence while it was known that she was currently back home in Sweden it would have spelled disaster.

Around the same time this information became known, a deal that Frank and Awad had been working on with a former Army man and now arms dealer by the name of Darrow was disrupted by none other than Jack Noble. What better way to pay the asshole back than by forcing him to come in, making him think he screwed up a hit ten years ago, then putting him in a no-win situation that would lead to him living the rest of his short and pain-filled life in a cell inside a prison that didn't exist as far as the general public was aware.

Only now Jack had disappeared and Frank had to grill Logan to figure out where unless his analysts could decipher that information from Brandon's computers.

"What will we do with them?" Ahlberg hiked her thumb over her shoulder toward the helicopter. The doors were open and Frank's men watched over Logan and Sasha Kirby, the MI6 agent.

Sasha's presence intensified the situation. They'd now abducted a member of British Intelligence, and she had seen Frank's face. She could not be allowed to live. However, Frank was aware that the only way he could get Logan to do what he said when he said it was if he could threaten the life of someone the big man loved.

"The car should be here any moment." He looked out into the dark woods where the narrow roadway snaked toward the airstrip. "We'll load them in separate vehicles to induce panic in Logan. The more worked up he gets, the more dangerous he'll be, and that will work to our benefit when the time comes."

"We should interrogate him," Awad said.

"And we will," Frank said. "Or I should say, I will. I don't want any of that jihadi stuff going on over here. This is business. Let's treat it as such."

Awad squared up to the man. "You and your kind do far worse than my brothers. We have Allah on our side. You pigs only do it for the fun." He spit on the ground between them. "Disgusting."

"The hell is up your ass?" Frank said. "Might I remind you that you really don't give a damn about any of that garbage you're spewing, you bacon-eating asshole. You are beholden to the all-mighty dollar. So here's a bottle of water." Frank tossed the open bottle and water sprayed forth on the Saudi. "Why don't you wash that righteous tone out of your goddam mouth."

Katrine smiled at Frank the way she used to ten years ago, and he remembered that it felt then much the same as it did now.

# 53

"I KILLED YOU."

I wanted to reach out and make sure the woman standing before me was real. The tattoo, the only thing I had to identify the women with, indicated that it was Birgit standing in front of me.

"I put a bullet in your goddamn chest and verified that you were dead."

She lifted her tank top and slipped her bra strap off her shoulder. She wound her slender arm through and then pulled the undergarment down so that it barely covered her. She came close to me again. I smelled the fish she'd had for dinner on her breath. She grabbed my hand and placed it on her breast at the site of a mass of knotted skin.

"And I have the scar from it. You feel that? You did that to me."

She held onto my hand as I pulled it back, so I pushed her away. She stumbled backward, tripped over her foot and fell to the ground. Before I could turn, someone slammed into my lower back and drove me forward. We landed inches from Ahlberg, hitting the ground hard. The air was expelled from my lungs. Fire rampaged through my ribcage. The son of a bitch was heavy. And unbalanced. I worked to my base, ready to reverse the guy.

"Enough," she shouted, hopping to her feet. She delivered a barefoot strike to my side and pulled the man away. "Get that chair off of him."

The guy grabbed my right leg and unsheathed his knife. I looked back and saw it glinting in the dim light. He brought the blade up and in one swoop severed the ropes that bound me to the chair.

Slowly I pulled my knees under me and stood, facing Ahlberg. She stood back near the boat slip now and aimed a handgun at me.

"Are you ready to see if you can live through a fatal wound the way I did?" She took a step forward, remaining well out of range. "Aren't you the least bit curious how I survived?"

I nodded and said nothing.

"You knew nothing about me. Never anticipated that you'd encounter me. Right?"

"That's right. Katrine was our target."

"I never came up in your planning or in the intelligence you sifted through?"

"You overestimate me," I said. "I was the trigger man. Nothing more."

"You underestimate yourself," she said. "I know all about you, Noble."

I shrugged the suggestion off. "You never came up. I knew nothing about you then, and all I know about you now is that your sister should have been living your life. I'm tempted to think I did kill her that night, but you're the one with a scar in the spot that I remember my bullet tearing through."

She smiled, took another step closer. It was as though she were daring me to take her out. The effects of the drugs they had given me had worn off. I could see the man in my peripheral. He had that look on his face that said he was waiting for me to try something. Anything. He'd act before I had a chance to take a second step. I was close to welcoming the challenge.

Ahlberg stopped and lowered her weapon, keeping both hands wrapped around the grip. "I trained in pharmacy and anesthesiology, and I induced a coma before you arrived. That's what saved my life. Well, that and the advance warning I had of the switch and setup. It wasn't the first time my sister tried to have me killed. She's such a jealous bitch."

"Who warned you?"

Ahlberg's cheeks darkened as she smiled and looked away.

"Who was it? Someone in the Agency? SIS?"

"My lover," she said. "You know him as Awad."

I sifted through the intelligence I had committed to memory a decade before as well as what I had reviewed the other day in Frank's old SIS office. Nowhere did I recall ever hearing or seeing or reading that Birgit Ahlberg had an affair with her sister's husband.

"You're lying," I said. "Who the hell told you?"

"You would be wise not to spit accusations at me. You know what it takes to survive ten years underground? Not giving away a single hint that you're alive?"

"You screwed up somewhere, otherwise your body double would still be alive."

Her upper lip curled and her nostrils flared.

"Christ, you put her in the line of fire by changing your look and hers. And for what, a million dollars?"

"That is not your concern. She served me and served me well. I have to deal with the fallout from that. When this is all over, she will be properly mourned."

I wasn't sure I cared to hear more of the story. "So what now? Why are we doing this? Why am I here?"

"I slipped up. This is true. I reached out to him—"

"Awad."

"Yes, Awad." She sighed. "I let him know that I was alive and had been in hiding all these years. He knew my sister's fate was to be reclusive for some time. Had to be after the way things went down and the assumptions our family made."

"Where did you go all these years?"

She shrugged as if to say it wasn't important. "Here and there and everywhere in between."

"Back to your contact with Awad," I said. "What did he say?"

"Everything a woman would want to hear from her lover."

I struck with the coldest words I could think to use. "And you fell for it." I paused a beat and waited for her to look at me. "Again."

The icy stare remained fixed on me, but this time it was buffered with a thin layer of tears that Ahlberg blinked away. "I took the bullet once, and they designated another for me on the streets of Leiden. If not for Martina, I'd be dead right now. I can only assume that they've figured out it was the body double who perished, and that I'm still alive, and they will soon attack with everything they've got. That, Mr. Noble, is why we picked you up and dragged you here."

I debated whether to tell her.

"Do you have something to share?" she asked. Her body relaxed for a moment.

"I put it together at the morgue. Everything was near-perfect, except for that." I gestured to the tattoo on her leg. "You should have replicated that on your double."

"She was scared of the needle, but had finally relented to have it done. We were going to start this week."

"Bad timing."

"Exactly." Ahlberg tugged on the hem of her shorts.

"I told Skinner that it was you in the morgue. The job was complete."

"Then why not just leave?"

"He wanted us to stay put, and without his help, getting back home was going to be a bitch. And I had to figure out what was taking place behind the scenes. Who was the woman on the table? So I went to Germany after our talk with the witness was cut short by a couple guys in the woods."

"Her bodyguards," Birgit said.

"Katrine's?" I said.

She nodded. "They were on the street that day. It was her that pulled off that shot. Did you know that?"

I shook my head.

"I also saw the witness the day he was murdered in the woods."

"That was you? At his house that morning?"

"I went to question him. He was scared, of course, as he had seen the shooter on the roof, as well as me and Martina. I suppose we all looked the same, and he wasn't sure if he was looking at a killer or a ghost." She smiled for a second. "Guess I'm both."

I studied her, trying to ascertain whether what she had said was bullshit.

"How did you feel talking to her weak husband?" Birgit said.

I shrugged. She had the man pegged. "Did she really have cancer?"

Ahlberg smiled again and shook her head. "We conceived that well before she ever mentioned the fake symptoms."

"Who was she?"

"Someone who meant a great deal more to me than you do. She grew to be more than my body double. Much more than my friend. So don't you forget that

I stood there and watched as she was executed in broad daylight. If it serves my purpose, I will gladly smile as you suffer the same fate."

"Why not just get it over with?" I stepped toward her. The man to my side started moving. Ahlberg held up a hand to stop him. "We're here now, all alone. Kill me now. I'm tired of these games."

Ahlberg, to her credit, did not back down from me. We stood toe to toe. I stared down at her. Smelled the mix of sweat and soap and the fish on her breath.

"I'm not going to kill you. Yet." Her smile faded as the door covering the boat slip rose out of the water. It made a hell of a racket as it cranked up. Ahlberg took a few steps back, turned away and greeted the man piloting the small craft.

There was something familiar about him. He cast a quick glance at me but did not hold my gaze. Instead, he looked toward the entrance, nodded, and stepped to the edge of the boat. The door slid down and hit the water.

I studied him as he conversed with Ahlberg. He was shorter than her, but well-built. His dark pants matched his t-shirt and the cap on his head. They spoke in her native Swedish at length. He nodded as she unleashed a series of questions. A broad smile crossed her face as she turned and flashed a thumbs-up to the man behind me.

The man stepped off the boat and that's when I saw it.

Ahlberg walked over to me, standing in roughly the same spot as before. The sweat and soap mixture wafted past, and between that and my revelation about the man, I found it hard to concentrate.

She leaned in and whispered in my ear. "Before I decide your fate, Mr. Noble, you need to finish the job you started ten years ago."

I acknowledged the words I hardly heard. I was too busy staring at the thousand dollar pair of shoes worn by the man who had just arrived.

# 54

WITH THE HEADACHES AND SUBSEQUENT DOCTOR VISITS, ANOTHER PART OF Bear's life had died. Namely the panic and anxiety that had stricken him since he was a child. Not one to let anything interfere with his plans and job, he learned early how to overcome the affliction. However, it never fully went away and had a habit of roaring to life at the most inopportune times. But for the past few months, whether it was the peace and tranquility of the estate, or the possible prognosis he faced, the general buzz he normally felt had disappeared.

It came back with a vengeance as they pulled Sasha away from him and stuffed her in a car with Frank Skinner and Katrine Ahlberg. Bear almost would have preferred she be seated next to the terrorist Awad. The bastard was soft. He funneled money, not jihadists, through training camps. The guy would fold at the sight of a pair of pliers anywhere near his fingertips.

At the end of the winding woodlands road, the vehicles split up. Sasha's went right. Bear and Awad turned left.

The terrorist had lowered his weapon after they left the single-lane road. Complacency? Concern that he might be seen by a passing motorist? It didn't matter because the flex-cuffs around Bear's wrists prevented him from unleashing his fury on the man who sat opposite. Although, if the guy moved one foot closer, he'd find himself wrapped between Bear's thighs in a scissor move that no man had ever escaped. Awad would suffocate slowly, unless Bear decided to end it quickly by snapping his neck.

When he could no longer take the racing thoughts, tight chest, and pounding heart, Bear said, "Where're they going?"

Awad didn't glance up from his phone.

"Hey, asshole," Bear said. "I'm talking to you."

Still no response from Awad.

"Towelhead."

Finally Awad looked up with a slight grin. "Do you have any idea who you are talking to? Another insult like that and I'll see to it you are brought back to Saudi Arabia if you somehow manage to survive the next twenty hours."

"Please," Bear said. "That's like a friggin' country club spa."

The man returned his attention to his device. Bear leaned forward. The Saudi lowered his phone and raised his pistol.

"Where are they going?" Bear slowed the words down as though he were talking to a five year old.

"What does it matter?" Awad said. "You're not going to see her again, I can promise you that."

Bear looked down at his bound hands, shook his head. He heard Awad's short laugh and that was enough to send Bear's rage-meter into the red. He lunged forward using the top of his head as a weapon intended to strike the terrorist dead in the middle of his face, leaving a crater where a nose had once been.

The blinding pain started at Bear's temple and stretched past his ear. The Saudi moved with speed and efficiency that Bear had not imagined the man possessed. He looked weak and slow. Bear summed him up as sagging. But the guy had managed to get the best of him in the current conditions.

Bear dropped to a knee. How had it happened? He had launched like a missile and out of the corner of his eye he saw the pistol striking him.

It wasn't enough to stop him though.

Bear pressed his head into Awad's gut. He planted his feet against the rear seat and used his massive quads and hamstrings in an effort to push Awad's stomach and intestines out of the man's mouth. The terrorist struck him again, on the back of the head. And again, at the base of the neck. Bear was struck in the same spot twice more and he felt his extremities go numb. He collapsed on the Saudi's lap.

"Stop the car," Awad said.

The tires screeched. Bear felt himself shift forward then slump back onto the space between the two rows of facing seats.

The front doors opened, closed. Awad kicked him in the face. The rear doors opened. The men leaned in. They grabbed Bear under his arms and dragged him back to his seat. The flex-cuffs were removed. Damn his muscles. Nothing fired when he wanted it to. Why didn't they work?

His arms were pulled behind him. The cuffs went back on. He heard the scraping sound of duct tape being pulled from the roll, ripped off. They planted it over his mouth. Simply struggling against it pulled the surrounding hairs out.

After the car was in motion, Awad leaned forward. He placed his elbows on his knees and wrested his right arm over his left wrist. The pistol aimed dangerously at Bear's head.

"Another outburst and I'll finish you myself," he said, smiling. "After you watch me have my way with your woman."

Bear settled in for the remainder of the ride, positive that if the right opportunity arose he would snap the Saudi's neck.

Sometime later the car left the road and bounced and dipped and swayed. The first sliver of the sun rose above the horizon, casting the field of lavender in an orange-ish wash. The vehicle came to rest in front of what appeared to be a six-foot high mound of dirt with a door stuck in the middle.

*What the hell was next on the itinerary?*

# 55

Frank decided that silence should rule the drive. He had instructed Katrine to ride up front despite the tug in his chest to have her next to him. He wanted the time alone with Sasha to see if the woman would offer up any information. He knew that pairing Jack with Logan would result in one of the men — most likely Bear — informing Sasha of what they were doing. The intelligence operator in her programmed to follow orders would not be able to override the analyst that wanted to come out and play. She would begin to dig and would come upon a whole host of facts that would help Frank wrap this mess up once and for all.

Somehow, though, the two assholes had gone far longer than he expected before involving Sasha. By the time they did, Frank could no longer contain Katrine and Awad. Sasha had found the information, but it was too late. The plan had already progressed to the point where they wanted to take action and Frank could not stop them. If he hesitated, they would be like frenzied Makos with severed limbs floating about in the water. And it would have been him who would feel their fury.

Halfway through the ride the car pulled over to refuel. Katrine took the opportunity to join Frank in the backseat. She offered a cool smile to him and a deathly glare to their guest seated opposite and facing them.

For whatever reason Katrine attempted to launch into her own interrogation of Sasha, who seemed amused more than anything by the line of questioning. The woman never answered a single one, although she made several well-placed facial expressions.

Frank found it amusing as well. Katrine had never spent a day in the field or in an interrogation room or even behind a terminal sorting through chatter to uncover the validity of a lead. Yes, she had killed, and turned out to be quite adept at it. It had been her that pulled off the hit of Birgit's body double. But aside from being a beautiful murderer, Katrine's job was money. Raising it. Managing it. Doling it out. She decided who to collect dollars from and who to dole out the funds to. It was the same now as it had been years ago.

When Katrine had finished unsuccessfully questioning Sasha, she leaned into Frank and placed her mouth next to his ear. Her lips grazed his neck, sending chills through him.

"Did you have any luck with her?" Her husky whisper was an even stronger turn on.

Frank shook his head as much at himself as her. *Get the damn broad out of your mind.* There would be time to rekindle their affair when the situation had resolved itself.

"It was never my intention," he said, making no attempt to lower his voice while pulling away from Katrine, "to do so in here. She's got fifteen years of service in British Intelligence. At least half of that in the field. She'd rather die than offer up any clues as to who, what, why, when and how. Isn't that right, Sasha?"

Sasha arched an eyebrow and shrugged as if to say screw you both.

"Let's hope the ride loosens your lips, dear," Katrine said. "We have ways of making you talk, and they are unlike anything you've imagined."

The words failed to impress Sasha, who rolled her eyes and turned toward the window.

Those were the last words spoken until the vehicle came to a stop next to Awad's outside the old wine cellar. Frank had purchased the property twenty years ago after an operation that had him spending considerable time in Tours, France.

He exited the vehicle and greeted two men from SOG who had ridden in the other vehicle. One stepped aside and opened the door to the cellar. Frank walked in and descended into the lit room below. He stepped over the old rusted Studebaker bumper. He hadn't the heart to throw it out after the old woman he purchased it from told him it was the vehicle her husband had passed away in three months after the war had ended. He was an American soldier who had been on the shores in Normandy. They met shortly after, fell in love, and had a brief but powerful romance. She never found herself in the arms of another man.

Frank had removed everything else but the old winemaking equipment for no reason other than he liked the look of it. Over the years he'd visited the place at least once every six months. He and Katrine had spent time here, too, on three separate occasions. But hell, he never expected the cellar to house a prisoner or be the place where he would iron out the details of a job with a known terrorist.

"Glad to see you made it," Awad said, rising from the stool. "And Katrine is OK?"

Frank gestured toward the worn stairs. "She's up there if you want to see her."

Awad shook his head. "That is not necessary right now."

"How'd things go with the big guy?"

"He gave me a little trouble, but I put him in his place. What do they call him? Bear? I showed him that he belongs in a circus, not the field."

Frank felt that somehow Awad was embellishing slightly, if not outright lying. Given a fair fight, there was nothing that would stop Bear from ripping the Saudi's head from his shoulders.

The door opened and Katrine's slender silhouette soaked up all of the light in the room. She bounded down the steps. They didn't creak or groan under her slight frame.

"Your men have everything under control up there," she said, looking around the room curiously, as though she had never seen the cellar before.

"They didn't put the two of them together, right?" Frank said.

She shook her head as she pulled a stool up to the wine-barrel pub table where Awad was seated.

Frank reached into a dark cubby and pulled out a bottle of cognac. He poured himself four fingers and drank it in three gulps with his back to the others. He tucked the bottle away, then turned and joined them.

Leaning with his arms over the table, he said, "This is how it's going to go down."

# 56

AHLBERG LEFT WITH THE MAN IN THE EXPENSIVE SHOES. HE WASN'T THE GUY WHO had stared me down on the sidewalk, or threatened to shoot from the docks. But he had been there. The way things had played out, it was easy to assume that Birgit had advanced notice of my arrival and the tail started then. She didn't have all the details ahead of time, though, and that was the reason why Bear and I managed to slip out of England on the boat Frank had arranged. All I could take from that was that her information had not come firsthand from Frank.

Who the hell was the secondhand then?

For four hours I tried to sleep on the rickety wooden chair. They'd cuffed and secured me again. The boat rocked and banged against the mooring. Every hour some new man came in, splashed water on my face and took his seat ten feet away where he could watch me and the door. The little sleep I managed was filled with thoughts of what would happen next. To say it was restful was like saying an amateur stepping in the ring with Ali had a chance.

When Birgit returned with the man in the expensive shoes we piled into the boat along with two armed guards. First we headed about a mile out, then turned north. The air was cool and heavy with mist. It coated my skin and dampened the change of clothes they had provided me. The chinos were loose, the shirt tight, and the shoes the right size. I supposed that mattered most.

We turned into the rising sun and pink and purple and red clouds, making our way to shore and awaiting an SUV. I was directed to the middle seat and allowed to occupy it on my own. Birgit made no qualms about her willingness to allow the men behind me to shoot me in the back of the head — and the front of it — if I got out of line. Asking how far out of line was so underappreciated that I received a punch to the gut by Mr. Fancy Shoes. As I leaned forward, I let loose with a gob of spit that just missed his toes. He hit me again, at which point Birgit intervened.

The ride was long and boring and quiet. The SUV dampened road and wind noise. And Birgit had something against the radio. Occasionally she would flip on a bulky scanner and listen in on three channels that were filled with static and not much chatter.

Three hours in I started recognizing landmarks and exits along the A10. The highway led to Paris by way of Tours.

It turned out the latter was our destination. We exited the highway with approximately fifteen miles to go to the city. The backroads we took were no faster, but much less traveled. We drove past farmland and fields of lavender, eventually reaching the area where the rural stopped being rural and turned into housing developments.

We stopped at the edge of town and exited the vehicle. I was led half a block to an alley. From there we entered a building, climbed three flights of stairs. It smelled like a colony of stray cats lived within the confines of the stairwell. At the end of the hall, across from the stairwell, Birgit stuck a key into a lock and turned. We piled into the small apartment with a spectacular view of a brick wall. She drew all the blinds, checked the fridge, pulled out a bottle of milk and emptied it into the sink. Solid chunks splattered and were broken into pieces small enough to slide down the drain. The awful smell passed after a few minutes.

They gathered around the island that separated the kitchen from living area. Birgit pulled some papers from her bag and spread them out. They spoke quietly in English, presumably the only common language between the four. I hadn't heard a word out of the guards and couldn't pinpoint their nationality. The man in the expensive shoes, who I'd heard Ahlberg call Thomas, was from Anywhere, U.S.A. I assumed he was ex-military, perhaps even ex-CIA, now engaged in contract work.

I picked up bits and pieces of their conversation, but much of it was spoken in code, which kept me in the dark as to their plans.

Several minutes later, Ahlberg and Thomas left the apartment. The guards stayed put. I attempted to engage them in conversation, but got nowhere. I wondered if they came as part of a package with Thomas.

The sun now shone in through the cracks in the blinds. Dust rose and fell in the fingers of light with the cycle of the oscillating fan. The clock on the stove read eight-thirty. Where would the day go from here? And what would my role be in whatever operation they discussed?

The front door opened and Birgit entered carrying a brown bag. She reached in the bag and pulled out a hunk of bread, which she tossed in my direction. She hadn't been gone long. The bakery must've been pretty close by. "Eat up. I don't want you passing out from low blood sugar when we need you."

I sniffed the bread to see if she'd coated with some chemical. I couldn't pick anything up and proceeded to fill my mouth with a large hunk of bread. There was something about the food over here. It was simpler and not made with a bunch of modified crap.

"What exactly do you need me for?" I said.

She set the bag on the counter and motioned for the guards to help themselves. Not sure why she thought that was a good idea, as it left her vulnerable to attack. I rose to test the men. One dropped his food and drew his weapon.

"Easy," she said, looking back at the man. I spotted the bulge of her pistol at the small of her back. Then she turned to me. "You are going to finish the job you set out to do ten years ago."

I glanced at the ceiling as though I were thinking her offer over. "Thanks for bringing me all the way out here, but I'm going to have to decline."

Smiling, she moved within a foot of me. Her scent was less soapy and more natural now. Still smelled good. Her hair was pulled back tight. She had the same tank top on, but had covered it with an unbuttoned white blouse, and had switched out her shorts for a pair of tan pants. The soles of her boots echoed off the walls.

What was this woman capable of? Had she always been dangerous, or had I set her on that path when I pulled the trigger that night, thinking I was carrying out a sanctioned hit on Katrine?

"I thought you might tell me that, Noble." She placed her hand over my heart. "But I know you have weaknesses and—"

I reached up with my right hand, secured her wrist and pulled back hard. Unprepared for the attack, Ahlberg twisted awkwardly at the knee. Her feet remained planted for a second. I brought my left hand up her backside and felt along her waist until I had the pistol secured. At the same time I brought my right arm around her front and gripped her chin in the crook of my arm. She dug her short fingernails into my forearm. Probably drew blood. I only squeezed harder.

The paper bag fell off the counter as the guards sprung into action. The contents of the bag spilled all over the floor. The man closest to us kicked a pastry toward the door. It hit hard enough that the insides exploded.

Both men reached for their weapons but halted.

"Don't do it." I held Ahlberg's pistol to her head. The move was risky. She seemed to be a capable fighter and with the right combination of moves could reverse on me.

I instructed the guard in the kitchen to come out and tie up the other man to the post holding up the ceiling. He balked at first. I dropped my right arm an inch and squeezed Birgit's neck. The man threw up his hands and then did as instructed.

"Now strip down to your drawers and toss them over here."

The man complied, cursing at me in his southern drawl and telling me what he was going to do to me when I was at the other end of the barrel.

"Go put yourself in the bathroom." We had full view of the room. "I want you to cuff yourself around the toilet."

He stood there for a moment. Ahlberg struggled against me to nod at him. The man slinked into the bathroom and dropped to his knees. He wrapped his arms around the toilet and slipped the cuffs over his wrist. His last act was drawing his arms apart to tighten the cuffs.

"You and I are getting out of here." I nudged Ahlberg toward the door. I didn't have a plan beyond leaving the apartment. Thomas would be back at some point, though, and we had to get moving before he arrived.

"This will be easier," she said in a strained voice, "if you let go of my neck."

I ignored her request, pushing her toward the door. The men in the room posed no threat right now. I assumed they were experienced enough to get out of their situations within five minutes. We had to push on quickly after leaving. I considered dumping Ahlberg at the stairs and fleeing on my own.

Only problem was the stairwell door opened before we got there. And Thomas stepped into the hall.

## 57

THE CIA'S DIRECTOR OF OPERATIONS WAS A WELL-KNOWN MAN IN THE HALLS OF GWU Hospital. And in many other places. More than he cared for. He thought that an odd thing, as it put him at greater risk than in the eighties when he walked the streets of Beirut followed by living on the fringes of the war against the USSR and the Afghanis.

His visit today, as with most of his hospital visits, was not a pleasurable one. He entered the CCU amid the sound of a host of life supporting devices. The air felt and smelled different in here. Sadness, perhaps. A lower-than-normal chance of survival. All who worked and visited the unit felt it.

A familiar-looking nurse forced a slight smile and nodded at him as he approached his destination room. He stopped at the door, grabbed the chart and had a read through it. By no means was he a medical professional, but he'd seen enough over the years to comprehend what was written.

No one waited at the bedside of the dying man. Crumpled tissues were found on one of the chairs next to the bed. At least someone cared. The window revealed a dark sky and lamppost-lit parking lot filled with a handful of cars.

The director of operations towered over Brandon Cunningham's lifeless body. The machines kept him alive at this point. He had been told there was a ten percent chance of survival. The director had responded by saying he wanted that at fifty percent by noon.

He had recruited Brandon when the guy was an eighteen-year-old caught hacking into systems he had no business in. The police arrested the young man. The judge found him guilty and sentenced him to fifteen years. What in the hell would the guy bound to a wheelchair do to survive fifteen years in the pen? Not to mention the taxpayer burden of keeping him alive, though the director did not mention that to Brandon when he had him brought to the Farm and made him an offer that was too good to refuse. The arrogant young punk agreed to put his talents to use for the Agency. And the director, who never fathered his own children, had another "son" to watch over.

He reached down, grabbed the dying man's bony hand and squeezed it.

"Hang in there, kid. We still need you."

# 58

THE SUN ROSE OVER THE KNEE WALL, PENETRATING THE SHADED POCKET OF COOL air. Bear assembled the M40 sniper rifle that he had found on the roof where Frank Skinner had said it would be. To say Bear was intimately familiar with the Marine Sniper's weapon of choice was an understatement. Though he had spent relatively little time as a Scout Sniper, Bear had pulled off several assassinations during his military career and contractor years.

Every kill left its mark on his soul. He often wondered if his current condition reflected that fact.

The small earbud emitted a burst of static and then Frank spoke. "How's everything going up there?"

"Fine," Bear said. "Starting to get a tan, though."

"Enjoy it. You're gonna be waiting for a while. The meeting isn't until ten a.m. and you won't do your part until they leave. So ready your weapon, steady your mind, and keep your big head down and out of sight."

The line fell silent again, giving way to the steady breeze. Bear leaned back against the wall and laid the rifle across his thighs. The smell of fresh bread filled the air. At the corner of the roof a smokestack rose and faded into the blue sky, merging with the passing clouds. He reached into the bag they had provided him and pulled out a protein bar and bottle of water. The bar tasted like dirt and the water like piss, but he ate and drank and stuffed the trash back in his bag.

Few details had been provided. Frank told him it would be doled out on a need-to-know basis. The most critical piece of information Frank left him with was that Sasha would be covered with at least two weapons at all times and his failure to act on their instructions would result in her being killed without hesitation. Bear had carried out assassinations for worse reasons before. Rarely under as much stress, though. The endgame had always been defined in previous situations. He worried that Frank and Awad would continue to move the goal posts today.

Bear disassembled the rifle and then put it back together again. The activity was meditative. It cleared his head of the tangled web of junk cluttering it. Figuratively and literally. "Don't go there," he muttered to himself. The test results were inconclusive and all worrying would send him down the dark path of anxiety.

He pulled the tripod from the duffel bag and attached the weapon to it. Bear rolled onto his stomach and practiced with the sight. The M40 felt comfortable in his large hands. He gave the trigger a few practice squeezes, picturing random targets in his mind's eye.

His target today was the unknown piece. They had a meeting at ten a.m. That much he knew. And after the meeting is when the assassination was to take place. He assumed the shot was to strike outside the doors of the restaurant across the street.

What kind of support would he be given after that? So far there had been no mention of a waiting car, change of clothes, or anything else. The duffel bag waiting on the roof only had the weapon inside of it. The bag he carried with him had three protein bars and three bottles of water. They could have at least provided him with a hat.

He laughed quickly at the suggestion. Anyone who saw him enter the building would not be fooled into thinking he was someone else because he wore a cap on his head. Not a man of his size.

The earpiece burst into static and then gave off the electrical hum he had grown accustomed to, knowing it meant it was connected.

"What?" he said preemptively.

"I love you, Riley," Sasha said.

The connection then went dead.

# 59

"As long as he does what we instruct him to, you're gonna be OK." Frank Skinner ripped a piece of tape from the roll and applied it to Sasha's lower back, securing the tracking device against her spine near the waist.

The room they were in was warm, dim, and smelled like rotten eggs. She stared at a stack of plain boxes that stretched floor to ceiling. The walls had the remains of the glue that had once held wallpaper.

"You know the trouble you're going to be in when this is all said and done?" She turned her head far enough to make eye contact. His grin was enough to tell her he had no plans on being caught. Did that mean he was never returning to DC? She doubted that. If anyone was never going home, it was her.

He applied another piece of tape to her back and then pulled her shirt back down, tucking it into her waistband. She wanted to say something about his fingers traveling further inside her pants than necessary, but figured he'd get off on hearing her complain.

"Why not just kill me now?" She pulled away and spun around to face him.

"No one is gonna kill you if that big oaf does his—"

"Cut the crap, Skinner. I've been in this business long enough to know that we can't coexist after this."

He hiked his shoulders an inch into the air as if to say why not. "Sure we can.

You're a grown woman who is more than capable of keeping her mouth shut. My friends can make it worth your while to do so."

"Even if I agreed," she said, watching his reaction closely, "Bear would not. He'd rather dip the money in a vat of acid and eat it than spend it."

Frank laughed. "You obviously don't know him very well. I can't begin to tell you the things I've seen that man do for far less than what we can offer to keep your mouths shut."

"It'll never happen."

Frank's demeanor changed. He reached behind his back and pulled out his concealed handgun and aimed it at her head, cautiously keeping a few feet of distance between them. He knew Sasha had field experience. Their paths had crossed before when both were younger.

"OK," he said. "If you want to die I can make that happen now."

Slivers of light cut across his arm and the pistol. The weapon was ready to fire. If he was bluffing she hoped he had a steady finger.

Ahlberg entered the room wearing a knit dress that stopped above her knee. A tattoo peeked out. She stared at Sasha. "Not yet, Frank. We need her alive for a little bit longer."

Frank returned his sidearm to its holster then walked over to Ahlberg. He wrapped his arms around her waist and drew her in. As they kissed, Ahlberg's fingers tightened into a fist around Frank's short hair.

"I've missed you," Ahlberg said after pulling away a few inches.

Frank released her and gestured toward the door. "He's nearby."

"I know. I passed him in the hallway." The smile on her face made Sasha feel that Awad might join her in a shallow grave later that day.

"Let's stick to the plan, OK? Soon he and your sister will be out of the way and you'll be in Washington with me."

"What about her?" Ahlberg jutted her narrow chin at Sasha.

"No, she can't come with us." He smiled at both of them. "Unless you want her to?"

"She just heard everything we said. Perhaps we should rid ourselves of her?"

"As you said a moment ago, we still need her if we're going to get Logan to take the fall for the hit."

Katrine Ahlberg looked disappointed as she left the room. Was it an act?

"No hard feelings," Frank said.

Sasha parted the blinds with her thumb and forefinger and stared out the window at the French flag dancing in the breeze. She contemplated that this was how she would spend the last minutes of her life.

# 60

I TIGHTENED MY GRIP ON AHLBERG AND THE PISTOL WHILE KEEPING MY FOCUS ON Thomas. I knew little about the man and had to rely on the assumptions I had made about his past. Instinct told me he had a similar skill set. He was a dangerous man. He held one hand in front of him as if to tell me to settle down. In reality his intent was to distract me as he dropped his other hand to his side and inched it around his back.

"Both hands," I said. "Let me see them."

"All right." A little bit of his Chicago accent emerged. "Just don't do anything stupid. You gotta trust me on this, Jack."

"Don't use my name."

"Fair enough. Look, I'm not sure what you're—"

"Shut up." I lifted the pistol so the first shot would land between his eyes.

His gaze flitted to Ahlberg for a second. How well did they know each other? Could she shoot him a look that said 'stand down' or 'attack now'? The muscles along his jaw rippled as his posture grew rigid.

"There's something you need to know," he said.

"I thought I told you to shut up?"

"You recognize me, right? I was there in England. In town and at the marina."

I pulled Ahlberg in closer. Squeezed tighter against her neck. He glanced at her, licked his lips nervously.

"I had a partner," he said, gesturing with his hands. "You remember him, don't you? The trigger happy guy?"

I expected Thomas's partner to pop out of the stairwell with a semi-automatic ready to gun me down. It took all I had to keep my focus on Thomas. A second was too much time to gift to a guy like him. He could be on me before I had time to readjust.

Thomas reached for his pocket.

"Get 'em up," I said.

"I'm only going for my phone. You're gonna want to see this."

Ahlberg grunted, swallowed hard, sucked in air with a deep groan. Thomas looked up from his phone at her. The whites of his eyes looked blue due to the glow of the screen. His eyes widened in response to Birgit's reddening face.

"Easy, Jack. Easy." He held his phone so we could all see. A couple taps later and there was an image. He double tapped and the image zoomed close on a face. "You know who that is right?"

"You motherfucker." I squeezed hard enough to cut off Ahlberg's air supply. She scratched my forearm and struggled against my body.

"That's where my partner is now." Thomas zoomed out a little. "He's been watching them for the past twelve hours outside their rental. If I give the word, he'll kill your brother and daughter and the rest of them."

I stared at the image of Sean and Mia, holding hands and walking along the beach. The dense foliage in the background made me think of Central America. Costa Rica, perhaps. I had told Sean not to tell me where they were. If I were ever caught and tortured I could truthfully deny their whereabouts.

"Let her go." Thomas reached out with one hand. "Then place the weapon on the ground and step back."

I held onto Birgit and my sidearm.

Thomas switched to his messaging app and started typing. "If I send this, they're dead, Jack."

Was he bluffing? He'd be dead if he sent it. Perhaps he didn't care.

His thumb hovered over the send button. "Last chance."

I relaxed my grip on Ahlberg, She twisted and dipped and pulled away from me, turning back toward me after she was out of arm's reach. Her face was dark red. She swallowed a huge gulp of air. Hatred filled her eyes. As the oxygen took hold, she balled her fists and bounced on her toes. Looked like Ali ready to throw down. Thomas placed his hand on her shoulder and pulled her back.

"We still need him," he said.

"We can do it ourselves," she said.

"What if we get caught?" He tugged on her and she faced him. "Remember, he's taking the fall here. We don't care what happens to him."

I squatted halfway and dropped the pistol then stepped back. "I'm not doing a damn thing for you."

"Then I'm texting my partner and your family will be terminated. The little girl will watch as her aunt, uncle, cousins, and grandfather are all shot in the head. Then she'll get the same. Perhaps we'll apply a few of the tricks we leaned over in Afghanistan and make her—"

"All right," I said, keeping my voice a notch below the roar that fought to come out. The fire engulfed me. I almost snapped. But it wasn't the right moment. Yet. I had a vision of how to end this. And it would happen soon. "I'll do it."

Thomas smiled for a second. "Nothing in your file ever suggested you would fold so easily." His gaze shot over to Birgit. "Sucks having a weakness, doesn't it?"

We went back to the apartment where I was forced to free the two guards. They were instructed that I was off limits until this was over. And even then, they should resist making an attempt on me until it was certain that the police were not going to get involved. I would make sure it never got that far.

Thomas and Birgit stood across the kitchen island from me. They detailed the plans for the following hour and my role in what was to happen.

"Can you handle that?" Thomas said, wrapping up the briefing.

"You read my jacket," I said. "Right?"

He nodded and said nothing.

"Then why ask?"

He turned to Birgit. "All right, princess. Get ready."

# 61

Birgit Ahlberg entered the restaurant wearing a blue dress that clung to her slender figure. The horizontal slits along the right thigh offered a glimpse of the intricate piece of artwork that adorned her leg. It was one of two in the world, and when placed side by side, it told the story of two sisters and the intricate web of deceit they had woven over the years.

She scanned the mostly empty dining room until her eyes met those of the blonde woman who shared the same face, body, and tattoo.

The sisters hadn't seen each other since that night ten years ago when Birgit took the bullet that had been meant for Katrine. If Katrine's husband Awad hadn't given Birgit advance warning, she would have perished. Fortunately, Awad loved both sisters, and after making love to Birgit two days prior to the assassination attempt, he revealed Katrine's plan.

Katrine had an inside source at one of America's clandestine agencies who had given her advanced notice of the impending attempt on her life. She and the source hatched a plan to direct the assassins to Birgit instead of her. It was easy. After all, they were twins. Katrine's contact falsified the intelligence and made the hit team believe they had been tracking Katrine.

Birgit knew there was no way out. The killers were relentless bastards. If she ran, they'd follow. Furthermore, Awad had explained that Katrine had already initiated plans to assume Birgit's life. Either way, her life as she knew it was over.

While living life as a ghost was not in her plan, dying seemed the worse of two options. Awad funded a number of accounts in Switzerland with more than enough money to survive on for the rest of Birgit's life.

Using her knowledge of pharmacology, Birgit administered midazolam to herself the night of the hit and peacefully went to sleep. Awad had his cousin, a trauma surgeon, on standby. After the American assassins had left the scene, they loaded Birgit's limp body into the back of a car and brought her to the boat equipped with everything Awad's cousin needed to put her back together.

Birgit traced the scar through her dress as she crossed the room and walked into the outstretched arms of her sister. They kissed the air beside their cheeks the way women do when they're wearing make-up even though neither woman had a smidge on their faces. Despite being forty, neither needed it.

"You look beautiful," Katrine said. "I like what you've done with your hair."

"I suppose if I had not," Birgit said, lifting a sweating glass of water to her mouth, "it would have been me that was gunned down that day in Leiden."

Katrine offered a thin smile. "Dear sister, I had nothing to do with that."

"Spare me the garbage. I know you better than you know yourself."

Katrine nodded once, letting her sister know the same was true.

"How long have you known?" Birgit set the glass down using the ring of water it had left behind as a guide.

"I suspected early on but had no evidence that you were alive. But then a friend and advisor told me he had spotted me in Leipzig, Germany. I asked him where, then hired an investigator to follow up. It was not easy, as you might imagine. After all, I told him to look for a woman that looked exactly like me. I had no idea you had turned your hair jet black at one point."

Birgit smiled. She had rather liked the look she had assumed when she portrayed the role of Martina Kohl's natural healer.

"When he saw you at the gypsy shop, he snapped a picture and emailed it to me. Unfortunately, I was at an event with my family—"

"Our family."

"—and did not respond quickly enough. Whether you saw him or it was our twin connection that tipped you off, you disappeared that night. He waited another month and chased down four different leads but none panned out. Obviously."

The women changed the conversation while the waiter set the bread, butter, and cheese on the table.

"How is father?" Birgit asked.

Katrine smiled slyly. "Dead."

Birgit bit down on her tongue and fought back the few tears that struggled to break free. Two dozen memories raced through her head, from the first time she recalled him lifting her from her crib, to the hug he gave her after she graduated college. He was the only man who ever made her feel safe.

"It was quick," Katrine said. "Heart attack."

"What are we doing here?" Birgit asked after the waiter had returned to the kitchen. "Why after all these years did you want to see me?"

Katrine held her hand out. "I simply wanted to make sure you had no designs on returning home and making yourself known again."

She leaned back and crossed her arms over her chest. "It's my life. You stole it."

Katrine shrugged and looked toward the window at the end of the table. "You stole things from me, too."

Birgit's breath stuck in her chest for a moment. Katrine had never made mention of knowing about the affair between her and Awad. "I'm not sure what you mean unless you are talking about when we were kids and I stole your doll and drowned her in the lake behind our house."

Katrine's gaze slipped past her sister and landed on the door. "Speak of the devil and he will make himself known."

Birgit turned to see Awad for the first time since she left the boat. During her recovery, he had visited the boat often to check up on her. Once she was in the clear, he let her know that her account had been funded and provided her with the keys to an apartment in Milan that she never once visited. She was sure a device was present that would alert him she was there. Perhaps he would show. Or maybe one of his goons would.

She often wondered why he had warned her. Guilt, perhaps. Looking at him now, she was surprised that her feelings were not as they were so long ago.

Neither woman rose when Awad stopped at the foot of the table, seeming unsure where to sit.

"You couldn't choose then," Katrine said, sliding toward the window, "I don't see why I should expect you to now."

He looked taken aback by her accusatory tone. If he hadn't told her, who had?

"Birgit," he said. "After all these years, it is good to see you. I thought we lost you a decade ago. When Katrine reached out and told me that you had surfaced, we knew it was time to rejoin and put a new plan into effect."

A new plan? What was he talking about? They never had an old plan. And jumping into bed, metaphorically speaking, with these two was not in Birgit's future. She had no interest in becoming a terrorist even if she had once loved one.

Katrine glanced toward the entrance and cleared her throat. "I assume this one is yours?"

Birgit looked over her shoulder and saw Thomas enter the dining room. He requested a table on the opposite side where he was to keep watch over the proceedings.

Birgit signaled to Thomas that he had been made. They knew this was a possibility. If it happened he was to join them at the table so that Jack Noble would know where to shoot. The time it took Thomas to reach the restaurant should have been the same as Birgit, which meant three minutes had passed. Noble had instructions to wait fifteen total, and if he heard nothing from them, he was to take the three minute journey down the stairs, across the street, and along the sidewalk to the restaurant and enter with his weapon ready to fire.

Glancing around the room, Birgit noticed that one of the men in the kitchen was out of place. He was not a cook, server or part of the management. Not dressed like that. She found herself wishing she had not instructed both of the guards to remain with Noble. The way the meeting was shaping up, she expected it to break out into a gun fight. And right now she had less firepower on her side, especially with Katrine picking Thomas out so quickly.

But there was one final wrench to be thrown into the plans.

"If you'll excuse me," Katrine said, rising and dropping her napkin on the table. "I'm going to leave you two old *friends* alone to hash a few things out."

Awad slid off the bench seat and extended his hand. Katrine leaned close and kissed him. "Inform her of our plan." She pressed her lips to his ear and said barely loud enough for Birgit to hear, "Then escort her out."

# 62

Bear cleared his mind for the seventh time in six minutes while staring up at the racing clouds. He had tried mastering the mindfulness thing, but it wasn't working for him. There was always some problem lingering that his brain tried to find an answer for. When the static burst emanated from his earpiece, he nearly sat straight up, revealing himself.

"It's time." Katrine's breathing filled the void. "She will be exiting the restaurant in a few minutes. Ready yourself."

Bear rolled over on his knees and sank back on his heels. The breeze hit him in the face. He'd grown accustomed to the smell of the bakery. The sun glared down from his left. He set the short tripod on the knee-high wall and rested the barrel of the M40 on top. A few slight adjustments and the concrete landing in front of the restaurant's entrance was perfectly aligned in his sights.

*The deadline.*

That imaginary line outside of a prison that guards used to determine whether a prisoner would be given another chance to get back inside or be shot dead.

Bear marked his own deadline a few feet in front of the doorway. God help anyone who passed it.

"I see you are in position. Be aware that you will be visible to anyone on the ground, not that they have a reason to look up. So take care to conceal yourself until the last possible moment."

Bear was comfortable enough with his abilities that leaving the perch was OK. He closed his eyes and visualized the target exiting the restaurant. Lining up his shot. Squeezing the trigger. Breaking down the weapon. Descending the stairwell. Ditching the weapon.

Where was Frank? Given the man's position now, he was likely a block away, monitoring the radio and keeping tabs on the chatter to see if anyone had picked up on the meeting. It wasn't everyday two dead women met for brunch.

"Two minutes," Katrine said. In the background he heard Sasha say something but couldn't make it out.

The taste in his mouth soured. He knew he should have turned this damn job down. Sasha could have protected him while Jack faced the consequences on his own. Perhaps it was his stubbornness that led him to this mess. Loyalty was to blame as well. Why'd he have to be so damn proud that he couldn't let her help him more?

The damn tumor in his brain was the only answer he could think of. Staring down his possible death — one that would have him rolling in his own feces like a babbling idiot — he needed to control what remained of his life because it sure as hell seemed like there was a good chance there wasn't much left.

And that was why Bear decided right then that he would kill whoever they asked him to, then he'd make sure every last one of the sons of bitches paid for what they had done.

Or he'd die trying.

# 63

The call from Thomas never came.

"It's time," the guard said.

On the counter were two Berettas, two extra magazines, one suppressor and a tactical knife. I put the magazines in my right pocket. Tucked one of the Berettas behind my back. I held the suppressor in one hand, the other sidearm in the other.

"Just thread it on?" I said, acting like I was having trouble with the device.

The guy rolled his eyes and nodded slowly as though he were dealing with a fresh recruit who had never handled a gun. He stuck out his hand. "Let me see it."

"Sure thing."

I squeezed the trigger and placed a single round between his eyes. His ass hitting the floor made more noise than the shot. As expected, his partner jumped off the couch and ran toward me while attempting to free his weapon from its holster. I squeezed the trigger twice, hitting him dead center. He went down hard on the glass coffee table. It shattered under his weight. Fragments scattered across the floor. I walked around the couch and placed one more round into the back of his head.

I took each man's cell phone and emptied their wallets of cash and IDs. The latter I threw out the window into the alley. They were fake, so it really wouldn't matter if the officials found them. There was enough cash to get on a train.

I only had three minutes to make it to the back of the restaurant, so I made the phone call on the way.

The man answered in his native Spanish. He was an old friend of mine from my days in the Marines, working with the CIA SOG. We spent plenty of time in Central America. Javier supplied us with shelter and supplies anytime we were in his country. He was a high-ranking official in Costa Rica, and had always been friendly to our cause. He had an affinity for me and Bear after we'd spent our leave one summer rescuing his daughter from a local drug lord.

"Javier," I said. "It's the Nobleman." He'd always called me that. "Look, I need a favor."

The call took no more than twenty seconds and I was off the phone by the time I left the apartment building. I dismantled the cell phone, tossed the sim card in the trashcan, the battery into the gutter, and the phone itself onto the top of a two-story building that housed a florist, butcher, and a massage parlor.

While the street smelled of the bakery, the alley behind the restaurant smelled like burned grease and trash. An interesting combination that always seemed to be present at the rear of every restaurant I'd had the pleasure of standing behind.

A young woman wearing a blue shirt and black apron with flowers on it and an older man wearing an apron covered in blood were smoking cigarettes. They took one look at me, smiled, then noticed the weapon in my hand.

"Don't worry," I said, holding my free hand up, waving at them. "It's not for you."

They dropped their cigarettes where they stood and fled into the back of the two-story building I had thrown the phone on top of a minute ago. I wondered why the masseuse hadn't joined them for a break. Guess her clients didn't like smoky hands on their asses.

The cigarette smoke wafted past me, tempting me on some level. It had been long enough that I really didn't want to smoke anymore, but damn if it didn't smell good at that moment.

I stopped at the back of the restaurant. The screen door hung open an inch. It sounded as though there were two radios playing, one with something akin to a man battering a steel trashcan with a club while screaming his head off, and the other baroque piano. Combined, it was an interesting combination that got my blood flowing even more that it already was.

I hadn't felt this way in some time. The thrill of the hunt had returned and electrified me. My heart pounded against my chest, and I liked it. I felt alive. I was not running now. I had no fear of what would happen to me or my brother, father, sister-in-law, nieces, and even little Mia.

Every single one of these assholes was about to die.

I would leave no one in my wake.

# 64

"We want your help," Awad said. "Both of you, actually."

Thomas shifted in his seat and bumped into Birgit, causing her to spill some water in her lap. The mercenary placed his hand flat on the table. "While I do have a certain amount of moral flexibility, I will not participate in any terrorist activities that result in the death of innocent women and children."

Awad barely glanced at the man. "I think you'll do whatever your boss tells you to do."

"I am under no obligation to—"

Birgit placed her hand on Thomas's. "We haven't heard the facts yet. Let's hear the man out. If I know him as well as I believe I do, then there will be plenty to gain."

For the next five minutes Awad detailed a plan for which he was the primary source of financial backing. Birgit's accounts, which were controlled by her sister, were liquidated in order to contribute. As the money rightfully belonged to the sister seated across from him, he considered that her buy-in. Thomas, for his part, if he chose to go along, would be compensated accordingly. Birgit knew that if Thomas refused, Awad would have him killed. Today, most likely. He'd seen and heard too much.

"I'll expect your answer when I return." Awad excused himself from the table, leaving Birgit and Thomas alone. Birgit glanced at the out-of-place man in the kitchen. He made no effort to conceal his effort to watch the pair.

"What do you think?" Thomas asked.

"I think you should reconsider what you are thinking right now."

"How do you know what I'm thinking?"

She hadn't removed her hand from his. She squeezed and looked him in the eye. "Somewhere outside this restaurant is a sniper whose job it is to remove evidence from the scene. We have been told of a terrorist plot with the potential of disrupting the European and perhaps all western economies. Awad may present himself as a financier, but trust me, I have known the man for a long time and in many ways, and he will not shrink away from bloodying his hands. He is an extremist. Worse, he has wealth beyond most people's imaginations. If he can visualize it, he can make it happen. And his visions are of the worst kind."

She paused to allow Thomas time to respond. No words escaped his clenched lips. Perhaps the reality of the situation was setting in.

"If you refuse," Birgit said, "you will be killed. Even if Noble comes through and completes his part, we will not be able to stop them from ultimately carrying out our executions and this attack."

Thomas pulled his hand away from Birgit and leaned back. "You want to take part in this?"

She shook her head. "I am not saying that. But I do believe that the proper course of action at this time is to say that we will. We will then wait for the right opportunity to leave."

"What about Noble?" Thomas glanced toward the kitchen. "He's due to show up any second now and do what he does best."

"We will see him before anyone else does. When Awad returns, you will rise to use the restroom and instead go to the kitchen to stop him."

Thomas cleared his throat and gestured quickly toward the dark hallway. Awad emerged, shaking the remaining water from his hands. He returned to the table and sat.

"Have you made your decision?" Awad said.

"We have," Birgit said. "We're in."

"Excellent."

"If you'll excuse me," Thomas said, standing. "I need to use the restroom now."

He walked past the hallway that Awad had emerged from and went to the yellow smoke-stained swinging door that separated the dining room from the kitchen. He glanced back and nodded at Birgit. A move that resulted in him not seeing the moment that Awad's guard posted in the kitchen went down.

# 65

One tap.

One shot.

One man down.

It was easy to pick the guy out in the room of cooks. If they had wanted him to blend, they should have dressed him somewhat like the others. Clad in black gear and holding a pistol at his side made it too easy.

The bullet slammed into the back of his head. He never had a clue. Never heard me enter. Probably pegged the thud of the shot as one of the cooks' spatula on the flattop.

The other men in the kitchen took notice one by one. I aimed the Beretta in their direction and held my other hand to my lips for a beat, then gestured for them to file past me and exit. The first of the cooks hadn't reached me yet when I noticed the next out-of-place visitor to the kitchen.

Thomas stared at the fallen man with a look of confusion. It didn't appear that he recognized the guy or cared that he was dead. Perhaps he'd entered the space with the same idea I had.

He looked up at me, threw his left hand up in a gesture that said stop now. But his right hand went to his side. I had a bead on him so I paused long enough to see what he'd do next.

Thomas took a few steps toward me. He stopped, glanced backward, then spoke. His hands remained in the same positions. "Calling it off."

"Why?"

"Birgit's orders." He lowered his left hand. "Not mine."

"You call your guy in Costa Rica?"

"I have." He glanced quickly to the left, back at me. His lack of questioning me verified I had the country correct. "He's bailing out now."

"Lies." I squeezed the trigger three times with no more than a half second between shots. The first hit dead center, creating a dark red circle that spread rapidly across his white shirt. The next created an effective tracheotomy in the soft fleshy part of his neck. His head dipped back so the third round hit under the chin and exited through the top of his skull, sending bits of blood, bone and brain into the air, coating the upper wall and ceiling.

I spat on his shoe as I walked past on my way to the dining room. Glancing toward the cooking line, I saw a young man cowering near the fryer.

"The hell is wrong with you?" I said.

The cook looked like he was about to cry.

"Didn't you hear me tell you to get the hell out?"

He shook his head. One of his hands was behind his back.

"It never crossed your mind to follow the others out the back?" I flicked the pistol up and down. "Get up, asshole."

The young guy grabbed hold of the top of the fryer. He dipped his fingertips into the boiling grease and let out a scream. A second later the door to the dining room burst open and a woman not much older than the cook froze in place, her gaze fixed on my Beretta. The door swung back and forth, colliding with her ass.

"Christ." I pulled the non-silenced pistol and aimed it at the cook while shifting the first Beretta toward the waitress. "Join him."

She didn't move.

"Now!"

Her gaze was fixed on the cook. Her eyes grew wide, as did her mouth. I don't know what she wanted to say but a sort of shrill yet soft scream came out.

The cook skipped forward on his knees and brought his arm around from his back. Son of a bitch thought he was going to be the hero. He flung the chef's knife at me in an underhanded sort of motion that a softball pitcher uses when they want to throw a curve.

I sidestepped the blade. Before it collided with the steel walk-in door and bounced off, skating across the floor, I fired a shot at the man. Fortunately for him I placed the bullet near his knee so it would be non-fatal. Probably.

Unfortunately for me, I used the naked Beretta and it sounded like a rocket exploding in the mostly metal kitchen.

The waitress fell to her knees and crawled toward the boy, muttering something. Presumably his name. I didn't stick around to see. Kicking the door open, I saw Awad and Birgit seated at the table. He was twisted at the waist, his left arm draped over the chair next him and his right arm reaching inside his lightweight herringbone coat.

I surveilled the rest of the room and determined no other immediate threats.

Without hesitation I squeezed the trigger. The first shot hit Awad in the left arm at the tricep muscle. It likely shattered his humerus. He fell forward. The table stopping his progress. He grabbed his arm with the opposite hand. Blood spilled through his clenched fingers. His sidearm fell to the ground. I sent another round into his lower back. I decided at that moment then to use the entire magazine on the guy before launching the final fatal shot into the top of his head from a distance of only two feet away.

Why?

Because fuck that terrorist son of a bitch.

His body jerked with each shot. His screams grew weaker.

Across the table Birgit flailed her arms back and forth in front of her, crossing them.

"It's off, Jack," she said. I swear I heard it in slow motion. "The whole thing is off. Thomas was supposed to tell you."

I stopped behind Awad and grabbed a handful of his hair. I glanced at Birgit.

"He told me."

She shook her head, tears streamed down her cheeks. "What? Why, then?"

"I didn't like the way he said it." I placed the Beretta on the back of Awad's head. "So I killed him."

Birgit pushed away from the table. Her chair tipped and she fell backward to the floor. The woman managed to turn as she went down and landed hard on her right side. She crawled away from the table, then got to a knee and stumbled toward the ground again.

Summoning his last bit of life-force, Awad screamed out. "Get out of here, Katrine!"

I yanked back hard so the son of a bitch was forced to look me in the eye. Noticed the curly flesh-colored wire hanging out of his ear.

"Until we meet again in hell."

I squeezed the trigger, sending the round through the back of his head. His forehead ripped open and the bullet smashed into the light hanging over the next table.

Birgit tripped over the step up to the front door. She clawed her way to her knees, looked back at me. As she moved to her feet, she fell forward again.

I was closing the distance between us fast.

She rolled over and scooted on her ass until she reached the door. Unable to open it, she settled for leaning back against it. It cracked slightly, creating a howling wind tunnel.

"There's probably a sniper," she said, her voice shaking.

I aimed the un-suppressed Beretta at her head and said nothing.

"Please, I have millions and can pay you whatever you want if you just get me out of here."

"Tell me a number."

She blinked and shook her head and spat out the first thing that came to mind. "Ten million."

I lowered the weapon, still keeping it aimed at her, and acted as though I were thinking it over. A moment later, I gave her my response.

"Not good enough."

She stared at the rising pistol as though it were a snake about to reach out and bite her.

"I'll give you all I have," she said, both hands extended, pleading for me to take it. "Every last cent. Twenty million."

"You think twenty million is enough to buy off the souls of all those you have had a hand in killing?"

"What?" She searched the ceiling for an answer. "I never took part in any—"

"Shut up! I don't want to hear your lies."

"Please, just let me go."

I knelt down in front of her and jammed the pistol against her forehead. She reached up and grabbed the barrel. Fear sapped her strength. I heard her skin singe on the scorching barrel. She gritted her teeth.

"I only wanted to stop them," she said.

"And you were willing to kill my child to do so."

I fired the final round into her head before she had a chance to respond. She jerked back and then slid to the right, leaving behind a trail of blood on the wall.

# 66

“WATCH THE DOOR.”

Katrine Ahlberg repeated the phrase three times in rapid succession. Bear had no doubt the urgency in her voice was tied to the gunshot he’d heard moments prior.

The sun hovered to his left and reflected off the floor to ceiling windows that lined the front of the restaurant and allowed passersby to get a look at the day’s offerings. The glare prevented Bear from seeing inside the building. Who was the shooter? Had they been detained? Why hadn’t Frank come on the radio?

In the final seconds Awad shouted something, but the feed in Bear’s earpiece was too corrupted for him to make out the words. Perhaps they weren’t even in any of the languages he knew.

The door cracked open a couple inches. Bear leaned forward and pressed his face to the scope. The magnified view of the entryway revealed a pistol’s barrel poking out. Through the reflection of the street in the glass he made out the shape of a man just inside.

“Take the shot!”

Katrine’s outburst caused Bear to flinch. It sounded like she stood over him with a bull horn. He shook off the distraction and sighted the door again. It had closed and the person behind it had disappeared.

“What are you waiting for?”

Bear did not respond. The woman could pound sand. He'd complete the job they had told him to do only once he had a visual of the target. The last thing he wanted was to kill an innocent person who had the misfortune of eating a late breakfast at the restaurant.

The door flung open as though the person inside had kicked it. Two pistols emerged, one with a suppressor fixed to the barrel, the other without. The man's right arm swung to the side, covering the street. His left remained straight out. A swift movement reversed the order.

Then the guy stepped out from the shadows.

"Shoot him now."

Jack Noble stood some forty feet across and fifty feet below Bear. Whatever had happened in that restaurant — and Bear assumed it was much more than the single shot he had heard given the suppressed sidearm — had taken place at Jack's hand. Given that the only person on the line was Katrine, Bear realized that Jack might have already handled everyone else, including his primary target, Birgit.

"What are you waiting for?"

He grew tired of the woman's Saudi-influenced Swedish accent. Shoot Jack? She could go to hell.

Jack stepped away from the door. It fell shut behind him. He noticed a woman's face press up against it before retreating back into the dining room. Her eyes were wide and she watched as Jack walked into the middle of the road, pistols extended and ready as they had both been trained years ago.

That told Bear that not everyone was dead. If it were police Jack were concerned about, he would have escaped through the rear of the building and disappeared through the network of alleys and apartments and offices.

No, the man was looking for someone and practically begging for them to come to him.

"Look across the way to your left." Katrine paused a beat. "On the rooftop."

Bear pulled his head back and pivoted the rifle and stopped at the sight of the woman. Leaning forward, he corrected his aim until he had her in his sight. Except what looked like a single woman was actually two, with one pressed close behind the other, slightly off center by four to six inches.

Sasha stared in his direction. It felt as though they made eye contact through the scope. Behind her stood Katrine. The Swedish woman held a gun to Sasha's head. Though Katrine was taller by at least three inches, they now appeared to be the same height.

"If you don't shoot him in the next seven seconds then I'll kill her."

The sights centered on Sasha's chest. Bear held them there momentarily as Katrine started her countdown, then he swung the rifle toward the street.

"Six."

He located Jack. He'd managed a good ten yards since Bear last spotted him.

"Five." Her counting was deliberate and slow. At least three seconds had passed since the previous number. Or Bear had reached the point where he was dialed in and the world around him operated in slow motion.

Bear jerked the weapon forward and locked in on Noble's back.

"Four."

Could he do this? Could he kill the man he'd identified as his best friend since the age of eighteen? The guy he'd bonded and bled with? They'd done unspeakable things, but also great things in their time together. Could he end it all now?

"Three. I'd encourage you to get this over with now!"

Christ, the pounding flooded his head. Not now. Anytime but now. Why couldn't it just be him down on the street? Let Jack be the one to take him out instead of this cursed softball living and breathing inside his cranium.

"Two."

To hell with her.

Bear pulled his face back an inch and swung the rifle toward the rooftop. He leaned in and lined up a shot. He could only see a small portion of Katrine, and if he managed to hit her with a clean shot it would not do the kind of damage he wanted.

"One. Time is almost up. Do it now."

She hadn't seen him adjust the rifle because she had focused her attention on Jack. It was a good thing she only held a pistol, otherwise she might have taken Noble out.

Bear took a breath and held it. In the second that followed he didn't blink, his heart beat one and a half times, he cursed Jack for showing up at his door, and he prayed forgiveness from Sasha for what he was about to do.

"Last warning, Logan. Or else your woman dies here and—"

Bear squeezed the trigger. The round left the weapon traveling at over twenty-five hundred feet per second, making its journey near instantaneous. By the time he locked in on the target again, the bullet had hit Sasha on her left side above her chest and under her shoulder, placed precisely in the only spot that would not result in her immediate death. Sasha's eyes widened and her chin dipped to her chest as she glanced down at the hole in her body. The gun barrel pressed to her head slipped off and aimed skyward and discharged a round that would sometime soon land near them. The hand around Sasha's arm fell to the side. Sasha dropped to her knees, her stare now fixed on Bear.

Katrine remained on her feet. Bear smiled briefly. His plan had worked. A red stain formed near the Scandinavian Princess's ice-cold heart. He adjusted the rifle a fraction of an inch and squeezed the trigger again. The bullet entered the front of Katrine's head and tore off the back of it. She dropped where she stood.

Bear pushed the rifle aside and pressed up against the knee wall.

"Sasha." His shout echoed around the buildings for a moment. He yelled her name again.

A slender arm stuck into the air and she raised her thumb.

Bear sighed a breath of relief, then grabbed the rifle and put into action his escape plan, only now it included retrieving the woman he loved.

# 67

The shots from above didn't give me a single moment of pause. If they were destined for me, so be it. At this moment my world could be crashing down. I wouldn't speak with Javier until this was over, and probably even a while after that. Every second that passed provided the opportunity for Thomas to miss a call to his partner, who was watching my brother and his family, my father, and my daughter. If anything happened to them, all I would have left to live for was death. My own, and several others.

And the man who was first on the list stood a block away, defiant in the middle of the road. His hands were loose at his side. He had a sad sort of smile plastered on his nodding head.

He met me halfway. Looked me up and down, taking note of the blood-soaked clothing. "Put the guns away, Jack."

I didn't.

He glanced down at the Berettas I had aimed at the ground. "You got her, right?"

"Birgit is dead." I paused a beat. "So is the man working for her. And so is your buddy Awad."

He licked his lips and raised his left hand, extending it out to the side a foot. The ploy was meant to prevent me from seeing him sneaking his right arm towards his sidearm.

"Thank God. That son of a bitch was—"

I fired an unsuppressed round into his foot.

Frank toppled over onto his side. He brought his knee up and wrapped his hand around his wounded extremity. "Goddamn you son of a bitch." He fumbled around his waist and pulled his Sig.

I shot him again in the right forearm. The sound of the weapon firing echoed off the street and buildings. He dropped the weapon behind his head. He rolled on his side and reached for it with his left hand. I dashed forward, kicked the pistol away. It skated along the asphalt and ricocheted off the curb.

Frank continued onto his stomach and crawled a few feet before getting to his knee. Blood pooled around his foot. His right arm hung limp. He held out his left hand once again, this time imploring me to stop.

"I get the point, Jack."

"Do you?"

"Yes!" He dropped his head back and blinked at the sky a few times. His chin dropped to his chest. Frank looked up at me. "You're pissed. And, hell, if I was in your position, I'd be pissed, too."

"Glad to hear it."

I lifted both pistols and aimed them at his face.

"Christ, Jack. Hear me out, would you?"

"There's nothing you can say, Frank. I haven't quite figured out who's in bed with who here, and honestly, I don't fucking care. But they had to get Mia's position from someone, and the only person I know who can get that information is you."

"I didn't, Jack. I didn't tell them."

I took a step forward. Worst case if he lashed out at me was I'd shoot a round into the asphalt. I could live with that. At that moment I wanted to smell the fear emanating off his body in the moments before I took his life.

Frank sank back on his heels. He lowered his left arm and pretended to use it to support him. I had no doubt he was going for a knife hidden under his pants leg. "We both know you won't do this, Jack."

"You think you know what I'm thinking?" I squeezed the trigger and a bullet dug into his left shoulder.

The small knife clanked as it fell to the street.

"You couldn't pull the trigger last time."

"I think I've already shot you three times."

"Yet I'm still alive." Frank forced himself upright. Even managed to bring his bloodied foot forward and rose. Blood dripped off his fingertips and puddled on the street. It looked almost black. "I know you want to kill me. Believe me, Jack. I've been there before. In this business, no one's your friend. Can't trust a damn soul. I know I don't. Except for you, Jack. And I trust you'll do the right thing here and hand over your weapon."

I had to give it to him for standing through his speech and managing to hold one hand out. I looked up at the sky. Thought I saw an arm hanging over the ledge of a building. I shook the image free and brought my gaze back to Frank. I reached my arm out. He grabbed hold of the barrel. I shoved my hand forward and fired a round into his stomach.

Frank's eyes widened. He stumbled back and dropped to his knees again.

I walked forward and placed the pistol a foot from his head.

"Hear me now, Frank. The only reason you survived last time we were in this position was because my little girl was looking on from the car. I couldn't allow her to see that. Couldn't have her know that I'm a killer." I leaned forward, looked him in the eye. "But that's what I am."

I pulled the trigger as though it had violated me personally. At point blank range, I wouldn't miss, so it didn't matter. Frank's body jerked and then fell backward. His lifeless eyes stared up at the passing clouds.

"No!"

I spun in the direction of the booming voice, ready to shoot. Bear raced toward me. He held a sniper rifle close to his chest with one hand. The other he extended and aimed his large finger down the street. I turned in that direction and was prepared to face an army of Frank's SOG operators.

Instead I saw three Chinese women, an old bald man, and two local teenagers standing not too far off. They all had one thing in common.

The cell phones they aimed in my direction.

I'd been filmed killing one of the CIA's top men.

# 68

JAVIER ANSWERED HIS CELL PHONE WITHOUT SAYING A WORD. HE DIDN'T WANT to wake his sleeping granddaughter. It amazed him how she looked so much like her mother as a young child.

"We got him," the man said.

Javier placed the sleeping girl on the couch and walked into the kitchen. He leaned against the counter as he stared out the back window. "Dead?"

"Alive."

"Perfect." He thought about the ways they could torture the man. The intelligence they could glean from him. "And the family, they are OK?"

"Yes. Everyone is safe if not a little spooked by the takedown."

"I want you to stay behind and personally keep an eye on them. My associate said he is going to be sending a communication that we must deliver to them, so it is important they do not leave your sight."

"Understood."

Javier hung up and placed his cell phone on the counter. As he watched the little girl sleeping and thought of his daughter, now all grown up, he wished he could get ahold of Jack Noble to let him know that the man's child was safe.

# 69

The first time Brandon opened his eyes, he was greeted by a woman he wanted to call Bruhilda. Fortunately for him, he didn't. She smiled briefly and said, "You're going to be OK."

He passed out immediately after.

The next time he opened his eyes he saw two faces staring back at him. The only thing they shared in common was that in the past few years he hadn't seen either in person.

"Good to see you up, young man," the CIA's director of operations said. He glanced at the woman seated next to the bed, then back at Brandon and gave him a wink. "I think I'll come back and check on you a little later."

Brandon tried to lick his lips but his mouth was parched. The woman held a cup of ice to his lips and tilted it a notch too far. Round ice cubes pelted his face. She laughed. He smiled. Their gazes were locked on one another.

"I'm glad you're OK." She inched her wheelchair forward until it pressed into the bed. Her hand fit perfectly in his.

"Kimberlee." His voice sounded like he had gravel in his throat.

"This isn't the way I envisioned our first face-to-face going." She grabbed the bed's remote and checked out the controls. "I think we can work with this, though."

Brandon forced a smile as he traced the long line of staples in his chest. "I think we're gonna have to wait a little bit."

Kimberlee squeezed his hand. "I've got all the time in the world. I'm not leaving your side again."

# 70

THE MAN ARRIVED AT THE SMALL HOUSE AT A QUARTER PAST NOON. RIGHT ON time. He stepped out, came to the door and dropped an envelope on the ground. He retreated back to the car and drove off. I climbed down from the attic and read the note. He would be back in thirty minutes after he had ensured he was not being followed.

A week had passed since the day I killed Frank, Awad, Birgit Ahlberg, and the others. I'd learned that Bear had taken out Katrine, too, using an intriguing shooting technique. Guess we could put the ten-year-old hit to rest.

As I had stared at the crowd of people filming me on the streets outside Tours, the voice inside my head screamed 'run.' So I did.

When I looked back at Bear, he gave me a simple gesture that told me he'd find a way to get in touch. All I needed was a phone. He would take care of the rest.

A couple days had passed before I heard from him. During that time the footage had been all over the news and in the papers. I faced the stark realization that I might never be a free man again, whether bound by chains or the inability to move freely.

I heard the vehicle approaching and saw the twin spires of dust kicking up as the guy returned. I glanced at the clock. Thirty minutes exactly. He looped around the front of the house and parked close to the door. The windows were coated in dust and I couldn't tell if it was him or not, but I jumped in the passenger seat anyway. He nodded once, reached across my lap and opened the glove box. Then we sped away.

Inside the compartment I found a Glock 19 and a concealment holster, a Garmin watch that was equipped with GPS and an altimeter and barometer, a passport, cash and credit cards, and a numbered account.

"We're not going to see him?" I asked the guy.

"That's for just in case," he replied.

I held out hope that nothing would happen during the trip to Bear's location. With my luck, it was hard to imagine that it would work out OK.

Two hours later we were close to the French-Swiss border. The mountains rose out of the earth like giants and dominated the skyline. We rolled down the windows and sucked in the crisp air.

A short distance further we turned off on a dirt path and pushed forward until the road was out of sight. We came to a fork, veered right and went on until we reached the small square house. It was white with blue shutters. The guy parked in front and exited the vehicle. I followed his lead, tucking the holstered pistol behind my back as I stepped outside.

The front door opened and a tanned man with a full head of gray hair exited the home. He walked up to the driver and they shook hands. The driver leaned in and whispered something. The older man watched me, nodded his head and walked over with his hand extended.

"Doctor Vasseur," he said.

"Jack." I gripped his hand in mine.

He patted me on the shoulder. "Come with me."

I followed him into the house, down a set of stairs and through a door that looked like rock on one side and reinforced steel on the other. I saw Bear sitting in a chair, head slumped on his shoulder, asleep. Next to him on a hospital bed was Sasha. She held a book in her hand but quickly tossed it aside when I entered.

"That was some trick shot," I said.

She smiled. "I can't say I would have done the same thing, but it was effective at getting that wench's hands off of me."

I leaned over and kissed her on the cheek.

Her expression soured. "You're in a lot of trouble. You know that, right?"

I nodded and let my frown speak for me.

"The CIA wants blood. And as bad as that sounds, there are some terrorists who want even more than that. Between Frank, Awad and that mess in Texas, you've pissed a lot of people off."

"So things are normal is what you're telling me."

"Your face is everywhere." She bit her bottom lip. "It's probably best that you disappear for a long, long time."

"I can fight back. We both know what I did was the right thing."

She grimaced as she sat up straight. "Perhaps, Jack. But this is about vengeance now. The CIA has men who will operate outside any semblance of the law. And the terrorists, well, I don't think I need to tell you more about that. At least an Agency man might kill you on sight. Those other bastards will keep you alive for as long as you can withstand their tortuous methods."

I glanced over at the slumbering Bear. "I might need to borrow him for a few weeks."

Sasha looked away, tears filling her eyes.

"He'll get back to you." I ran my hand along the back of her head. "I promise. I just need a running start, and he'll be helpful there."

"It's not that, Jack." She drew in a deep breath and pushed it out quickly. "He's going to be pissed at me for doing this, but here goes."

"What is it?"

"There's a tumor."

"What?"

"In his head."

"Bear?"

"Yes, Riley...Bear. He has a brain tumor and one doctor says it's inoperable and another says we can operate but the chance of survival is not even fifty percent. Well, they both bloody say that."

The words were worse than any sucker punch, blade, or bullet that I'd ever been on the receiving end of. Bear, the guy larger than life, my best friend, dying? "This can't be happening."

"I know what you mean."

The big guy groaned, stretched his arms out and sat up. He looked at Sasha, then me. His forehead bunched up. He scratched his beard. "Where's the funeral?"

"We're just saying our goodbyes," Sasha said, wiping the tears from her eyes.

Bear rose and reached for my hand. I met his half way. He pulled me in and wrapped his arms around me. He was more of a hugger than I was. Given the circumstances, I let him hang on as long as he wanted.

"This isn't goodbye," I said. "I'm gonna set this right."

Bear pushed me back with his massive hands on my shoulders. "I know you will." He dropped one arm and reached into his pocket. He placed the piece of paper he withdrew into my hand.

"What's this?" I said.

"Safe house," he said. "It's in the middle of Italy on the west coast. The owner is only there on the weekend and no one else knows about the place. Figure it's a good spot for you to lay low for a bit, maybe figure out your next step while the attention fades."

"Herman," Sasha said, "the man who drove you here, will get you past the border and arrange for transportation for the rest of your journey. He should have already provided you with your passport and so on."

I nodded while looking at the couple in turn. The big guy's face was etched in my brain, but I wanted to hang onto the image of him sitting there with Sasha, happy. I had a ton left to say, but decided to keep it in. Suppress and repress. My mantra.

We shook hands once more, then I left the room, perhaps laying eyes on Bear for the last time.

# 71

Javier personally delivered the communication to Sean Noble. He remarked how the man looked like his brother. It only took a few minutes to clear up the confusion regarding Jack's current situation and then present the information as he had instructed.

"Here is the signed form releasing Mia to your custody. It is your brother's wish that you raise her as one of your own."

Sean read the paper with the intensity of a lawyer, then set it down. He scrutinized Javier, as the official had expected Jack's brother would.

"This is the information regarding her trust. You will now be the executor." Javier placed another packet on the table. "These are three separate bank accounts for your use in taking care of her and the rest of your family. One is in the Caymans. Another in Europe. And the third is virtual. Petty cash, I suppose. Mr. Noble, it should go without saying that you should not return to your home in the United States. Jack has provided you with close to eight million dollars between these accounts. That should be enough to ease the suffering of leaving your business behind and uprooting your family, which unfortunately you must do."

The older Noble brother clenched his jaw and narrowed his eyes, but he nodded and signed all of the documents.

"I would offer for you to remain in our lovely country, but just the other night we dispatched a man who had been sent here to execute you all. I feel it is in your best interests to leave immediately. I have arranged for a Gulfstream to carry you to the Caymans. Once there you will receive directions to the home you have full use of for as long as you need until you are settled elsewhere."

Sean shuffled through the papers until he arrived at the three deeds, each for a house in different parts of the world.

"I guess I know what it's like to be my brother now," he said.

Javier smiled, full well knowing that this lawyer-man had no idea. But he looked like a decent fellow, and obviously Jack trusted him enough to have the man raise his little daughter.

An hour later the family was packed into the Gulfstream. Javier sent a coded message that notified Jack Noble his loved ones were safely on their way out of the country.

Javier's debt to Jack Noble was partially repaid. In some ways, he hoped he'd have the opportunity to fully repay the man. At the same time, he prayed he'd never hear from him again.

# 72

After crossing the border into Italy, Herman navigated to a small town and stopped in front of an abandoned warehouse. He cut the chain around the doors with a pair of bolt cutters. The chain piled up like a snake in waiting in front of the door. The building was fifty feet long and thirty feet wide. And there was only one thing inside.

He started the BMW motorcycle and then asked me if I knew how to ride. I nodded. He proceeded to punch the coordinates of my destination into the GPS unit, then fixed the device to the bike.

As we changed positions, he placed a cell phone in my hand. It was a simple device unlike the massive tablet looking things people carried around these days. "Don't get pulled over."

"I'll try not to."

"If you do, kill the cop." He smiled and half-heartedly shook his head.

I pulled out of the warehouse and followed the digital map. I thought about Bear a lot for the first part of the trip. I knew if anyone could beat the odds, it was him. And as much as I wanted to send all the positive vibes I could, I had to focus on staying alive. There would be time to contemplate my old friend's future. Just not right now.

The ride took close to five hours and ended with me ascending a long hill into a town that had been built into the cliff. I parked the bike and set out on foot with the GPS now in hand. The worn streets grew narrower until they reached a size no automobile could pass through. There were several steps along the way. The shadows grew longer and longer until the sun disappeared behind the mountain. Voices erupted from the windows of every home I passed.

Sunday evening dinner. I could smell the bread. The sauce. Taste the wine.

I climbed the final set of cracked steps to my destination. The white house had yellow trim around the windows and a door that was now red but looked as though it had been painted several times over the last couple centuries. I reached out and rapped my knuckles against the weathered wood. A paint chip fell and spun as it drifted to the ground.

The door opened and I stood face-to-face with the woman who for so long had been a major part of my life. Her hair was different, blonde. But her eyes were the same emerald green.

"Jack?"

"Clarissa." I looked past her to see if there was anyone else inside. The room was deserted. "I guess Bear didn't call first."

She bit her bottom lip. Shook her head.

Bear had said she was only there on the weekends. "Does anyone else know about this place?"

"No."

"Look, I wouldn't have come here if I had known. They said this was a safe house, and I'm in need of a place to hide out for a while."

She reached out and gestured me inside. "Say no more. I'm rarely here and no one knows I own the house. Stay as long as you need."

I grabbed a large bottle of red wine as I passed the kitchen and collapsed on the couch. A moment later, Clarissa joined me, setting two glasses on the wooden table in front of us.

Our reunion only lasted for a few hours. She left before midnight, had to get back to Rome for some big job. I watched her disappear into the darkness, then settled into my temporary home.

Only one thought remained on my mind.

I had to clear my name.

At any cost.

***Jack Noble's story continues in End Game, links and an excerpt below!***

Want to be among the first to download the next Jack Noble book? Sign up for L.T. Ryan's newsletter, and you'll be notified the minute new releases are available - and often at a discount for the first 48 hours! As a thank you for signing up, you'll receive a complimentary copy of *The Recruit: A Jack Noble Short Story*.

Join here: http://ltryan.com/newsletter/

I enjoy hearing from readers. Feel free to drop me a line at ltryan70@gmail.com. I read and respond to every message.

If you enjoyed reading *Never Cry Mercy*, I would appreciate it if you would help others enjoy these books, too. How?

**Lend it.** This e-book is lending-enabled, so please, feel free to share it with a friend. All they need is an amazon account and a Kindle, or Kindle reading app on their smart phone or computer.

**Recommend it.** Please help other readers find this book by recommending it to friends, readers' groups and discussion boards.

**Review it.** Please tell other readers why you liked this book by reviewing it at Amazon, Barnes & Noble, Apple or Goodreads. Your opinion goes a long way in helping others decide if a book is for them. Also, a review doesn't have to be a big old book report. If you do write a review, please send me an email at ltryan70@gmail.com so I can thank you with a personal email.

**Like Jack.** Visit the Jack Noble Facebook page and give it a like: https://www.facebook.com/JackNobleBooks.

# ALSO BY L.T. RYAN

## The Jack Noble Series

The Recruit (free)

The First Deception (Prequel 1)

Noble Beginnings

A Deadly Distance

Ripple Effect (Bear Logan)

Thin Line

Noble Intentions

When Dead in Greece

Noble Retribution

Noble Betrayal

Never Go Home

Beyond Betrayal (Clarissa Abbot)

Noble Judgment

Never Cry Mercy

Deadline

End Game

## Mitch Tanner Series

The Depth of Darkness

Into The Darkness

Deliver Us From Darkness - coming soon

## Affliction Z Series

Affliction Z: Patient Zero

Affliction Z: Abandoned Hope

Affliction Z: Descended in Blood

Affliction Z Book 4 - Spring 2018

# END GAME: CHAPTER 1

**January 17th, 2010**

*The following takes place between Thin Line and Noble Intentions, books 3 and 4 of the series.*

I stood at the corner of East 72nd and Third Ave. A frigid wind whipped from the direction of the Park. The cold rendered my nose useless in picking up the smells from the bakery behind me. Even the exhaust from the line of cabs didn't register.

The message had come in late last night from a random 212 number to meet Charles at this location. The big oaf acted as a buffer between me and the Old Man whenever he needed me for a job. I figured by now trust would've been earned. For the past couple of years I'd taken every job thrown my way. It didn't matter the target or the scope of work. Whether information or extermination, I completed each without a single thought otherwise. No hesitation.

The moral compass that once guided me had faded into the nether. Not much of a conscience ever existed, but at least there was some semblance of right and wrong guiding my actions. As long as I could justify taking a life, I did it. After being set up one too many times by those I trusted most, I'd had enough and decided that no one else mattered. The size of the paycheck was often the driving factor now.

The white Mercedes screeched to a stop in between two yellow cabs. A woman driving a blue minivan laid on her horn as she swerved to miss the back end of the luxury sedan. A cigarette butt flew out of the cracked window, soaring end over end toward me. The wind intervened and sent it fluttering to the ground.

"Getting in?" Charles said from behind the glass over the high-pitched wailing of an opera singer and a heavy club beat. "Or do I gotta open the door for you like I do the Old Man?"

I stepped off the curb, crushing the lit cigarette in the process.

Charles hiked a thumb over his shoulder. "In the back, asshole."

I peeked through the window and saw one of Charles's new goons occupying the passenger seat. The rear seat was empty, and so far neither man made any move to disarm me. So I opened the door and slid to the middle. Charles looked up at the rearview and made eye contact for a moment. His gaze shifted and the Mercedes jolted forward to a chorus of horns. I glanced over my shoulder and saw two cars behind us stopped at an angle, inches from one another.

"Jack," Charles said. "This is Matt, he's new to the inner—"

"Yeah, I really don't give a shit." I stared out the window at a woman jogging in shorts and a vest, her cadence almost in perfect time with whatever weird techno music Charles was blasting. "The hell are you listening to?"

Charles swatted his goon on the shoulder. "You believe this guy? I swear, what the Old Man sees in him, I don't get it. You could do the work he does, and do it better."

"Then why am I here?" I said. "You wanna replace me with this chump, then let me out now. I got plenty of other people I can get work from."

"Chill your damn goats, Noble. I'm just bustin' your balls, man."

Twenty minutes later we pulled to the curb in front of a renovated brownstone on Hicks Street. A stack of bricks piled as tall as a man stood to the left of the sweeping steps leading to the entrance. The salvaged windows wavily reflected the bleak day.

Charles led me inside the building while Matt remained with the car. He'd been given instructions to cooperate should a cop poke his nose into their business. Usually they'd do so looking for a handout. Even the ones on the Old Man's payroll were always on the lookout for a few bucks more. The old guy didn't mind. He used it as a qualifier to know who he could trust, and who he could consider killing.

We huffed it up three flights of stairs and stopped in front of an unassuming apartment. Charles placed one large hand on his belly, the other on the doorframe, sucking in deep breaths of air. I knew of at least five properties owned by the Old Man, and was sure he had several others. Some for meetings. Others for out of town associates to stay when they visited. And at least a few used as safe houses for his guys, and himself, when necessary. While I had no desire to run a business on the scale of the Old Man's, I adopted his practice of buying real estate. Together with my old partner Bear, we owned seven residences spread throughout the city, and a few houses in northern New York.

"You know the drill." Charles had one hand on the knob, the other extended toward me. Collecting my pistol was a formality. We both knew that once inside, I'd be out-manned and outgunned. No chance I'd reach for my backup piece.

He cracked the door, put his big hand on my back and pushed me inside. Two bodyguards dressed in black and wearing black gloves with cutout fingers turned their attention to me. The third remained perched at his lookout spot, watching the road below. The Old Man spun a quarter-turn in his office chair. A lit cigarette dangled from his fingers. Smoke slipped from his parted lips, catching the sunlight and creating a haze between us. As the smoky veil lifted, his yellow teeth shone through his crooked smile.

"Mr. Jack," he said, tipping his ash into a ceramic tray. "So good to see you. Feels like it's been forever since we last met."

"A month," I said. "Last time we saw each other was a month ago. Remember, you needed help making that woman disappear. Something about a paternity suit, if I remember correctly."

"So recently?" Smiling, he shook his head and gestured for me to take a seat opposite him. "Perhaps I am slipping in my old age."

"Perhaps." I stood firm, waited to see if he'd get to the point of the meeting.

The Old Man waved at his bodyguards and they dispersed, leaving him, Charles and me as the sole occupants of the room. The door slammed shut, and we waited amid the thundering silence.

I broke the first rule of negotiations. "What's this all about?"

The Old Man took a final drag off his cigarette, then extinguished it in the tray. Exhaling, he said, "An associate of mine, a businessman, made a rather large and costly mistake, putting himself at risk in the process. Which puts me at risk.

And when I'm at risk, my entire organization, including my contractors, is at risk."

"What kind of dealings do you typically have with this associate?"

Charles leaned forward. "That's not for you to worry—"

The Old Man sliced his hand through the air between us. "Please, Mr. Charles, allow Mr. Jack to ask whatever questions he wants. After all, he is the one who is going to help us solve this problem."

"Yeah, Chuck," I said. "So back to my question."

"He's a businessman, so business dealings. As you know, a good portion of what I do is on the right side of the law. I have many associates who do not delve into or share our view of the world."

"And this guy?" I said. "What's his worldview?"

The Old Man smiled, answering the question in the process.

"What do you need me to do?"

"Find him. Find out what he knows, what he's said, and what he's planning to do." The Old Man reached into his breast pocket, producing a bullet. He placed it flat on the table, spun it with a flick of his finger. "And once you've got every last bit of information out of him, kill him."

I nodded, said nothing.

"One more thing." The Old Man lifted his eyebrows. He spoke through clenched teeth. "Before killing him, Mr. Jack, make him hurt."

# END GAME: CHAPTER 2

The rest of the meeting was more of a formality than anything else. Matt showed up around this time. The guy stood in the corner and kept his mouth shut while Charles, the Old Man and I continued on with the kind of mindless banter that occurs in boardrooms across the country. Throughout our bullshit conversation, the missing details of the job nagged at me. What had this man done that left the Old Man wanting him not only dead, but also tortured? I preferred hitting hard and fast and getting the job done. Torture wasn't my thing, but for the payday the Old Man was offering, I couldn't refuse the job or his requests.

After we wrapped up, Charles led me out of the building. His new associate Matt stayed behind. Perhaps he had his own private meeting upstairs. What was his role within the organization? Had it been coincidence that we were in the same car together that morning? Or did they want him in there with me for a reason?

"Everything you need's in here." A worn leather messenger bag dangled from Charles's fingertips.

I slung the lightweight bag over my shoulder and protected the zippered opening with my left arm. I felt a pistol inside the bag.

"What do you know about this guy?" I shot him a sideways glance to judge his reaction as we stepped out into the cold.

Charles's expression revealed nothing. It rarely did. His face was made of stone. "Just some guy who got on the Old Man's bad side."

"You never met him?"

Charles shrugged, his bottom lip poked out, pushing his upper lip into his nose. Was he telling me something, or was it a reaction to the frigid air freezing his nose hairs together? "What's it matter? Guy could be my best friend's cousin's lover and he'd still be gettin' whacked. Know what I mean?"

Once the wheels were in motion, there was no stopping the hit from taking place. It was only a matter of deciding on the trigger man. For some jobs it could be anybody. Others required a specific assassin. I'd take just about any job these days. That hadn't always been the case, though. Morals and ethics, as shifty as they could be, played a part at one time. Too much had happened to me over the years to care anymore. But I still had two no-gos. Kids and dogs. Not a chance I'd harm either. Everyone else? Better not do something that gets me sent to your front door.

"True enough," I said. "Anything I should be aware of with him? Military background? Security?"

He pointed at the bag. "It's all in there."

We slipped into the idling Mercedes. The heated cabin was a relief from the arctic assault happening outside.

"You believe this flippin' weather?" He blew a puff of hot air into his clasped hands then rubbed them together before slipping on a pair of black leather gloves. "Where's this crap come from?"

"Canada, I guess. Maybe Alaska."

"Weatherman Noble." He looked at me. "You'd be real cute on television. You know that? Maybe get you one of those skirts to put on, maybe a wig to help cover up that ugly mug of yours."

"I don't think I could sleep at night if I knew you were jerking off to me on the eleven o'clock news."

Charles chuckled. "You wish, Noble."

We headed back to Manhattan, the Upper West Side this time. As we approached the drop-off point, I scanned the street for threats and flagged anyone who looked out of place. On this morning where temperatures had only just reached zero, that was pretty much everyone. In the end, though, no one stood out enough to warrant concern.

"This job could go a long way for you in our organization," Charles said as he pulled to the curb, rubbing the tires against the concrete. "Maybe get you a full-time gig."

"Why would I want that?"

"Why wouldn't you?"

I acted as though I mulled it over for a couple of seconds. "For starters, I don't like following the orders of underlings. I can handle a boss, some of the time, as long as he leaves me the hell alone. So really, the only job worth having would be yours. My first act would be to take you down so I could slide into your position. From there, I'd work on taking over the whole organization."

Charles laughed. "You? Right. A guy who likes to live in the breeze and pick up work when it suits you. You wouldn't want to take on the Old Man's responsibilities." He paused a beat. "Mine either."

"Like you do anything important on a daily basis."

"You got no idea, Noble." He shook his head. "You really don't."

"Just busting your balls, man. I don't want your job. I certainly don't want to run an enterprise like the Old Man's." I cracked the door open, inviting a steady gust of wind inside. "And I have no desire to be a part of your organization."

"Solid pay for a guy like you. No more drifting. And you'd have the full protection of the Old Man. Right now you're pretty much in danger every second of every day. With his backing, you'd be almost untouchable."

"Untouchable...right. Except to the same people I already have to watch out for. Like you said, every second of every day, I'm watching my back for the criminals I put away, and the agency I put them away for. Let's not get into other organizations and the Old Man's rivals I've weakened in the past."

"But if you're with us, you'll be avenged. If someone got you right now, you'd be a dead asshole with no one mourning you."

I sat there for a moment, my grip loose on the door handle. He was right. If someone took me out right then and there, no one would mourn my passing.

And I was happy with that.

**Click here to purchase End Game now!**

# ABOUT THE AUTHOR

L.T. Ryan is a *USA Today* and international bestselling author. The new age of publishing offered L.T. the opportunity to blend his passions for creating, marketing, and technology to reach audiences with his popular Jack Noble series.

Living in central Virginia with his wife, the youngest of his three daughters, and their three dogs, L.T. enjoys staring out his window at the trees and mountains while he should be writing, as well as reading, hiking, running, and playing with gadgets. See what he's up to at http://ltryan.com.

**Social Medial Links:**

- Facebook (L.T. Ryan): https://www.facebook.com/LTRyanAuthor
- Facebook (Jack Noble Page): https://www.facebook.com/JackNobleBooks/
- Twitter: https://twitter.com/LTRyanWrites
- Goodreads: http://www.goodreads.com/author/show/6151659.L_T_Ryan

Made in the USA
Columbia, SC
13 March 2020

89147953R00183